STRANGLED INTUITION

"An endearing cast with their own codes of conduct."
—*Mysterious Women*

"Cally is a very refreshing and likable character."
—*The Romance Reader's Connection*

BODY OF INTUITION

"Fans of Jaqueline Girdner's Kate Jasper series will relish Claire Daniels's new Cally Lazar series. Cane-wielding Cally and the rest of the cast are a delight."
—Jan Dean, editor of *Murder Most Cozy*

"Prognosis: original, innovative, and unique. Don't miss Cally Lazar's fresh approach to problem-solving. Claire Daniels creates an 'energetic' plot with captivating characters. *Body of Intuition* will open up your mind to new perspectives."
—Janet A. Rudolph, editor of *Mystery Readers Journal*

"A riveting plot. Absorbing and endlessly entertaining."
—Lynne Murray, author of *A Ton of Trouble*

"Whether your aura is serenely silver or your karma needs a tune-up, you'll enjoy following intuitive healer Cally Lazar as she uses her unusual talents to find a murderer at a Love Seminar."
—Kate Derie, editor of *The Deadly Directory*

"Daniels's portrayal of the New Age milieu is both realistic and a bit tongue-in-cheek." —*The Drood Review of Mystery*

"Hilarious and outrageous . . . Murder is no laughing matter, but in Claire Daniels's capable hands, catching a murderer has never been so amusing." —*I Love a Mystery*

"Claire Daniels has written a creative New Age psychic mystery starring a heroine that it is impossible not to like."
—*Midwest Book Review*

Karma Crime Mysteries by Claire Daniels

BODY OF INTUITION
STRANGLED INTUITION
CRUEL AND UNUSUAL INTUITION
FINAL INTUITION

FINAL INTUITION

CLAIRE DANIELS

BERKLEY PRIME CRIME, NEW YORK

THE BERKLEY PUBLISHING GROUP
Published by the Penguin Group
Penguin Group (USA) Inc.
375 Hudson Street, New York, New York 10014, USA
Penguin Group (Canada), 90 Eglinton Avenue East, Suite 700, Toronto, Ontario M4P 2Y3, Canada
(a division of Pearson Penguin Canada Inc.)
Penguin Books Ltd., 80 Strand, London WC2R 0RL, England
Penguin Group Ireland, 25 St. Stephen's Green, Dublin 2, Ireland (a division of Penguin Books Ltd.)
Penguin Group (Australia), 250 Camberwell Road, Camberwell, Victoria 3124, Australia
(a division of Pearson Australia Group Pty. Ltd.)
Penguin Books India Pvt. Ltd., 11 Community Centre, Panchsheel Park, New Delhi—110 017, India
Penguin Group (NZ), Cnr. Airborne and Rosedale Roads, Albany, Auckland 1310, New Zealand
(a division of Pearson New Zealand Ltd.)
Penguin Books (South Africa) (Pty.) Ltd., 24 Sturdee Avenue, Rosebank, Johannesburg 2196, South
Africa

Penguin Books Ltd., Registered Offices: 80 Strand, London WC2R 0RL, England

This is a work of fiction. Names, characters, places, and incidents either are the product of the author's imagination or are used fictitiously, and any resemblance to actual persons, living or dead, business establishments, events, or locales is entirely coincidental. The publisher does not have any control over and does not assume any responsibility for author or third-party websites or their content.

FINAL INTUITION

A Berkley Prime Crime Book / published by arrangement with the author

PRINTING HISTORY
Berkley Prime Crime mass-market edition / February 2006

Copyright © 2006 by Jaqueline Girdner.
Cover illustration by Griesbach / Martucci.
Cover design by Lesley Worrell.
Interior text design by Julie Rogers.

ISBN: 0-425-20855-9

BERKLEY® PRIME CRIME
Berkley Prime Crime Books are published by The Berkley Publishing Group,
a division of Penguin Group (USA) Inc.,
375 Hudson Street, New York, New York 10014.
The name BERKLEY PRIME CRIME and the BERKLEY PRIME CRIME design are trademarks
belonging to Penguin Group (USA) Inc.

PRINTED IN THE UNITED STATES OF AMERICA

10 9 8 7 6 5 4 3 2 1

To my husband, Greg,
who still laughs when he reads my first drafts

ACKNOWLEDGMENTS

My thanks to Bill Girdner, Lynne Murray, and Eileen Ostrow Feldman for lighting my way with your inspiration, imagination, and generosity.

CAST OF CHARACTERS

THANKSGIVING DAY DINNER GUESTS AND HOSTESS

Geneva Lazar: The eldest of the five Lazar siblings, clothing designer, and hostess for Thanksgiving and sudden death.

Cally Lazar: The youngest of the Lazar siblings. She's a recovering attorney, a "cane-fu" master, an intuitive energy healer, and a very reluctant sleuth.

Roy Beaumont: Cally's sweetie. An accountant, he loves Cally even though he sees "darkness" near her.

Warren Kapp: Geneva and Cally's octogenarian attorney friend, billed as the "Melvin Belli of Glasse County."

Zoe Jackson: Rising star in Geneva's clothing design business.

York Lazar: Cally's brother. His life's work is teaching martial arts.

Daphne Dupree: Aunt to the Lazar siblings, sister to their late mother. A former legal secretary, she's cheerfully dying of cancer.

Pilar Vaughn: Daphne Dupree's sixteen-year-old caretaker. But who is Pilar related to?

Bob Ungerman: Aunt Daphne's beau, a tax attorney with heart.

Earl Lazar: Uncle and godfather to the Lazar siblings, brother to their late father, and a former firefighter.

Victor Dupree: Uncle to the Lazars, brother to their late mother. He's a former English professor who now owns a bookstore.

Linda Dupree-Salcedo: Victor's daughter, and cousin to the Lazar siblings. She programs computers when she's not busy complaining.

Fern Salcedo: Linda's daughter, who's glad to work in her grandfather Victor's bookstore.

OTHERS

Melinda Lazar (with Zack, Cole, and Jessie in tow): Cally's sister, a cartoonist. She came with her husband, Zack, and her children for late dessert at Geneva's.

Arnot Lazar (with Barbara and Kinsey): Cally's brother. He also came with his wife and daughter for dessert. They all got a taste of murder instead.

Tom Weng: York's sweetie, an artist who visited Geneva's the day after Thanksgiving.

Virginia McFadden: Cally's client, friend, confidante, and a guest on Cally's massage table before Thanksgiving. A lucky woman, she never visited Geneva's home at all.

SPOKEN OF, THOUGH UNSEEN

Hugh Lazar: Deceased father to the five Lazar siblings. He was a scientist and inventor.

Simone Lazar nee Dupree: Deceased mother to the siblings. She was an artist.

Ingrid Lazar: Uncle Earl's wife, gone to her grave long ago.

Mary Dupree: Uncle Victor's more recently late wife.

Natalie Dupree: Another member of the family. They *think* she's still alive.

THE POLICE

Chief Kaifu: Of the Estados Police Department.

Sergeant Quantrill, Officer Rossetti, and Officer Khashoggi: Also of the EPD.

ONE

"So, Cally, who're these people you're sharing Thanks-giving with tomorrow?" Virginia McFadden demanded as she sat straight up on my massage table and looked me in the eye. The lilac overtones of her antiperspirant sat up with her. It seemed that her session was over. I checked my watch. It was eight P.M. Virginia was right on the dot.

A smile worked at my mouth as I returned Virginia's look. We were in my small house's warmest room, where I practiced my intuitive energy healing. I was feeling better than I had before I'd begun to help Virginia clear her meridians and smooth the ragged edges of her aura. My energy work seemed to do as much for me as it did for my clients some days.

Virginia McFadden was a longtime client who'd first come to me with liver problems. Those had cleared as her deep well of anger had emptied. Then the grief had appeared, like a child looking out from behind her mother's skirts, grief hidden for years by anger. Virginia had lived more than eighty years and had her ample share of grief. Though you wouldn't have guessed it as she cocked one white eyebrow and grinned at me. Whatever else Virginia's energetic body told me, her face told me she was curious. And I was ready to spill the beans. Virginia had become a friend over the years, and she was a good listener.

"Mostly, it's my family that's coming," I began. My almost smile stopped before it ripened. I let out an involuntary sigh. And I wondered why my family reunion would make me sigh. *Because both of your parents are dead?* a small voice suggested. I shook my head as if to will the voice away.

"The five lurid Lazars?" Virginia prodded.

"Yes, that would be us," I agreed, a second prospective smile tugging at my mouth with her description of me and my siblings. "My sister Geneva's hosting dinner. My brother York's coming. And Melinda and Arnot are putting in late appearances with their families. They have other obligations, too. See, Geneva set it up as a sort of reunion for the family members that are left. The uncles and aunts and stuff. We haven't seen each other in years."

"Hmm . . . not seeing family." Virginia tapped her temple and pretended to ponder. "Good idea," she concluded and winked.

I laughed aloud. Virginia probably knew my family as well as I did, after talking to our mutual friend, Warren Kapp. Kapp was as least as old as Virginia, a notorious attorney, and my cane-sparring partner . . . if you count sneaking up behind a person and trying to whack them as sparring. If he hadn't worn the same aftershave all these years, my whole body might have been dented from his attacks. I never knew if he would really hit me or not. I'd always used my own cane to stop him. And worse yet, he was a true gossip. He savored gossip the way some people savor good food and wine. And he always had plenty to enjoy. I was looking forward to seeing Kapp. It was the rest of the extended family that was bothering me. Though I couldn't have told anyone, especially myself, exactly why.

"Actually, I guess we all have seen each other, but mostly at different times," I mused. I looked around my cozy space, at the bookshelves, stuffed chairs, and artwork in the former living room. Somehow, these objects grounded me. *This is my home,* I reminded myself. *I'm not just a Lazar. I'm an individual. I'm me.*

Virginia cocked her other eyebrow. I wasn't the only intuitive person in the room. I was just the only professional.

"I see my brothers and sisters all the time," I explained. "And I see my uncle Earl fairly often, even though he lives in Los Angeles now—"

"Isn't he your godfather?" Virginia asked.

"You *have* been listening to Kapp!" I accused.

She just nodded.

"So, I suppose you know my uncle Victor's coming, too, with his daughter and granddaughter."

"Yep, Linda and Fern," she replied smugly. "From Colorado."

"And my aunt Daphne—"

"Poor thing's sick, isn't she?"

"Yeah, cancer," I muttered and sighed again. Maybe Aunt Daphne's illness was pulling all of those sighs out of me.

"You gonna work on her?" Virginia inquired.

"Only if she wants me to," I answered, bringing my mind back to the present. "I doubt that she will. Anyway, she'll be going back to Oregon after the visit. They'll all be going home. Daphne, Earl, Victor, and their families all used to live here in Glasse County, you know."

"I know," Virginia informed me. "How about York's new boyfriend, Tom Weng?" Virginia looked up as if seeing something beyond the room. Her voice deepened. "I went to his gallery showing downtown. His paintings seem absurd, but they're strangely moving."

"Tom might come," I told her, as my own mind's eye flashed on one of Tom's works, a woman stretched pietà style across a duck's lap. Weird, but compelling. Virginia was right. As usual. "And Kapp's coming. And this woman, Zoe, who works for Geneva. And a couple of people who're with Daphne. Anything else you want to know?" I grinned her way to soften my last question.

"Sure," Virginia snapped back. "What's the deal between Kapp and Geneva anyway? The old dog won't tell me."

"I don't know," I replied truthfully. I wanted to sigh again. "Geneva doesn't talk to me about important stuff. Our family isn't good about sharing secrets."

"Hey!" Virginia rasped. Then she patted my shoulder. "That's why they're called secrets. All families have them. Believe me."

"Yeah, I guess so," I muttered. I really was heading into a bad mood. Even in my warm room, I felt chilled. Secrets, the lurid Lazar legacy.

"How about Roy?" Virginia asked. "He's coming, isn't he? Aren't you two lovebirds together again for good?"

I blushed and nodded, my cold hands coming back to life with the mention of Roy's name.

"How about you?" I asked Virginia, putting some enthusiasm back into my voice. "What are you doing for Thanksgiving?"

"Yikes!" she squeaked. "The whole stinkin' family's coming to my house. Four generations' worth." She batted nearly invisible eyelashes. "Guess which generation *I'm* in?"

I chuckled dutifully.

"Gotta run, Cally," Virginia told me. Then she jumped off the table and did just that. I hoped I'd have that kind of energy in my eighties.

She was almost to the door when she spun around and loped back to hug me.

She held me for a while before letting go. Criminy, I loved Virginia. Then she sped out the door as I called out "Happy Thanksgiving" to her back.

I grabbed my cane and walked into the former dining room that currently held my business office. The cane was just insurance. At thirty-seven years of age, I shouldn't have needed the cane at all, but there was always the chance of my leg buckling, as it did every once in a while, and as it had the first time on the day my parents died more than twenty years ago. My leg had buckled before I'd even heard they were dead—

I stopped my thoughts right there. I knew they could circle for hours on the subject. I searched a wooden four-drawer cabinet and found Virginia's file, then sat down at my desk to add a few notes.

"Cally, darlin'," I heard from behind me. "Is Virginia gone then?"

It was my sweetie, Roy. He'd moved back in with me a few months ago. His presence made my small house on the hillside a home again. Even without turning, I could visualize him, small and slight with reddish brown hair, freckles, and features that were almost as sharp as mine, in a narrow face. And those intense golden eyes. My own hair and eyes were dark, my skin fair. And I wore glasses. Still, we might have been twins but for those and a few other differences. So our friends Joan and Dee-Dee told us. I breathed in, smelling his scent. My cat, Leona, slithered up before I let my breath out again, looking for something to shred, preferably a lap. If we'd had the three goats from the back hill there, we'd have had the whole family.

"Virginia is gone, indeed," I answered, trying to lend a little seduction to my tone. Roy put his hands on my shoulders as Leona leaped for my lap. Yes, I was home.

"I'm melting," I whispered. Can the Wicked Witch of the West sound sexy? I thought so.

"Cally," Roy breathed. Did he think she was sexy, too? "I gotta tell you something."

"Tell," I ordered languorously.

"Cally, it pains me to speak of it, but I see the darkness near you again."

All lusty thoughts fled my mind. Leona dug her nails in, then jumped from my lap, sensing the change in direction. "The darkness." Roy hadn't spoken for months of the darkness he used to see so regularly. For a long time, he'd thought the darkness was something harmful that he brought to our relationship, but I'd come near to convincing him otherwise. I'd hoped he wasn't seeing it at all anymore. I slowed my breathing and tried to think of light.

"Cally, are you all right, darlin'?" Roy asked softly, but then went on before I could answer. "I'm sorry I had to say so, but I truly do see darkness again—"

"I know," I cut him off, keeping my tone as light as the rest of me felt heavy. "It's my family."

"No, really—" He tried again.

"Really," I interrupted once more. "I hate these get-togethers. You're just feeling that."

"But—"

"Kiss me," I ordered, turning my chair around.

He did, and my working day turned into night. And the night was beautiful.

The next day we set off to Geneva's house in my old Honda Accord. I drove, and in a grocery bag on his lap, Roy held the eggplant dip, whole-grain bread sticks, and vegetable enchiladas I'd made for the feast. My brother York was a vegetarian as well as a martial artist. I wanted to compensate for the turkey that Geneva had insisted on cooking.

"It's strange to be going back to Geneva's," I told Roy.

Roy hadn't spoken of the darkness again, but I could see by the circles under his eyes that he'd been thinking of it when he should have been sleeping.

"How long did you make your home with your sister?" Roy asked.

I thought for a moment. "Three years, I guess," I calculated. "From age fifteen, when my parents died, till I went to college at eighteen."

"Cally, I know you worry about your parents passing the way they did—" Roy began.

"And it doesn't do me any good," I interrupted.

"Sometimes it does do good, darlin'," Roy argued softly. "You're a healer. You know you can't just pretend to forget these things. You know that's what's wrong with your leg."

"Oh, Roy," I whispered. "You're probably right. But today, I need to be here for Geneva. She was there for me."

"But these visits make you miss your mama and your papa," Roy went on. "I can see that."

As if a movie was suddenly projected onto my windshield, I saw my parents gardening together, laughing, as Pop pretended to be a tree, twisting in the wind. Then the image was gone again.

"It seemed like my parents were always laughing," I said to Roy.

He reached over and stroked my leg silently, encouraging me.

I told him more: about Mom's surreal artwork, light within light; my father's science experiments (he never quite got the solar oven going); our raucous dinners; family vacations. My throat was sore by the time we reached Geneva's. I wasn't sure why. It had only taken a few minutes to drive to her place, a few sentences. My sister Geneva and I both lived in the same town in Glasse County, after all. Estados, the same town my parents had lived in.

It was two o'clock when we walked up the familiar gravel driveway to Geneva's home under the clear, cold sky. Then we saw them. Two turkeys. Only they weren't stuffed. They were wild. Their bodies were dark with shining bands of bronze, silver, and cream on their feathers. The markings reminded me of a tabby cat's markings, but these guys were a lot bigger than most tabbies. At least in body. Their heads were tiny, and their legs looked like bent pencils.

"The Turkey Sisters," I breathed in awe.

"Who?" Roy asked before he saw them, too.

"Geneva's been talking about them for weeks," I whispered, tiptoeing now. "They took up residence a couple of months ago. They like to peck at her gravel."

The Turkey Sisters ignored us as we slipped past them.

"Are they safe on Thanksgiving, do you think?" Roy asked.

"Safe as we are," I answered. "Just don't eat any stuffing mix."

Roy let out a laugh, and the Turkey Sisters glanced up.

"Sorry," he apologized, and the Sisters went back to pecking.

We walked past flowering purple cabbages, rose-colored sweet alyssum, and late-blooming chrysanthemums in all the shades in between purple and rose. Those were my sister's colors.

If Roy and I hadn't guessed her color preferences by her garden, we would have been sure when we stepped through the front door into her expansive living room. Purple, magenta, periwinkle, ruby, lilac, orchid, berry, plum, mauve, and grape were all represented in rugs, wall hangings, and the fabric of the couches, love seat, and numerous chairs that circled the vast coffee table. The only earth tones were in the wood. My brother Arnot's custom-made coffee table, shelves, and side tables were all in cherrywood. The inherited piano and grandfather clock were walnut.

The design of the room was much like Geneva herself: neat, simple, and beautiful. Geneva owned her own clothing company, for which she happily designed, even in colors other than her favorites. And she managed her own company, too, although not quite so happily.

I stood still for a moment after we entered the living room, enjoying it as the work of art that it was. I ignored the people that were also collected in the room, then took a breath.

Roy put his free arm around my waist, still holding the grocery bag in his other hand. Whoa. I could smell the turkey cooking. I was ready to mingle.

"Happy Thanksgiving!" A wizened woman I didn't recognize greeted me. Her narrow face was gaunt, enlivened by eyebrows drawn in black and a black wig. She held the hand of a young woman, a teenager whose plump, bland features only served to highlight the elder woman's emaciation. I tried to open my mouth.

"This is Pilar," the elder woman went on, indicating the teenager whose hand she held. Pilar nodded, raising plucked russet eyebrows over makeup-laden eyes, but her mouth didn't smile. Then she turned back to the elder woman, a look of concern peeking out from her bland face.

Finally, I realized that this wizened woman was my aunt Daphne. Her aura winked at me and I saw death.

My leg buckled beneath me.

TWO

My cane might have just been insurance, but I was profoundly grateful for it in that moment. If I hadn't been holding my cane, I might have hit Geneva's mauve carpet the hard way. Or maybe not. Roy still held me around the waist. And he was looking at me with something verging on panic in his golden eyes. I pulled my features back together and stood up straight, breathing in and out slowly.

"Dack, I must have tripped," I said to my aunt Daphne after a few breaths. The room felt hot.

She smiled as if she believed me. Pilar frowned next to Daphne as if she wouldn't believe anything I had to say.

I didn't tell either of them that I'd seen death winking my way. My aunt Daphne knew she was dying. And she was okay with it. I saw it in her eyes, that look of joyous acceptance that some people have when they face death with courage of spirit.

What I *had* seen had shocked me far worse than my aunt's impending passage. I'd seen the death of my parents. As if in a dream, images of the explosion, the fire, and the instant of their startled faces had danced in my mind. I clenched my fingers around the handle of my cane. My mouth tasted sour. It was impossible for me to remember that stuff. I hadn't even been there when they'd died. I had no real visual memories. So what had I seen?

"Cally?" Roy tried from my side. For a moment, I wondered if he'd seen what I'd seen in that wink of time. I looked at his face and only perceived confusion. Of course, he hadn't seen what I had. He'd just seen my leg buckle.

"I'm fine now," I lied gently, swallowing the sourness in my mouth.

I smelled a familiar aftershave. I turned out of Roy's grip and raised my cane to meet Kapp's. Once I'd parried his strike, I whipped my cane around and tapped him lightly on his head where he combed his hair over his bald spot. I smiled for real, this time. Finally, I did feel better.

"Hooboy, Lazar!" Kapp barked. "Still as mean as ever, hitting an old man when he's down." He screwed up his bulldog face and scowled at me through his steel-rimmed glasses.

Aunt Daphne laughed. Kapp laughed back and reached for her hand.

"Ah, the charming Daphne Dupree, I presume," Kapp cooed and bent down to kiss the hand he held. Kapp could be a class act when he wasn't trying to bop me with his cane. I'd met him years ago when I'd been liberating some rose cuttings from the edge of his garden by moonlight. He'd raised his cane then, too. We'd become instant friends as we'd sparred and shouted at each other: Kapp shouting out penal and civil codes; me shouting that the cuttings in question had been drooping over the sidewalk and were fair game. Many years and cane battles later, he'd met my sister Geneva. I wasn't sure what they'd become exactly.

Kapp dropped Daphne's hand as a man that looked about ten years younger than Kapp's eighty-some walked up to join us. He had a wide, happily wrinkled, dark-skinned face, a broad nose, intense eyes, and gray, cropped hair that looked more like a halo than a natural. He viewed Kapp quizzically.

Kapp turned to him and stuck out his hand. "Warren Kapp, attorney at law," he announced. "Call me Kapp."

"Bob Ungerman, tax attorney," the other man parried. His voice was firm despite a slight tremor. "Call me Bob."

"Hah!" Kapp bleated. "The rooms are crawling with legal vermin."

Bob grinned for real.

"Bob's Daphne's dude," Pilar announced, looking up with affection as Bob slid in on Daphne's other side, his large hand slipping around her smaller one. Daphne leaned her head against his arm.

Kapp sighed theatrically. "Damn, the good ones are always taken," he complained. He threw his hands in the air.

A hint of pink colored Aunt Daphne's cheeks.

"She's spoken for," Bob declared affectionately.

"And this is my niece Cally," Daphne introduced me. Then she looked pointedly at Roy.

"Oh," I mumbled, taking my cue. "And my dude, Roy Beaumont. Glad to meet you, Bob."

Bob held out his hand and I shook it as Roy greeted Daphne. I could feel a tremor beneath Bob's firm grip. Was he ill, too? Parkinson's disease?

Then I heard Uncle Earl's voice. I looked up and saw him speeding toward our group. My stomach clenched. In my father's brother, Earl, I always saw what my father might have looked like if he'd been allowed to age as long as Earl. Uncle Earl had the narrow Lazar face and my father's bone structure. But he didn't have Pop's animation. Instead, Earl's eyes were puffy and dim, his wavy hair gray and styled, his long-nosed, thin-lipped smile wooden.

"Cally, you're prettier every time I see you," Earl told me. He coughed behind his hand before continuing. "And probably smarter, too. Give your old godfather a hug." He extended his arms to embrace me. I leaned into his embrace and smelled smoke as usual. My uncle Earl was an ex-firefighter and a smoker. Go figure.

Once out of his embrace, I worked up a smile for Earl. My uncle Earl had tried his best to be a true godfather after my parents had died. He'd helped all five of us siblings with finances, education, everything. And he'd agreed that I should live with my sister Geneva after my parents' deaths. For that and more, I owed him. But he wasn't my father. He was only my father's brother. As usual, I wished I could love him more than I did. I worked harder on my smile.

"Uncle Earl," I said. "This is my boyfriend, Roy." I didn't tell my uncle that Roy was my roommate, too. My godfather was old-fashioned about some things. Actually, he was old-fashioned about a lot of things. "Roy, this is my uncle Earl Lazar."

"Well, it's good to finally meet you, young man!" Earl told Roy, his voice booming suddenly. It always seemed to me that there was something wrong with Earl's sound system. One minute his voice would be quiet, the next it could blast you out of your chair. And the fluctuations didn't seem to depend on content. Maybe it was all the years he'd spent bellowing out orders as a firefighter.

"Good to meet you, sir," Roy answered. The "sir" was a good touch, just the thing to get on Earl's good side, not that Roy was capable of manipulation. He just respected his elders. Actually, Roy respected just about anyone who didn't give him reason to do otherwise. Roy was a good man. He couldn't help it any more than Earl could control his voice.

"Well, you'd better treat our Cally right, or you'll have this Lazar to answer to," Earl went on, his voice quiet again. He smiled, but there was no doubt in my mind that he was giving Roy a serious message.

"Oh, foot! Cally's too wonderful to treat any other way, sir," Roy responded. "She's very precious to me—"

"Hah!" Kapp snorted from our side. "Roy's good to Cally because she'll bash him with her cane otherwise."

Roy laughed before I could object to Kapp's words. "Bash" Roy, indeed! It was Kapp who needed bashing. But Bob and Daphne were laughing, too.

Earl didn't laugh though. He pulled a pack of cigarettes from his pocket instead, eyeing Kapp suspiciously.

My sister Geneva showed up the minute Earl pulled out the cigarettes, her finger pointing at him.

"Outside with those things, Uncle Earl!" she commanded.

"This is a smoke-free environment. And even you will abide by the rules."

I thought I heard Earl mumbling something like "Still as bossy as ever," as he exited the door we'd entered.

Geneva turned to me and gave me a hug. I returned *her* hug with enthusiasm. Bossy, yes, but Geneva had always loved me. Some qualities are hard to beat.

Geneva looked me up and down when she'd released me from her hug.

I wriggled in my thrift-shop turtleneck, fleece jacket, and jeans. Geneva designed clothing for a living. Her own silk outfit suggested a tuxedo, but not a man's tuxedo. The cutaway jacket rippled far too sensuously to be male as she stepped back to take a better look at me.

"At least the turtleneck's purple," she finally concluded.

I breathed in relief. Geneva had been my surrogate mother for years, but her opinion still mattered to me. She was fifty-two this year and proud of it. Geneva had the same narrow face and sharp features that all the Lazars (and all the Duprees, for that matter) shared, but her full lips and haughty eyebrows gave her a regal presence no matter what she was wearing.

"And Cally's comfortable," Aunt Daphne threw in. "That's always a point for style."

Geneva grinned, looking slightly less regal for a moment. "Ah, Aunt Daphne, how well you know me," she purred. She stood even a little taller and shook her long mane of salt-and-pepper hair. "Simplicity and comfort. Those are what I strive for in my clothing. Feminism and elegance united . . ."

Geneva was still lecturing on clothing design when Earl came back through the front door, smelling smokier than he had before.

My uncle Victor Dupree joined the group of us at the door. I had to remind myself that he was in his late seventies, pushing eighty. He looked a bit like a bespectacled elf with what was left of his silver hair, his age-spotted skin, and the twinkle in his Dupree eyes. Or maybe he simply

looked like the retired English professor he was, with his
long nose and raised brows. Uncle Victor didn't smell of
smoke. He smelled like undiluted herbal tea.

"Earl, are you still smoking?" Victor demanded, reaching over his shoulder into his ever present backpack. "You
must realize that smoking's not healthy. I've got something
here that will help you quit."

"Please, no more herbs!" Daphne pleaded unconvinc-
ingly. "Don't tell me you have more herbs than you've already offered me."

"I always have more herbs, little sister," Victor assured
her with an evil grin, pulling out a bottle and brandishing
it. "And this one is to help Earl quit smoking."

But Earl had already drifted away from the group. I
hadn't seen him go. Maybe the firefighting had taught him
the art of hasty retreats.

"More herbs, more interests, more theories," Daphne
added with affection for her brother. "How's your bookstore doing, darling?"

Victor shot a look over his shoulder to where his daughter Linda and granddaughter, Fern, sat on a plum-colored
sofa.

"I ain't getting rich," he answered in a Bugs Bunny
voice. "But it keeps Fern off the streets, if you know what
I mean."

"Is Fern working in your bookstore?" Bob asked.

"Yes, and she's writing a novel, too," he told us proudly.
"Not bad for a recent college graduate. She's actually got
some very good themes going. You see, her novel's a biotech
thriller with some really great subplots concerning viruses,
the higher self, and martial law."

"Any herbs in it?" I couldn't help but asking.

Victor chortled and rubbed his hands together like a
maniac. "There will be if I have anything to do with it!
How's your energy practice doing, Cally?"

"Energetic as all get-out," Kapp answered for me. I
might have been quick with my cane, but Kapp's mouth
was the fastest in the West.

I laughed with the others. Maybe this family get-together wouldn't be so bad after all.

"Hey, Cally," I heard from behind me. It was my cousin Linda. I could recognize the constant complaint in her voice anywhere. I turned. "So, I guess your uncle Earl still thinks you and the rest of the Lazars can do no wrong," she dug in, jealous as always of the Lazar siblings.

Maybe the get-together *would* be so bad after all. I decided to ignore the dig, looking into Linda's face. Linda had the long Dupree nose, but her features weren't as narrow as the rest of ours. Her cheekbones were sharp but wide. Her mother, Mary, had been of Scandinavian descent. Linda's large, blue eyes were as discontented as usual. I knew she was about Geneva's age, but Linda didn't wear her age as well as my sister did, for all the style of her bleached, cropped hair and her carefully layered clothing.

"How are you?" I asked politely. I could feel my shoulders bunching up with the effort. "How's your husband . . ." I floundered. I couldn't remember her husband's name.

"We're divorced," she told me, crossing her arms. At least I didn't have to remember his name.

"Are you still in computer programming?" I tried again.

"Yeah, I'm working for a start-up," she said, the vocal whine lessening. "One of the start-ups that didn't go under."

"Yet," Victor muttered.

Linda ignored her father. "State-of-the-art stuff, you know," she expanded. "Big bucks."

"Great," I told her.

"So, is this the boyfriend?" she demanded, pointing at Roy.

"This is the boyfriend," I conceded. "His name's Roy. Roy, this is my cousin Linda."

"Glad to meet—"

"So, are you still doing all that weird 'healing' stuff?" she interrupted him.

Same old Linda. I'd wanted to kick her when I was a baby, and I wanted to kick her then. My leg was actually twitching. I reminded myself that there was a good person somewhere inside Linda, obviously somewhere very deep inside. And I remembered Linda's older sister, Natalie. She'd been even worse. Natalie was a terror. I just hoped *she* wasn't here. Given that I hadn't seen Natalie at a family get-together for more than twenty years, I figured my hope wasn't unrealistic.

"Yes, I still have an energy practice," I muttered.

"So, whaddaya do, like talk to ghosts or something?"

I took a deep breath. A new voice answered for me.

"Oh, Mom. Chill, okay?" I saw Fern beside her mother. It was hard to believe they were related, except for the shared long nose. Fern's face and body were round, her skin toast-colored, her hair black, and her eyes happy.

"Hey, Cally," she said in greeting. "How are you doing? I can't remember the last time I saw you. I wanted to talk to you about viruses."

"Told ya!" Victor crowed.

Fern grabbed me by the hand and dragged me over to the plum-colored sofa where she and her mother had been sitting, introducing herself to Roy along the way. I couldn't help but remember the last time we'd met, even if she didn't, at the funeral of her grandmother Mary, Victor's wife. The herb thing had come to Victor after his wife had died. And the pop psychology. And the philosophy. Sometimes I wondered—

"So, the real question is: Are viruses intelligent?" Fern announced the moment my bottom hit the plush sofa. Roy sat on her other side, still holding the grocery bag we'd come with. Turkey smells wafted our way, and I remembered why we were here again.

I thought for a moment. "Well, I've never talked to one, but if you look at the actions of viruses, they seem intelligent—"

"Yeah, yeah! That's it exactly," Fern interjected. She nodded frantically. "They mutate if they're in danger; they win the battle with drugs. But people think that they're incapable of intelligence because they're small."

"And simply because folks can't see them clearly," Roy put in. "Because our microscopes aren't good enough to really study their complexity. People underestimate things they don't understand."

Fern looked at Roy with adoration in her eyes. Little did she know when she'd grabbed me that she'd gotten a die-hard sci-fi buff in the bargain. Roy lived and breathed science fiction.

"Yeah!" Fern agreed. She shifted on the sofa to give Roy her undivided attention. I smiled behind her, glad that Roy had someone to talk to. "People keep telling me I should write about bacteria because they're more intelligent, but if they're so intelligent, then how come antibiotics work against them? The viruses are totally in the driver's seat, even if they are little. . . ."

Roy lowered the grocery bag onto the floor as Fern went on. And Fern did go on. I was glad to hear it. She'd been quieter before, lost in her dreams. It sounded like her dreams were going on paper now.

Roy was talking about the potential complexity of quarks when I looked up and saw my brother York standing alone in the far corner of the room. As usual, York stood in a martial arts stance, balanced and centered, his arms hanging lightly by his sides. And as usual, there was no smile on his handsome Lazar face. He wore jeans and a work shirt, his long dark hair tied back in a ponytail.

I got up from the sofa. Roy and Fern were deep in excited conversation. I picked up our grocery bag and walked over to York, keeping my back straight and my stride even. I could feel his eyes evaluating my moves.

York had taught me cane-fu. His Zartent studio, where he trained the disabled in customized martial arts, was flourishing. I'd been his first guinea pig. I was the baby of the family. He was the next up the sibling ladder from me. York and I were about as close as siblings can be, but our relationship had its prickly side.

"Where's Tom?" I asked.

York shrugged noncommittally. "Tom had his own family thing to do," York answered slowly and deliberately. "He might show tomorrow."

"Come help me with the food," I suggested, and York shrugged again. He liked family get-togethers even less than I did.

At least he followed me when I walked through the dining area to the adjoining kitchen. The turkey was cooked and seated on a platter atop a sky blue table, among crockery in a multitude of colors as bright as a crayon set. I took in the smells through my nose: not just turkey, but potatoes, yams, sweet pumpkin, and broccoli. I set out the eggplant dip and bread sticks. The vegetable enchiladas needed heating, so I stuck them in the microwave, hoping York wouldn't object. He didn't. Then I got worried.

"Those are your enchiladas in the nuker," I pointed out. York hated microwave ovens.

He shrugged for the third time.

"York, are you—"

But Geneva burst into the kitchen before I could ask York anything. And she wasn't alone.

"Cally, meet Zoe, my new designer," Geneva ordered, practically shoving a tall, slender woman near my age into my arms. Zoe could have been a clothing model for her own designs. Her face was fragile, with dark eyes under tiny, jeweled glasses, her nose perfect, and her lips fashionably bee-stung. Her hair was a fountain of black, gold-tipped tendrils. She wore a black cotton shirt, with sewn-in necklaces of gold and pearl and jewels, over black cotton pants.

"Oooh, is this your little sister?" she asked Geneva, her voice girlish. Then she turned to me. "Geneva talks about you all the time," she told me.

"Oh . . . um, thank you," I said, not knowing whether her words had actually been a compliment. Geneva might have been complaining or worrying or both when she talked about me for all I knew.

"Don't you love Zoe's outfit?" Geneva demanded. "It's one of her own designs."

"Gorgeous," I replied honestly. I was ready to love Zoe's outfit even if I wasn't ready to love Zoe.

York said nothing. Maybe he'd met Zoe before. Or maybe he didn't like the clothes. With York, it was better not to assume anything.

At least Zoe was good at preparing a meal for service. In fifteen minutes, she, Geneva, York, and I had the food on the long cherrywood table, which had been set ahead of time in the dining room. It smelled and looked wonderful.

Geneva took her seat at one end of the table, and York took his at the other end. I sat next to Geneva, with Roy on my right and Earl across from me. Then everyone seemed to be eating and talking at the same time.

I told Geneva that Roy and I had spotted the Turkey Sisters.

"Aren't you tempted to pluck 'em and eat 'em?" Zoe asked, then giggled.

York glared her way in vegetarian menace.

But it was Daphne who spoke, next to Zoe.

"Don't I remember you?" Daphne asked, pinching together her drawn-in eyebrows. "Your name is Zelda. Now I remember. Zelda, that's right."

"My name is Zoe!" Geneva's new designer snapped back. Whoa. I wondered what that was about.

Apparently, Daphne didn't. She just went on. "So, York," she said pleasantly. "I was hoping to meet your friend Tom."

"He couldn't come," York answered briefly. Then he looked up and attempted a smile for my aunt. "Maybe he'll be here tomorrow."

"Oh, that would be so nice," Daphne said. "I've seen his artwork. I like it very much."

York nodded, blushing. His social skills were improving.

I took a bite of stuffing. Geneva made it with almonds and raisins. Yum.

"I painted a watercolor for you, Aunt Daphne," Fern spoke up. "You know, flowers and stuff. I'm no Tom Weng, but I thought you'd like it. I've got it in the car."

"Have I told you that you're my favorite grandniece?" Daphne replied. "I can hardly wait to see it."

Daphne blew Fern a kiss, and Fern mimed catching the kiss and depositing it onto the tip of her nose. Pilar frowned as most of us chuckled. Linda just rolled her eyes.

"Victor, I haven't seen you since Mary passed on," Earl offered up as I took a bite of coleslaw.

"Yes, indeed," Victor murmured, and his smile was momentarily gone. "It was rough to lose her. Even now, after five years. But you know that. How long has your Ingrid been gone?"

"Must be twenty-five years now," Earl calculated. "But I always had the children. That helped." He looked fondly at me, then Geneva, and then York. My arms went up in goose bumps. I swallowed the coleslaw left in my mouth. It might have been made of rocks and mayonnaise. Earl and his late wife, Ingrid, had never had children of their own. When he said "children," he meant us. "I couldn't be more pleased by the way these youngsters have turned out. All so successful in their own fields. Melinda and Arnot, too."

"And you always loved Simone, didn't you?" Daphne murmured. "Always Simone."

"We all did," Victor added and shook his head.

I stopped even trying to eat then. Simone was my mother's name. I hadn't heard it used like that in years. Daphne pronounced it the French way, See-moan. And my memory saw and my mind moaned. Roy reached for my hand under the table.

From my blur of thought, I heard a chair being pushed back. Linda rushed from the room.

THREE

"The change," my uncle Victor pronounced. There was awe in his voice. He held a forkful of coleslaw suspended in the air. "My own daughter's going through the change of life. Would you believe it? And she has a bladder infection as well."

With a look on his face that was almost reverential, he stared past Linda's chair to the bathroom where she had escaped. Holy menopause? Then he seemed to shake himself out of his own thoughts.

"Listen," he continued, whispering. He bent across the long table conspiratorially, his eyes alive with ideas under his wire-rimmed glasses. "I have a theory that the bladder infection is really her mind/body rebelling from the change. She's afraid of her bodily dynamic just when she might be rejoicing. Menopause can be a time of glorious transition, when a woman comes into her own. I've been reading up on it—"

"Reading may be groovy, Uncle Victor," Geneva cut in dryly while spooning cranberry sauce onto her plate. "But you're not the one having the hot flashes—"

"Or the mood swings," Daphne added. I saw that most of her meal had gone untouched. Maybe she'd have room for dessert. "As I remember, I was ready to shoot someone when I went through menopause."

"Not you, Aunt Daphne!" Fern objected. She bent forward, as if challenging her great-aunt to tell more.

"Oh, not really, my sweet," Daphne conceded. "But it certainly felt that way. I'm glad I didn't know Bob then. He would have been in fear for his life."

Kapp snorted appreciatively. Daphne chuckled and gently lay the back of her light hand against Bob's dark cheek.

"How long have you two been, you know, dating?" Fern asked.

Now, that was an interesting question. This was the first time I'd met Bob, or heard of his existence for that matter.

"Quite a few happy years," Daphne answered, or didn't answer, quietly. "Ah, so many happy times. Bob thought our relationship might not be appreciated because of his race, so we kept a low profile at first."

"We met when Daphne moved to Oregon," Bob offered quietly. I could see that he was uncomfortable with the topic. Bob's skin wasn't dark enough to cover the flush spreading beneath it.

There was a quiet moment. Then Kapp weighed in on the race issue.

"You might have been right to worry," he declared, tapping his fork on his plate, a serious look on his face for a change. "Sad, but true. Things have changed in this country, but not fast enough."

"My dad's Hispanic," Fern put in, through a mouthful of York's homemade nutloaf. "When I was little, some kids used to give me a bunch of . . . you know, stuff about it, but now everyone thinks it's cool. Everyone *I* care about, anyway."

"I know menopause can be difficult," Victor started in again. "But there are many herbs that can help: primrose oil, black cohosh, licorice, dong quai—"

"Dong quai for me, Argentina!" Kapp sang out.

I groaned as bursts of laughter filled the dining room. I began eating again. The stuffing *was* good. And the coleslaw. And my own vegetable enchiladas. And the yams . . .

Linda finally opened the bathroom door just as I tasted

the turkey. It was tender and juicy, perfectly done. I looked down the table to where York ate sullenly, and I took a bite of nutloaf as penance. It seemed to me that Linda had been gone an awfully long time. I glanced at her as she stomped toward the table. Her makeup was blurry around her eyes. Had she been crying?

She slammed into her chair without a word and stabbed at a piece of turkey with her fork. The rest of us went quiet, too. I felt a rush of compassion for Linda. It was probably bad enough just to be going through menopause. But having your father analyze it every hot flash of the way? I wanted to reach out to her. But when I turned to her and caught her eye, she glared back my way as if she'd heard my thought and didn't appreciate it. *Sorry,* I sent to her. If there was any chance she'd actually heard my first thought, maybe she'd hear my second.

Earl coughed, and Zoe started talking about fashion, as Geneva beamed. Zoe said that the country might be more conservative again, but that women still wanted elegance and simplicity. She might have been quoting Geneva. She probably *was* quoting Geneva. My belly was full. It felt stretched like over-tight clothing. I looked at Zoe's perfect face and listened to her high-pitched voice critically. Something about her made me cringe. *Jealousy.* The word slithered into my mind. I tried it on for size. Yes, jealousy. Geneva had adopted Zoe. Let the sibling rivalry begin. I took in a breath. If I was already having mood swings like this, I wasn't sure how I was going to handle menopause. I tried to think of something nice to say to Zoe. I was still trying when Roy spoke up.

"Well, I do believe you share Geneva's vision," he put in. "That must be very gratifying."

My face muscles tightened into an imitation smile.

"Oh, Zoe has her own vision, too," Geneva added. "It's like working with a better part of myself."

Keerups! Geneva was never cloying. What was wrong with her? *Jealousy,* I reminded myself. It wasn't what was wrong with Geneva. It was what was wrong with me.

"Oooh, thank you," Zoe cooed.

Linda caught my eye and raised an eyebrow. Did she understand what I was feeling? Or was she making fun of Zoe? Or of me? I didn't want to reach out to Linda anymore.

"Hooboy, I'm full," Kapp announced. "I feel like I ate a whole Turkey Sister, feathers and all. Or maybe both of them."

Everyone started groaning then. All that food, and we'd all done our best Thanksgiving duty. I knew I had.

"I am most surely well stuffed," Roy agreed. "Aunt Daphne, Linda? I'm wondering if you might be a tad more comfortable in the living room."

"What a lovely thought," Daphne replied. She turned my way. "You hold onto this one, Cally. He's got a sweet nature, through and through."

Roy blushed as I smirked.

"Just like you, Cally," she expanded. "You two make a fine pair."

It was my turn to blush. And Roy didn't even smirk. *He* was sweet.

Linda muttered something under her breath that I couldn't hear. I was just as glad I couldn't make out her words.

Daphne rose from the table, looking as frail as she really was. Bob and Pilar jumped up simultaneously, and each took one of her arms, guiding her into the living room. I picked up the nearest plates and began bussing them into the kitchen. Roy followed my example as Linda followed Daphne and her helpers into the living room.

"Cally, darlin'?" Roy whispered once we were in the kitchen. "How are you holding up?"

"Better," I told him honestly. I put my stack of dishes on the kitchen counter. "Thanks for being so sweet-natured." I pinched his cheek. "Cute, too."

"Aw, Cally," he murmured, embarrassed. But I knew, as embarrassed as he was, he was also pleased. I grabbed his stack of dishes and set them next to mine. Then I pulled him to me to give him a kiss.

It was one of those kisses that might have counted as a meditation if the content of my absolute focus had been a little different.

"Hey, you two, cut that out!" Geneva snapped from behind Roy.

I pulled back in record time, but Roy's lips came with me. We just missed falling into the sink before Roy stood up straight again.

I looked over Roy's shoulder to confront Geneva. I wasn't fifteen years old anymore! But my big sister was chuckling.

"That was fun," she cackled and started issuing clean up orders.

"I—" I began, raising my cane for emphasis, but then I thought better of it. Geneva had put a lot into this dinner. She deserved a little fun . . . but not too much.

Roy only said, "Yes, ma'am," and began scraping dishes.

I went out to the dining room table for another load, passing Zoe on the way.

I peeked into the living room. Bob, Pilar, and Daphne were all on the lilac sofa. Kapp was in the easy chair next to them, regaling my aunt with stories. Linda sat on the other side of the room, her arms crossed.

"I met your niece Cally while she was stealing flowers from my garden—" Kapp began.

"I wasn't stealing," I shouted. "And he didn't win the cane battle!"

"Hah!" he replied, and went on with his version of the story.

York sidled up to me, a serving dish in each hand. "Geneva in the kitchen?" he asked.

"Yep," I told him.

Fern and Victor were clearing the table, too, and chattering in happy bursts. Earl still sat at his place, his eyes out of focus. Poor Uncle Earl. I wondered if he was remembering better times.

York sighed and turned toward the kitchen.

"York, what's up with you?" I whispered urgently.

York turned back to me. "I don't know," he murmured. "But something's not right here. Maybe I just hate family gatherings, but still—"

"Is it 'cause Tom didn't come?"

He shrugged. "Maybe," he finally conceded. "But it feels like more than that. Like some kind of danger."

"You and Roy," I muttered.

"Did Roy say something?" York demanded. If he hadn't been holding those platters in his hands, he probably would have grabbed my arm.

"Just the darkness stuff," I said, waving my hand dismissively. I wanted to feel better about this day, not worse. I didn't tell York I'd seen death winking earlier. Instead, I turned to the table and began gathering silverware as fast as I could. York sighed again and headed toward the kitchen.

By the time I followed him in, everyone seemed to be doing an assigned task. Victor was on garbage and recycling detail with Fern. Roy was washing the dishes too big to go into the dishwasher, and Zoe was drying them, giggling. Yuk! Geneva was loading the dishwasher with rinsed dishes. And York was putting leftovers into the refrigerator. Zoe giggled again. I dumped the silverware and went back into the dining room, breathing deeply. The table was almost clear, but it still smelled like Thanksgiving. I found some napkins and stacked them. At least Earl was gone. I tried to think about what York had said, but my mind wouldn't stay with it. I felt the texture of the napkins. I knew they were linen, but they felt almost silken. Perfect. Geneva wouldn't settle for anything less, I was sure.

When I returned to the kitchen, Geneva was talking about her houseguests.

"So, Aunt Daphne, Bob, and Pilar are all staying here tonight," she declared. "I don't think Daphne should be in a motel."

"Are Bob and Aunt Daphne sharing a bedroom?" Fern probed.

Geneva laughed, shaking her head. "Don't you think that's their business?" she asked. Still, her voice was gentle.

"Fern doesn't think *anything* interesting isn't her business," Victor answered for his granddaughter. He reached for her, putting his hand on her shoulder. "She might use it in a book someday, she always tells me."

"Just wait until I'm famous!" Fern rapped out in a mock huff. Then she hugged her grandfather. "Boy, has he got me totally pegged."

I smiled, glad to forget York's worries . . . and my own.

When we were all finally done, Geneva declared it was time for drinks in the living room.

Zoe looked at her watch. "Oh my gosh, it's time for me to go!" she chirped. "I'm supposed to be at my aunt Jane's by now. She's a wacko, but she's fun."

"A little like our family," I offered.

She giggled at that one, but she didn't answer.

"It was good to meet you, Cally." She began her retreat and reached out to shake my hand. I could tell she wanted me to like her. I decided to try. I grasped her hand.

"You, too," I told her. Then she made the rounds, shaking everyone's hand.

Geneva and I followed her out to the living room, where she continued her routine. Until she reached Daphne.

"Ms. Dupree," she intoned seriously, looking at her fashionable shoes. "I apologize if I've been rude. The past—"

"Don't worry, Zoe," Daphne cut her off. "The past is the past."

Zoe gave Geneva a quick hug, and she was gone out the door. And just as quickly, the kitchen crew came pouring in.

"Who'd like a drink?" Geneva asked.

Earl coughed and said he'd be glad to pour. But he had a lot of competition. Victor offered his services. Kapp insisted on the duty. Even Roy and York got in on the act. Only Bob seemed to act counter to his testosterone.

Linda just shook her head and went back to the bathroom.

"Cranberry juice," Victor diagnosed. "Linda could use some cranberry juice for her bladder infection. I don't suppose you've got any?"

"Sure, I do," Geneva assured him. "In the fridge with York's water and Cally's apple juice."

"And crème de menthe?" Bob asked for Daphne.

"Of course," Geneva replied, her face beaming. "Wherever Aunt Daphne is, there's crème de menthe waiting. We all know it's what she loves. It's in the liquor cabinet in the dining room as usual."

"Me and only me for crème de menthe, I suppose," Daphne sighed. "Even Bob won't drink the stuff."

Four men ran off to pour it for her. Pilar followed them. Victor was already back in the kitchen scaring up some cranberry juice for his daughter.

We were all talking about our favorite tipples when Linda came out of the bathroom. Victor strode up to her with a glass of red liquid in his hand.

"Cranberry juice, honey," he announced to his daughter.

Linda took one look at the glass in his hand and started screaming.

"I suppose you told them all!" she started out.

"Well, I—" he tried.

"All right, I'm a menopausal maniac!" she went on. "Are you happy now? Oh, and let's not forget the bladder infection which I shouldn't have since I'm supposed to be happy about my 'glorious life transition.' I'm sure he told you all about that, too!"

I realized I was nodding my head and stopped. She didn't really have any evidence if we all kept silent.

"Well, fine," Linda muttered. "Enjoy yourself, Dad. The drink's on me." She turned to go to the bathroom once more.

"Wow, Mom's done it again," Fern stage-whispered. "A menoplosion!"

"Hee, hee!" spurted out of my mouth, and we were all giggling.

"She's really okay," Fern assured us. "She does the

explosion thing, and then she feels better. She may be my mom, but she's totally cool."

"I don't blame her a bit," Daphne agreed, and Pilar showed up with an etched glass goblet containing Daphne's crème de menthe.

Daphne thanked her, and York arrived with apple juice for me. He turned to Pilar.

"And what would you like to drink, Pilar?" York asked.

Pilar's face changed before my eyes. He might have asked her to marry him. No longer bland, her round features were radiant . . . and beautiful.

"Oh my God," she breathed. "Um, a diet cola."

"I'll find one," York told her. I was proud of him. He didn't say one word about the potential toxicity of diet drinks.

"Wow," Pilar breathed. She led me to a love seat and sat us both down. "Is your brother married or what?"

I almost said, "or what," but I couldn't bear to see the adoration on Pilar's young face vanish so quickly.

"He's not married," I told her instead.

"No lie?"

"No lie," I agreed. I didn't tell her that York was gay. But I didn't want her heart broken later. "I think he has someone he's interested in, though," I added.

"Still, I'm really psyched," Pilar chirped enthusiastically. "I think he kinda likes me."

"I think so, too," I compromised.

"Cally, I want to talk to you," she blurted out then, not looking me in the face.

"What?" I asked gently.

"I'm worried about Daphne," she said to her lap.

"Uh-huh." I wanted to touch her, but I wasn't sure she'd appreciate the gesture.

"You do some kind of healing, right?" she demanded, finally looking me in the face. Her fair skin was pale under her makeup. I could smell her perspiration over the cooking smells of the house.

"Yes, I do," I admitted, meeting her eyes. "But, Pilar,

you have to understand. I only do healing work on people who request my services."

Pilar looked back at her lap. I thought I saw tears in her eyes.

"Pilar, does Daphne want me to do a healing on her?"

Pilar shook her head hard. I could hear her sniffling. Then she wiped her eyes on the sleeve of her oversized shirt and looked back up at me.

"No," she told me, her voice clogged. "I even asked her. I told her I was stressing, that she shouldn't lose hope. But Daphne just told me she was fine. She says there's a time to die. That that's how it's gonna go down. But, I . . . I . . ."

"You don't want her to die," I finished for her, putting my arm cautiously around her shoulder. My heart actually hurt, just touching her. I tried to remind myself that the human condition wasn't unfair, just hard to understand.

She nodded, and edged into my one-armed embrace.

"Pilar, you love Daphne, don't you?"

She nodded again, her tears flowing.

"Then you know how much she loves you. Don't you think she'd work with me if she thought it could keep her alive?"

"Yeah, I guess so." Pilar's head came up, her eyes squinted in thought.

"Sometimes people just know it's their time to go," I murmured, holding her a little tighter and wishing I could tell her something different. "All I could do for Daphne at this point is to make her more comfortable. Do you understand?"

"Yeah." Pilar sighed. "That's kinda what she told me herself. Even Bob's just letting the Parkinson's thing eat him alive. I don't get it—"

"Does Bob have Parkinson's disease?" I asked.

"Yeah, I think so anyway. But Daphne's the one who's really sick, you know."

I nodded. Daphne was dying of cancer, and Bob probably had Parkinson's disease; who was going to take care of Pilar? I took a deep breath and went back into lecture mode.

"Pilar, Daphne has the kind of acceptance of her

condition that's like a healing itself. *She's* okay. I don't know exactly what you're going through, but I know how hard it is. You're the one who has to heal, to accept."

"That's what she says!" Pilar cried out. Then she lowered her voice again. "I'm like 'hel-lo,' aren't you going to try and do something, and she's all kinda serene or something. She's just worried about me."

"How do you know Daphne?" I asked.

Pilar shrugged. "I kinda take care of her and stuff." She looked at her lap again.

"Well, you're doing a good job. And part of your job is to take care of yourself."

"Like *I* need healing?" she asked.

I nodded.

"Maybe," she whispered.

"Listen," I told her, grabbing a business card from my pocket. "I'm going to give you my phone number. If you want to work with me, call."

"Me, but not Daphne." She raised her head again.

"Yep," I told her.

"I'll think about it," Pilar promised. "Maybe before we go back to Oregon." She took the card from my hand. Then she rolled toward me and gave me a real embrace before jumping up from the love seat and running back over to sit with my aunt Daphne. They were both strong women, I reminded myself, even if Pilar was only a teenager.

"Hey, Lazar!" Kapp shouted.

Geneva, Earl, and York all looked up at Kapp from the couch they shared with Roy.

"I mean, Cally," he amended. "Was this your father's clock?"

I ambled over to the eight-foot grandfather clock that was clicking away.

"Yeah, it was Pop's," I told him.

"What's this cord thing for?" he wanted to know.

"Oh, Pop rigged that up, so you didn't have to reach behind the clock to turn the chimes on and off," I explained. "He liked to hear the chimes, so he turned them on during the day. But he turned them off at night. See, you can tell by the red tag that they're turned off. If you pull the other end of the cord, a blue tag will show up to tell you the chimes are on again." I paused and added, "Don't pull it. You don't want to hear the chimes."

"Smart man, your father," Kapp muttered.

All I could do was nod. I looked at the walnut clock with its moon and sun, pendulums, day counter, and brass hands. Yes, my father had been a smart man.

"I remember that clock," Linda commented from behind me. "It's a beautiful piece of craftsmanship."

I turned and looked at my cousin suspiciously. Had someone taken over her body? She was being civil.

Fern walked up and put an arm around her mother.

"See," she crowed. "I told you Mom was really a human being."

"This from a girl who won't take computer courses," Linda returned, rolling her eyes. But a smile fluttered at her lips.

"I love you, too, Mom," Fern threw back and kissed her mother on the cheek.

"Pilar, can you take me to the bathroom, sweetie?" I heard Daphne's voice. It sounded strained.

Pilar took command, hoisting Daphne up and guiding her across the room. I wondered how old Pilar was.

"Who is Pilar to your aunt Daphne?" Linda whispered in my ear once the bathroom door was shut behind them.

"I don't know," I answered honestly.

"Are you sure?" Linda prodded. She narrowed her eyes.

"Mom, if anyone would know, I would," Fern put in. "And I haven't been able to find out either."

Linda turned to Kapp, her eyebrows raised in question.

He shrugged his shoulders.

We talked about Fern's job at the bookstore for a while. That was a relief.

Daphne and Pilar came back, and afternoon moved into evening as I made the rounds, chatting up Bob about tax accounting, Daphne about Bob, Pilar about movies, and

Victor about his newest theories on the corruption of the political establishment.

Daphne sounded spacier and spacier as we talked. She seemed to be having trouble breathing. Pilar looked at me. I looked back.

"Oh, sweet brother," Daphne crooned, looking at Victor.

"Are you okay—" Pilar began.

And Daphne fell off the couch.

FOUR

There was an instant of silence after Aunt Daphne hit the mauve rug, face down. Then everyone began moving and speaking at once.

"Daphne!" Bob shouted, kneeling next to his lover before he'd even finished her name. He grabbed her wrist and pressed his fingers against its underside. York was at Bob's side in a flash, his face worried and frightened.

"Daphne?" Pilar whispered, going down on her knees, too. She seemed to move in slow motion, as if in a dream. "Daphne?"

"She's alive," Bob announced, his voice shaking. "But her pulse is slow."

"But what—" Fern began.

"She isn't breathing right!" Pilar yelped, coming out of her trance-like state at full tilt. "Bob, she isn't breathing right!"

"No, honey," Bob said simply. "She isn't."

"Does anyone know first aid?" I asked, looking around the room. Nobody answered.

"I'll call the hospital," Kapp offered, and rushed to the kitchen for a phone. A call to the hospital was probably more important than first aid anyway, I told myself. But still . . .

"Should we get her comfortable?" I asked, keeping my voice calm with an effort.

Inside, I was screaming in fear and frustration. I knew how to heal energetically, but I didn't know first aid. I was useless. I'd taken a course once, but it had been a long time ago. My mind was a jumble of contradictions. *Don't move the victim. Tilt the victim's head back. Lay them on their sides. Make them vomit. Don't make them vomit. Give mouth-to-mouth resuscitation. Leave them alone.* But we didn't even know why Aunt Daphne had collapsed. How could we know what to do?

"Don't you think we should at least turn her over so she can breathe better?" I suggested. My mouth was sour with fear. Maybe I shouldn't have said anything. But it couldn't be right to leave her face down if she wasn't breathing right.

Bob stared at me as if trying to make out the meaning of my words. Then he nodded.

York knelt down by him, and the two men and Pilar gently rolled Aunt Daphne's frail body over so that she was stretched out on her back. Her eyes were closed as if she were asleep. I grabbed a throw pillow from a couch and put it under her head. As I did, I took notes in my mind. Daphne was barely breathing, her skin was flushed and warm. I sniffed for any scent that might be a clue to Daphne's condition, but smelled nothing except the perspiration of the people kneeling next to her and the ever-present food and drink smells.

Kapp came jogging back into the room, cane in motion. "They'll be here within minutes," he told us. He pulled off his glasses and wiped the sweat from his face with his cane hand.

"Thanks, Kapp," I murmured gratefully. Kapp could make those kind of promises happen. Not very many people could.

"Now what?" he demanded, looking at me.

"I think we should tilt her head back so she can breathe more easily," I recommended, starting to remember.

York rolled the pillow I'd brought and stuck it under Daphne's neck so that her nose pointed upward.

"Should I give her artificial respiration?" he asked me, his voice too high. I just wished I knew the answer.

"She's breathing," I thought aloud. "But she isn't breathing much. Is there anything stuck in her mouth?"

York ran his finger around the inside of Daphne's mouth. I held my own breath. If only it were that easy. A piece of food in her airway?

"I don't think so," he concluded finally.

"Maybe it would be a good idea to loosen her clothing," Victor tried. I turned at the sound of his voice. He didn't look like he felt very well himself—pale, his narrow face stretched by tension.

"I'll do it," Pilar offered, and gently undid buttons and smoothed fabric, her eyes flowing with tears as she worked.

I closed my eyes and tried to trace Daphne's life force. It was as hard to follow as her breathing, filled with bursts of energy and sudden dissipations. Still, a column of silver light seemed to anchor her, even then. I asked myself if she'd had a heart attack. *No,* my mind told me. Did she choke? *No.* My mind searched. *Medication.* The word came from nowhere.

"Is Daphne on medication?" I asked, opening my eyes.

Bob and Pilar both nodded. I started to ask exactly what medication Daphne was taking, but York was already in action.

He bent over Daphne and covered her mouth with his, pinched her nostrils, and began artificial respiration.

"But she's breathing," Victor pointed out, panic tingeing his words. "Maybe you should just leave her alone."

York pulled his face away from Daphne's. I hadn't seen that much uncertainty there since we were kids.

"Maybe Victor's right," Geneva put in slowly. "Her breathing isn't stopped. It's just too slow."

" 'Do no harm'?" Roy whispered. "Isn't that what the doctors say?"

"We can't just leave her alone!" Pilar objected.

"We're not leaving her alone, sweetheart," Linda soothed.

The gentle tone sounded strange out of her mouth. "We're just trying to do the best thing until the ambulance gets here."

"But—" Pilar began.

"Could it *hurt* her to do the mouth-to-mouth?" York demand.

"No," I answered without thinking. I had no idea if I was right.

York bent over Daphne and put his mouth over hers again.

"Thank you," Pilar whispered. "Thank you."

"What kind of medication was Daphne on?" I tried again.

"Pain medication mostly," Bob answered.

"Was she supposed to drink?" I asked eagerly, my mind's eye picturing a prescription warning I'd once seen on someone's pain medication.

"Her doctor said a little would be all right for the celebration," Bob told me, the tremor in his voice less pronounced. "Daphne was careful. She wasn't taking her maximum dose of medication anyway. And the doctor said one drink probably couldn't really hurt her. Her medications were much stronger than the alcohol."

"She only had one glass of crème de menthe," Pilar reminded us defensively.

"I'm just trying to think out loud," I assured Pilar. "Sometimes people shouldn't drink with their medications, but it sounds like Aunt Daphne had it figured out."

"Daphne has everything figured out!" Pilar snapped. "She's not stupid. This shouldn't be happening!"

"I know," I told her, keeping my voice soft. "Daphne's a very smart woman."

Still, Daphne was lying on the living room rug, unmoving as York tried to breathe more life into her. Actually, her chest seemed to be moving, but I was pretty sure that was York's doing, not Daphne's.

No one spoke. I could hear York's breath and the clock ticking. And the beating of my own heart. Daphne's heart had slowed down, and mine had speeded up, thumping in my ears.

I wondered if it would be good to take Daphne's pulse again. I closed my eyes for a moment, gathering the will to do it, gathering the will to see if she had any pulse at all.

Then we heard the siren of the ambulance.

I let out my breath. I was so glad that they were coming. Tears sprang to my eyes as my body went limp.

"They'll know what to do," Bob assured Pilar, grabbing her hand and squeezing it. "They'll do the right thing."

"I'm going with her," Pilar announced and stood up.

"No, honey," Bob disagreed, standing up himself. "I'm going with Daphne. You know we talked about this ahead of time."

"But I want to go with her!" Pilar insisted.

"Honey, you're too young," Bob held his ground. "Daphne gave me her medical power of attorney for just this situation. She wants you to stay. It's the right thing to do. You know that."

There was a knock on the front door.

Geneva speeded toward the door, but Kapp had already opened it.

The man and woman who came through the door were uniformed, loaded down with equipment, and fast. Kapp spoke to them first, pointing at Daphne and then Bob. They rolled a gurney over and lifted Daphne onto it, the uniformed man deftly taking over the mouth-to-mouth resuscitation from York, but using a strange funnel-shaped mouth condom. So York had been doing the right thing. I could feel a kind of relief flooding me. Whatever happened to Aunt Daphne, York had done the right thing. *We* had done the right thing.

"Oh, Daphne!" Pilar wailed. "I want to go with you!"

"Honey, you can't," Bob began again. "You know—"

"Sir," the uniformed woman broke in. "You have medical power of attorney?"

Bob nodded.

"Do you have a list of medical information, current medications, allergies—"

"Yes, I have all of that," he interrupted. "I carry it with me."

"Then we'll be going," she ordered. "Now."

"No!" Pilar shouted.

Bob looked around, his eyes wild for a moment.

I jumped forward and put my arms around Pilar. "No," she murmured again, but turned her face, leaning toward my chest and holding onto me as they wheeled Daphne out with Bob alongside. The uniformed man kept on with the mouth-to-mouth as they moved. And the woman was pulling out more equipment from her bag. They knew what they were doing. I let out a breath. My aunt Daphne was in good hands.

Pilar jumped from my arms when they were almost gone from view and shouted, "Bob!" He looked over his shoulder at her.

"I know you're cool, dude," she called out. "Take care of Daphne."

Bob saluted with a shaking hand and sprinted to catch up with the gurney.

Within a very few moments of Geneva closing the door behind Daphne and her attendants, the siren was screaming again. Then it moved away, the sound fainter and fainter.

All that was left in the living room was the sound of Pilar's sobs. I took her back into my arms. I just held her. What had Daphne been to Pilar? It didn't matter. Pilar loved her. That much was clear. Pilar cried, and I cried with her, for Daphne, for my own mother, for my own father. And I could hear someone else crying, too. Was that Victor?

After what seemed like a very long time, Pilar finally pushed away from me.

"What if it was you?" she asked, peering into my eyes.

"What if what was me?" I returned her question, puzzled.

"This isn't the way it was supposed to go down," she muttered as if to herself. Her eyes were red and disoriented. "There's something wrong here. This isn't—"

"Of course there's something wrong," Geneva broke in, laying her hand on Pilar's shoulder. I hadn't even seen Geneva standing near us. "Daphne's sick, maybe very sick. We all know that. But we have to cope. We have to—"

Pilar shook Geneva's hand off.

"No!" she cried. "You're not going to write her off. No one touches me until I figure this out."

"Figure what out?" Roy asked softly.

"One of you knows what I mean," she rapped out, shaking her finger in the air. Her voice grew louder. "She wouldn't try to kill herself. Not yet. Not here. It's one of you."

"Pillar, I know you're upset," Victor put in, his voice old and grief-sodden. "But we'll take care of Daphne. We'll take care of you. I promise. I have herbs that might help you—"

"No!" she shouted. She shook her head, then surveyed the room. "But why?"

"Why what?" Kapp demanded. "You've got to be more specific if you want us to understand you."

"One of you knows," she insisted. "One of you knows what I'm talking about."

"Oh, Daphne!" Victor cried out then. "Oh, Daphne, please be all right. I can't bear it if you're gone, too."

"Granddad?" Fern whispered, her body stiffening with fear.

But Victor was whirling into his own vortex.

"Simone and Daphne," he sobbed. "My beautiful little sisters."

Fern stepped forward to put a gentle hand on her grandfather's shoulder, but her mother beat her to it.

"Dad, just calm down," Linda suggested gently, enveloping her father in her embrace. "We're here for you, okay?"

"Yes, sweetie," he murmured and let himself be comforted. Linda seemed to tower over her father's crumpled form.

Fern stepped to the side and turned her attention to Pilar, anger in her stance.

"Pilar, how were you related to Daphne?" she demanded.

Pilar's eyes slitted in her round face.

"I'm not telling until Daphne is better," she declared.

"But—" Fern began.

"Is it you?" Pilar accused, pointing at Fern. "You want to inherit. Hel-lo! Is it you?"

Fern shrank back under Pilar's accusing finger.

"What do you mean, 'inherit'?" Linda asked sharply, over her father's bent head. "Are you accusing someone of trying to kill Daphne?"

Pilar only smiled. It wasn't a happy smile. It was a scary smile.

"You figure it out," she replied softly. "Daphne was sick, but she was in control. And now . . . now . . ."

Pilar's shoulders slumped. She began to cry again.

I moved toward the teenager, but she cried out before I could touch her. I stepped back, giving her space but staying close enough that she could reach for me if she wanted to.

"Oh, Pilar," Linda sighed. "Let Cally take care of you. I know you're in pain, but—"

"No," Pilar insisted, closing her eyes and shaking her head. "No."

"Pilar," Linda tried again. "I understand your anger. Believe me. Life is rough. The human condition is rough. But you've got to let us help you."

Pilar continued to shake her head.

"Victor," Uncle Earl cut in. "Maybe you and your girls and I should just leave. This young lady is obviously distraught. I don't understand what she's going on about. But she needs to calm down. And you could use some rest."

Victor shook his head as vehemently as Pilar. "I refuse to leave until we hear about Daphne," he pronounced blearily. "And we all must take care of Pilar."

"No one is here to take care of me!" Pilar shouted. "Daphne and Bob are all I have. Don't you understand?"

"But we want to help you," Victor whispered. "We all love Daphne. Let us help you."

Pilar shook her head again, but opened her eyes. She

took in a long breath, balling her hands into fists. "Listen, I know I gotta chill, okay? I know that. But it's not about me. It's about Daphne. What if she dies?"

Roy nodded earnestly. I hoped she didn't see him.

"Listen, Pilar," Linda tried again. "You're under a lot of stress. I can see that—"

"Of course, I'm stressing!" she shrieked. "One of you is trying to kill Daphne!"

Kapp stepped forward, his bulldog face intent.

"I'm listening," he told her, his voice booming with authority. "Now explain to me as clearly as you can just what you're trying to say. Then we'll be able to help Daphne."

Pilar looked at Kapp, wrapped her arms around herself, and lifted her head defiantly. Still, her voice was almost calm when she finally spoke.

"One of you poisoned Daphne," she pronounced simply.

FIVE

"What?" **more than** one voice demanded.

"You can't make an accusation like that—" Linda started.

"Let her talk," Kapp commanded.

"One of you poisoned her!" Pilar screamed, her momentary calm gone. Her round face was flushed, her arms waving spasmodically. "I don't have anyone else in the world, and one of you tried to kill her. What if she dies?"

"Pilar!" Kapp boomed. "Tell us why you believe someone poisoned Daphne. Let us understand. Where's your evidence?"

"I don't have any evidence," she sobbed. She wrapped her arms around herself and bent low as if her stomach hurt. It was becoming hard to understand her words. "I just, like, know. I know! Poison . . . one of you . . . I know . . . you knew how . . . it was one of you . . . oh, please . . ."

Geneva strode up to the teenager.

"Pilar, I hear you," she assured her. "Kapp and I hear you. Cally and York hear you. We all hear you. But you have to calm down now. 'Chill out.' It's the only way you can really help Daphne. What if she gets back and you're not able to help her? You've got to rest. You need rest."

Pilar just wept. Cautiously, Geneva put her arm around

Pilar's shoulders. Pilar didn't fight her this time. Slowly, Geneva guided her to the stairway that led to the upper story.

At the stairway, Pilar looked over her shoulder.

"But I know," she mumbled through clogged sinuses. "I really know."

"You need to lie down," Geneva soothed her. Geneva reminded me of someone at that moment. Or was it Pilar? Geneva had put her arm around my shoulders just like that when my parents had been killed some twenty years ago. She'd put her arm around me that way more times than I could remember as I grew through my teenage years under her care. My eyes fogged with tears as Geneva led the girl up the stairs, one stair at a time, probably to what used to be my bedroom. I pulled off my glasses and wiped them, as if that could wipe away my tears. Dack, I loved my sister. Poor Pilar. Who *did* Pilar have if Daphne died?

The minute we all heard the bedroom door close above, everyone began talking at once.

"Did she really mean to accuse one of us of attempted murder?" Victor asked the room at large. "Could she be—"

"She's upset," Linda cut in. "She wants to blame someone. When bad things happen, we blame others. I do."

At least she was honest.

"Teenagers have wild imaginations," Uncle Earl added.

"What if it's not just imagination?" Roy said slowly. "What is in that poor girl's mind that would lead her to suspect that Daphne was poisoned? There must be something. She was on the idea like a duck on a june bug."

"Maybe she's lying," Fern speculated. "I mean, she won't even tell us who she is. What's that about? What else is she hiding? If she was in a book, she might be an illegitimate daughter or something cool like that. But Aunt Daphne is too old to be her mother. That can't be it."

"Fern—" her mother put in.

But Fern just kept on talking. "I don't like the way she's keeping secrets," she added. "There's something uncool about the whole scenario. She accuses us, and yet she won't tell us anything. I don't trust her. Maybe she's just pretending to freak out to hide something that she's ashamed of."

"I'm not so sure," York murmured once Fern had run out of words. "Pilar may have a good reason to hide her connection with Daphne. Maybe she's protecting Daphne somehow."

I turned to Kapp. But he was uncharacteristically quiet, seemingly lost in thought. He frowned, staring out at the room, his eyes unfocused. He massaged his chin. I worried a little more. Kapp pondering was not always a good thing.

"Lazar," he finally spoke, turning to me. "Whaddaya think?"

I shook my head. I didn't even try. My mind was full.

Had Pilar really meant it? Attempted murder? Poison? I didn't want to think so. But then again, I was there. And people had been murdered in my presence before. Maybe this was the darkness that Roy saw. Maybe . . . My mind went into a loop. Daphne collapsing. Pilar screaming. Death winking. Who did I trust in this room? Who did I distrust? I felt cold and sweaty at the same time. Roy put his hand on my wrist tenderly.

"You'll be okay, darlin'," he whispered.

And I was. I popped out of the loop and back into my right mind. Daphne's life was still in jeopardy. But I trusted Roy. I would have trusted Roy with my life, even with my spirit.

Geneva came back down the stairs.

"What did she say?" Linda demanded.

"Did she accuse anyone specifically?" Fern followed up.

"Is she in distress?" Victor thought to ask. "Does she need any herbs?"

"Pilar is resting," Geneva told us stiffly. "She is as well as can be expected." Then she raised her head and straightened her back. "I suggest we talk about something else."

There was a stunned silence. This was Geneva's house. She was setting down the rules. No one argued with Geneva. Not even Linda.

Talk about something else? I was sure Daphne's collapse was out of bounds, too.

I waited. I heard the sound of a car in the far-off distance and the sound of the grandfather clock ticking nearby.

What would we talk about? The weather? Food? Fashion?

"Oh, come on, Geneva!" Kapp snapped, his voice slicing through the silence. "That young woman made a serious accusation. Holy Mother! Are we just supposed to forget about it?"

"No," Geneva replied with apparent calm. But her eyes weren't fully focused. I'd lived with Geneva long enough to know that she was fighting to hold down her feelings. "It would be groovy if everyone here could just forget, but I know that's not possible. Still, I don't think we should be discussing Pilar and her accusations without her here to defend them. Bob's gone. Daphne's . . . ill. And Pilar is hysterical. We need to wait until there is some clarity before we proceed."

"But what if Daphne *was* poisoned?" Kapp demanded.

"And if we sit here blathering speculations, are we going to learn anything?" Geneva shot back, her stiffness giving way to anger.

"It won't do any good to be fussing about something we don't know the answer to," Roy agreed mildly. Then he added, "Still, shouldn't the folks at the hospital know about the possibility of your aunt's being poisoned?"

Geneva's brows shot up. Her eyes focused.

"Son of a lizard," she muttered, bring her hands up to touch the sides of her own face. "Of course, they should be informed. Why didn't I think of that? I—"

"I'll call them," Kapp assured her and raced back into the kitchen to phone the hospital.

I walked up to my sister and took her hand in mine. I didn't want to see her facade crumble. Not then. Not ever. "Geneva," I whispered. "You did great with Pilar."

"Did I?" she asked, her voice no longer authoritative, but muddled.

"Very groovy," I expanded. It was her favorite word, after all.

Her mouth quirked in a half smile.

"Hah!" she snorted, coming back to earth. "What would you know of 'groovy'?"

"Don't forget, I was the one following you around and handing out the pamphlets while you were marching a hundred years ago."

She clasped my hand.

"Do you remember the little purple 'peace and equality' shirt I made for you when you were five?" she asked, her eyes actually alive again.

"I think you're doing better work now," I told her, straight-faced.

She laughed.

"What?" Kapp demanded, returning to the room. He looked ill, old.

"Girl stuff," I stage-whispered.

Kapp took a step back in mock fear. Or maybe he really was afraid. It was hard to tell with Kapp. Something was wrong with him, though.

I wanted to ask Kapp if he'd been successful in his call to the hospital. But I couldn't form the words. Maybe I didn't want to know why he looked so old. And Kapp wouldn't have returned to the room if he hadn't done his task. Still—

"So what are we supposed to do now?" Linda demanded, flinging her hands out. "Play charades?"

"Excellent choice," Kapp shot back. He straightened his back, took a deep breath, and brought his own hands up in front of his face and opened them.

"Book?" I guessed. I couldn't help it. My brain was tired. My emotions were exhausted. My angst was bone dry. I flopped down on the nearest chair. Roy pulled up another one next to mine.

Kapp touched the tip of his nose in confirmation of my guess and bowed in our direction.

Then everyone but Kapp seemed to drop: Linda and Earl onto the love seat; Fern and Victor onto the lilac couch; and Geneva into her orchid easy chair. Only York held his ground, standing straight with his arms ready at his sides, ever vigilant.

Kapp stepped into the center of the chairs and couches by the cherry coffee table, held up a fist, then flicked out all four fingers and his thumb.

"Five words?" Roy hazarded.

Kapp taped his nose again.

Kapp dropped his hand, then pushed it out in front of his torso, palm open, all digits extended.

"Fifth word," Uncle Victor declared.

Kapp touched his nose again, then reached his arms into the air and began swaying, cane and glasses and all.

"Whoa! A belly dancer?" I tried.

Kapp shook his head, squinting a nasty look my way, then began swaying again.

"Fire?" Earl hypothesized.

Kapp shook his head emphatically no.

"A ship at sea!" Fern shouted out.

Kapp sighed, stopped swaying, and stuck two fingers out.

"Drowning man?" Linda asked.

I sniffed sarcasm there, but Kapp just shook his head again.

"Second word," Roy said.

Kapp slapped his own nose so hard, he needed his cane to hold him up. Then he puffed out his cheeks until they were red and blew out with all his force.

Blowhard, I thought, but I didn't say it aloud.

"Air?"

"Blow?"

"Explosion?"

"A bull?"

I had to hand it to him. He had the audience.

"Wind," York opined casually.

Kapp tapped his nose wildly.

"Oh," York said. "The Wind in the Willows."

"Yes!" Kapp conceded ecstatically, and did his swaying willow routine again.

I lay my head back and laughed. Then we were all laughing to Kapp's mock pique. Well, maybe not everyone. But it felt good, no matter who I was laughing with.

"A willow in a tutu is more like it," Geneva commented dryly. ·

"Mother of God!" Kapp swore beseechingly, hand on his heart and eyes on the ceiling. "Try to do a favor for a fashion designer, and she dresses you in a tutu."

"But how'd you figure it out?" Fern demanded of York.

"Easy," he answered brusquely, "Wind, willows."

"Okay, now it's your turn," Kapp proclaimed, pointing at York.

"Oh, no," York argued.

"Oh, yes!" Kapp crowed, crossing the room to drag York to center stage.

York looked from one side to the other in panic. He could fell Kapp with both hands and one leg tied behind his back, but Kapp knew it was against York's principles to use violence to protest.

"You can't make me," York declared, but I could tell he was ready to run if he had to.

Then the doorbell rang.

The sobriety was instant. The sound track of the gathering stopped dead as we all looked at the door. Was news of Daphne on the other side?

Geneva got up and walked to the front door, her face grim.

"Happy Thanksgiving!" a chorus of voices greeted her.

I let my breath out. I recognized the voices. My sister Melinda, my brother Arnot, their spouses, and their children had all arrived as planned for Thanksgiving dessert. I looked down at my watch. It was seven-thirty.

"I brought cranberry cheesecake!" Melinda announced cheerily. Melinda was literally a space cadet, an artist and writer who earned her living from her "Acuto from Pluto" cartoon strip. Her short, cropped hair gave her face a crazed elfin look that was all too appropriate.

"Mo-om," Melinda's twelve-year-old daughter, Jessie, complained. "Are we going in or what?"

"Yeah," Melinda's seven-year-old son, Cole, added from behind. "I want pie and cake and ice cream."

"Heh-heh," Melinda's husband, Zack, responded. He was a big, bearded man who taught art and loved his and Melinda's children without reservation. Luckily, only two of their four children seemed to be present for the occasion. The other two probably thought they were too old for the celebration. They were teenagers, after all.

Melinda stepped through the doorway and tripped. Zack just grabbed the cheesecake and chuckled some more. Melinda snuggled up to him. "Good catch!" she whispered.

"My friend Kelda says Mom is an accident looking for a place to happen," Jessie told us, stepping around her parents with Cole in her wake.

I marched up to the door to exchange embraces with my clumsy, sweet sister. She even smelled of cranberry. I didn't think it was perfume. It was more likely mashed berries in her hair or clothing or— I just hugged her.

Arnot popped up after Melinda, his arms outstretched, a bag of pastries in one hand and a smile on his handsome face. He bowed and kissed my hand flamboyantly. Too flamboyantly for a custom-cabinet maker, but that was Arnot. Arnot was the only Lazar to go bald so far, but he even managed to do that handsomely. Arnot's wife, Barbara, stepped in next, with their goggle-eyed five-year-old, Kinsey. Barbara was a big, red-haired woman who still sported a tough, big-city accent, even though she hadn't tended bar in the big city for close to twenty years. She'd become a veterinarian instead. I looked around for their older son, Huey, but didn't see him.

A few rounds of hugging later, everyone was inside, chattering. And the kids had run off.

"Hey, hey!" Barbara erupted, looking around after a few minutes. "So, where's your Aunt Daphne? I thought she was coming. I love that old broad. She's a kick in the pants."

The room went quiet. Quiet enough that we could hear the three kids arguing over the desserts in the kitchen. So that was where they were.

"What's wrong?" Arnot asked, his smile disappearing. He lowered his voice. "Is she too sick?"

Uncle Earl elected himself spokesperson.

"We've had a pretty rough afternoon," he began. "As your godfather, I'm sorry I have to be the one to tell you. But your Aunt Daphne collapsed a while ago, after dinner. Now, I don't know what happened. But she's very ill. She's in the hospital now."

"Aunt Daphne?" Melinda whispered, looking confused. "Is she that bad?"

"Pilar thinks she was poisoned," Fern threw in helpfully. "She was accusing all of us and—"

"Poisoned!" Barbara yelped. "Whaddaya saying here?"

"Who's Pilar?" Arnot asked at the same time.

I looked around the room, willing someone to answer the second question. Victor looked down at his feet. Even Kapp wasn't guessing. Kapp? Did he know? Did Victor know?

"Pilar's the teenage girl that's been taking care of Aunt Daphne," I tried. "I'm not exactly sure what her relationship is to Daphne." I looked around the room again. It still wasn't providing me with any answers.

"I don't know why Pilar is with Daphne at all," Linda complained. "She has Bob to take care of her."

"Bob?" Arnot steepled his hands patiently, looking uncannily like Geneva in the gesture. "Is Bob taking care of Aunt Daphne or is this Pilar?"

"Bob is Aunt Daphne's sweetheart," I said. "Pilar calls him 'Daphne's dude.' I don't think he's related to Pilar."

"*Did* someone try to poison Aunt Daphne?" Arnot prodded.

I looked over my shoulder at Geneva. Were we still under orders not to talk?

"Pilar has made the accusation," Geneva took over. "But we don't know if it's true."

"It's just stupid," Linda offered. "Why would anyone here want to poison Aunt Daphne?"

"And yet, Pilar believes it happened," Kapp put in finally. "I tend to think she may have a reason for her belief."

"She's just a hysterical teenager," Earl argued.

"And she won't tell us who she is," Fern reminded us. Suddenly, I understood Fern's animosity toward Pilar. Pilar was a puzzle Fern couldn't unlock. And Fern had to know everything.

"Please listen, everyone," Victor interrupted, his voice tired. "We shouldn't be concerned about Pilar. She's resting as well as she can. We should be trying to help Daphne."

"Oh, come on, Dad," Linda snapped. She turned and headed toward the bathroom. "Aunt Daphne's at the hospital. They'll help her. I suppose you want to send her herbs or something. Well, forget it."

I was beginning to understand what Victor had meant when he'd talked about his daughter's mood swings. They weren't really bad mood swings. Linda had been unpleasant as long as I could remember. It was the kind human being peeking out that was different.

Victor stood his ground even as Linda slammed the door behind her. "Perhaps we might all sit down and concentrate on Daphne. We might send her healing energy. I've read that healing circles can help people who are sick. We have to do something. Cally, what do you think?"

"It couldn't hurt," I agreed. And it might heal us as well, I didn't add aloud.

"Thank you, Uncle Victor," Geneva said solemnly. "Let's form a circle right here. A circle of silent healing intent."

"I'm not so sure—" Earl began.

"Aw, why not?" Kapp argued. I was surprised. Kapp usually made fun of anything he couldn't see in evidence.

It was a tight fit for all of us to sit, even in Geneva's expansive living room. But we squeezed in, filling the couches and chairs. Even Linda, who'd returned from the bathroom looking relaxed, found a place between her father and her daughter. Had she swung back to the human side again?

Once we were finally seated, York asked Arnot where his son, Huey, was.

"Not coming," Arnot replied quickly, too quickly.

"Hey, he got popped," Barbara told us. "Our son, the jailbird. They took away his license after his last DUI, but he had to drive again, drunk." She shook her head.

Arnot frowned. He wouldn't have told us on his own, I realized. Even Arnot kept secrets. Something in me tightened with the realization.

"Oh, my," Uncle Earl pronounced, shaking his head along with Barbara. "How did that happen?"

Arnot's face reddened. "Huey?" he snapped. "He's just eighteen. He's a mess. Isn't everyone at eighteen?"

"Sorry, son," Earl said.

"Right," Arnot muttered. Arnot, the all-smiling life of the party, wasn't smiling. And I could smell his anger and pain from his seat across from me.

I opened my mouth to say something, anything to help his pain, but Geneva spoke first.

"The circle of silence," Geneva reminded us.

No one spoke. I closed my eyes. I tried to ground myself, to bring in light that I could send to Daphne. But instead, I saw a black band where light usually appeared. Death.

My eyes popped open. Was Aunt Daphne already dead? My heart was pounding in my ears again.

In the silence of the living room, I heard a wail. The hair went up on my arms. Was that the wail of death?

"What will I do?" the wailing voice asked. "What will I do?"

But the voice was Pilar's.

SIX

There was no doubt about it. There was at least one crazy Lazar in the room—me. I'd gone off my rocker, around the bend, and thrown myself headfirst into the waterfall of lunacy. I'd actually thought I'd heard death's voice. I wanted to laugh at myself, but I couldn't. And Pilar— What if Pilar had realized Daphne was dead, too? I shivered all over again. Whatever Pilar was going through, she needed help.

"Pilar," I whispered, stood slowly, and walked toward the stairway. But Victor beat me to the first stair.

"Let me try, honey," he offered gently.

"But—"

"Let Dad go up to her till Bob gets back," Linda interrupted. "Dad's good with kids."

"But—"

"He put up with me, didn't he?" Linda argued.

I closed my mouth. I wanted to say that I should go, that I was a healer. But I didn't feel like much of a healer then. Ever since we'd come to Geneva's house, I'd been more in need of healing than capable of healing. Even before my aunt Daphne had collapsed, I'd felt off, as if I hadn't had years of training and practice, as if I was some twenty years younger.

I looked around the room. I'd hardly noticed the states of the people in the room with me. I'd stopped observing.

I looked then, really looked. Everyone was in shock. They just expressed it differently. Geneva was stiff, Arnot angry, Melinda sad, York uncertain. We were all off. No one was acting like themselves. Criminy, Linda was being kind. Earl was quiet. Even Kapp was quiet. And the formerly serene Fern was twitching like a cat's tail. Only Roy seemed to be fully present, as he watched the room intently. He seemed more alive than ever, a dog on the scent. While I'd been spiraling into my own inner world, he'd been observing for me.

I walked back to take my seat again, and closed my eyes, rousing my inner self to do an aura check. If there was any truth to Pilar's accusation, I wanted to see what I could see. Not that I could necessarily spot a murderer, if there indeed was a murderer. In fact, I was more likely to totally miss a sign of murder, if past experience was any guide.

"Are we done with the circle of silence?" Fern asked.

I opened my eyes.

"It was your grandfather's idea, and he's gone upstairs," Linda answered. "What do you think?"

"But it was kinda cool," Fern pressed on. "I could put it in a story. You know, with everyone closing their eyes except one person. And secretly, that person—"

"Don't you think we have enough suspense around here?" Linda growled.

"Hmmm?" Fern murmured, putting her finger under her chin and widening her eyes as she looked at her mother. "Enough suspense? Enough suspense? Gee, I'm like, I don't know."

"That's not funny—" Linda snapped.

"The circle of silence is done," Geneva cut in.

I kept my eyes open and concentrated my energy, thinking about auras. Everyone's aura was different. One person's fury could look like another person's sensuality. And a peek would just give me a snapshot. The same person could be filled with despair one day and radiating joy the next. I spent long periods of time with my clients, learning to gauge what I saw and felt in terms of their particular circumstances. A peek was never enough.

"Is Kinsey still in the kitchen?" Arnot asked.

"I think they're all in the kitchen," York answered.

Arnot exchanged a glance with his wife, Barbara.

"They'll be okay," Linda told him. "Even Kinsey. There aren't any drugs in there, just dessert." Was she making fun of Huey's DUI situation?

Imperfect snapshot or not, I really wanted to peek. I had to peek. I did peek.

Linda's aura looked way different than I'd imagined. Though fairly balanced in color and shape, there were striking anomalies. The left side of her aura looked squashed, as if something was squelching her feminine side, squelching her ability to listen and receive support. I wondered if this was just a result of menopause or if she'd always had this chip on her aura. There were some hot spots, too. I felt them rather than saw them, but they were there. Some intense healing was going on in her body, or maybe anger. It was hard to tell. I might have been just feeling her hot flashes. Her third chakra was a sickly yellow that looked like debilitating fear to me. I breathed in some humility. I'd always thought that Linda was an angry person, but what I was seeing was a person who was very afraid and doing her best to protect herself. No wonder she was so off-putting. Some "healer" I was. Where had I left my compassion?

"Linda?" I began. "Thank you—"

"What?" she demanded before I could finish. There was anger in her voice, even if there wasn't much evident to me in her aura. Did Linda pretend to be angry out of fear? Or was my reading of her completely off? I decided to put any acts of compassion concerning Linda on hold for the moment.

"Nothing," I told her. "Nothing."

I turned to Fern. Whoa! I should have worn dark glasses. Fern's aura was bright and pulsing, especially at her throat chakra. A scuzzy green of frustration leaped out at me, and

a mingling of blues and yellows that looked like some kind
of intellectual argument. But from the knees down, her aura
was barely visible. I had a feeling she wasn't very grounded.
But she *was* shielded. In an instant, the aura was gone from
my vision. Some part of her had known I was there, observing, and had shut me off. I was sure of it.

Fern looked at me then, turning her head slowly. I heard
the theme song of *Jaws* playing on my internal CD.

"What are you doing, Cally?" she asked.

"Daydreaming," I lied and turned my head away as fast
as I could.

My gaze landed on Earl. I refocused. There, I saw the
blue of mourning, the red-orange flame of anger, and a
pastel apricot that felt like protective love. But they were
all compartmentalized. I looked closer. Earl's aura looked
like an obsessively neat sock drawer. There was frustration
there, too, and self-loathing, fear—all the usual suspects,
each in its own separate little space.

"So, who's for a walk?" Earl asked abruptly.

I jumped in my seat guiltily. Maybe Earl knew I was
studying him, too. Maybe it was because I was staring right
at him.

"Take the kids with you," Melinda suggested after the
short silence that greeted his invitation. "They're probably
stuffed with dessert by now. Don't let anyone barf on you."

"Heh-heh," Zack piped in. No wonder Melinda and
Zack were married.

Earl stood up and crossed the dining room to the kitchen.

"Hey, kids," he invited. "Want to go for a walk with
your old Uncle Earl?"

"I feel kinda sick," whined a tiny voice that had to be
Kinsey's.

Arnot started to get up to go to his daughter, but Barbara
tugged at his shirtsleeve.

"Hey, not so fast, Papa Bear," she put in. "Remember
what the family therapist said about letting the kidlins
learn from their mistakes?"

"But—" Arnot objected.

"But, nothing," Barbara corrected him. "Eat twelve servings of dessert, get sick. Them's the new rules. We told her on the way over to eat two small helpings. And she agreed. Does it sound like she ate two small helpings to you?"

Earl came back into the living room holding Kinsey's and Cole's little hands in his. Kinsey's face was pale under multicolored smears of ice cream and pie. At least I hoped they were ice cream and pie. The colors looked right. I didn't think she'd limited herself to two small helpings. Five years seemed young for Barbara's "let them eat cake" philosophy, but what did I know? I didn't have children. Cole just looked happily stuffed, his chin and shirt covered in berry stains. Jessie brought up the rear, her hand on her stomach.

"Yummo-malario!" she chirped. "My compliments to the gonzo-bonzo baker. Lots o' sugar. Whee!"

"Heh-heh," Zack chuckled. I was glad Jessie was his twelve-year-old to deal with. And after hearing her speak, there was no doubt that she was Melinda's child, too.

"Let's walk." Cole prodded his great uncle, and the foursome went out the door, whining, whooping, and belching.

"How about you, darlin'?" Roy whispered in my ear.

I peered at him for a moment, dazed. Did he want to have kids? Finally?

"A stroll, Cally," he explained more loudly. At least he didn't wave his hand in front of my face. "I think we could both do to stretch our legs a bit."

"Oh, right!" I agreed, and shot up, grabbing my cane. Maybe I'd stood up too fast, because I was dizzy for a minute.

Roy stood with me, putting his arm around my waist. "Anyone who'd like to come with us is surely invited." He addressed the room at large.

But he didn't have any more success than Uncle Earl. Everyone was still in their private mode of shock.

"Have fun," Geneva ordered.

Just before we closed the door behind us, I turned to see my sister shaking her head as if she couldn't believe she'd used the word "fun."

We walked down the gravel driveway in the dark. I could hear Earl's slow voice floating somewhere near us. Then I saw what must have been the light of a flashlight bobbing along at the corner. I was pretty sure I smelled cigarette smoke, too.

"It's okay to throw up," Earl declared. "I've thrown up lots of times."

"Really?" Kinsey's little voice came back. She sounded better.

"Oh, sure," he went on. I could barely hear him then. The flashlight had bobbed around the corner and out of sight. "Firemen have to do all kinds of things. Why, I had to hang upside-down once . . ."

Finally, I couldn't hear him at all anymore.

"Uncle Earl was always there for us," I sighed as we walked toward the trees. "He was a firefighter before he retired. A real hero. Listen to him with the kids. He's so patient. I guess he and my aunt Ingrid couldn't have kids because she was so sick before she died. I wish I could spend more time with him. But next to my parents . . ." I faltered.

"There's nothing like your own mama and papa," Roy finished for me. "I know you grieve for them. It's just natural, darlin'. Of course, you do."

I put my arms around him and hugged. His familiar body was warm and solid. I felt much better outside in the dark of the evening. I was glad Roy had dragged me out of Geneva's house. I hadn't realized how claustrophobic it had been in there. I breathed in deeply, smelling the cool night air and Roy. Grass, trees, flowers, and fireplace smoke from the house across the street flavored the air. I looked up and saw moon and stars. Yeah. I felt the muscles in my stomach relaxing.

"Thank you, Roy," I whispered as I let go of him.

I tilted my head toward his, mouth ready for a kiss.

"Cally," Roy stopped me before my mouth arrived. "There's so much darkness here. I think this is the place where the darkness comes from."

"What?" I stared up at him, wanting to howl.

"Listen, darlin'," he tried to explain. "I know you love your brothers and sisters, but don't you feel the evil in this place?"

"Don't be scary, Roy. There's no—"

"Hear me out, please," he went on, holding onto my arms. "I used to think the darkness was mine. You know how I fretted on that. But now I think it belongs to your family somehow. I can't put my finger on it exactly, but it's denser here than ever."

"Is it one person?" I asked, torn between arguing with him and accepting the information he might have gleaned from his peculiar dark perspective.

"No," he replied slowly. I could feel him thinking. "It's like all of you together. Even your mama and papa—"

"Oh, stop, please," I whispered. My stomach was tightening again. "It hurts too much to talk about them."

"That's what I mean," he plowed on. "It hurts all of you. Even I can feel that. That's why none of you talk about important stuff. I see how it is, all that polite stuff. All the laughing. All the hurting. Even that poor young one, Pilar, is part of it somehow."

"Oh, Roy," I pleaded. "This is too hard. I don't know if you're right or not, but I can't seem to keep my mind clear when you talk like this." I felt the cold air hit the wet spots on my face and realized that I was crying. Roy seemed to realize it then, too.

"Oh, darlin', I don't want to sadden you. I want to help you out of your sadness."

He reached around and pulled me to him, just holding me as I cried.

"Let's find somewhere to sit down," I suggested once my tears had run dry.

We walked by moonlight to the side of the house and found two old wooden chairs to sit in.

"Do you think Aunt Daphne will die?" I asked him when we were seated. "Do you think she might already be dead?"

"Yes, darlin'," he answered quietly.

"That wasn't very reassuring!" I yelped without thinking.

"I'd dearly love to be reassuring, but I do believe she's dead," he expanded.

"But why?" I challenged him.

"I just have a gut feeling. And there is the way she looked as they carried her out. To my way of thinking, she might have already passed on by then."

"That's what I thought, too," I mumbled. And the tear spigot was turned on again.

"There, there," Roy said soothingly. "Your aunt Daphne was happy, wasn't she? That's what matters when someone passes, isn't it? She was loved. She is loved. I saw that woman. She didn't mind the dying. It's us that mind."

"We don't know that she's dead," I tried.

"Maybe not," he agreed. "Maybe not."

For a long while, we just sat together in the dark. I heard cars on the main road, rustling in the bushes, and occasional bursts of voices from the surrounding houses. But mostly it was quiet. My hands were as cold as a frozen turkey. But the cold reminded me that I was alive.

I finally broke the silence. "I remember Aunt Daphne and my mother dancing the Twist together. They were always laughing and sharing secrets."

"What else do you remember?" Roy urged.

"They were both so pretty. Maybe I just think so because they were my family, but they seemed beautiful. And they were both funny. A legal secretary and an artist, you'd think they wouldn't have much in common, but they did. When the two of them were talking, the room sparkled."

I thought for a while, remembering. I always tried to avoid nostalgia, but these memories were softening the hurt. I could almost hear the high-pitched notes of their voices, chattering. And my father's deeper voice, joining in.

"Do you and your brothers and sisters *ever* talk about your parents?" Roy asked after a while.

"No," I muttered sullenly. "They just keep secrets."

"They care for you, Cally," Roy put in mildly. He stood up and leaned over the back of my chair, rubbing my arms. "They just can't speak for the hurt they feel."

"I know," I answered impatiently. I stood up. "We'd better get home before we're frozen to our chairs."

We were walking back up the gravel driveway when a short dark splotch loomed up before us. My eyes were used to the dark by then, but I was cautious all the same. Then the splotch moved. It was a turkey. A big turkey.

"Look, he's a male," Roy whispered in my ear as the turkey splotch made tracks toward the bushes.

I didn't ask Roy how he knew the turkey was male. Maybe it was something about being raised in rural Kentucky.

"He isn't as friendly as the Turkey Sisters," I complained instead.

"I think the poor guy's looking for the sisters," Roy guessed.

It was nearly ten o'clock by the time we got back to Geneva's house. Earl and the kids had come back a long time before, and the kids had already left with their parents.

"Kinsey didn't even hurl," Fern informed us and turned back to her mother where they sat on the plum couch. Victor and Pilar sat nearby on adjacent chairs.

"I was telling Fern about my sister, Natalie," Linda offered. So, the Jekyll of the Jekyll and Hyde Lindas was back, I realized. "She was a hoot. Did you ever meet her?"

I nodded. It had been a long time, but I remembered Natalie. She'd been scary, no question about it. And my cousin had been the stuff of family legend, in trouble as often as not.

"She hitchhiked to Alaska when she was thirteen," Linda reminisced. "She said she wanted a real Eskimo Pie."

Fern laughed. But Pilar frowned. And even Victor didn't smile. Roy tried to chuckle. Roy wasn't good at faking, though. But Linda didn't seem to notice.

"Hey, Dad," she went on, undeterred. "Remember when she stole all those books from the library and then broke back in to return them?"

"Linda—" Victor began.

But Linda was on a roll. "And she got that dead shark and put it in the town plaza fountain!"

"Hee-hee-hee!" Fern laughed uncontrollably.

I'd probably have been laughing, too, if it weren't for Pilar's sad face. She'd redone her makeup, but it just accentuated the pallor of her skin.

"How're you doing?" I asked Pilar as Linda went on about Natalie's exploits and Fern yucked it up.

"I'm chilling," Pilar answered quietly. Too quietly. I did a very quick peek and was blasted by fear, grief, and anger. Her emotions were appropriate, but that didn't make them feel any better to me . . . or to her.

"Can I do anything for you?" I pressed, feeling helpless in the face of her despair.

"Nah, I'm okay," she lied, looking at her lap as Victor looked at her face with concern in his eyes.

I opened my mouth to convince her that I could help, then closed it again.

"Thank you for checking, Cally," Victor put in.

I nodded and smiled as best I could, thankful for the old man's kindness. Then I looked away, scanning the room.

York sat across from Kapp, shaking his head.

"They don't eat it, exactly," York muttered.

"Hooboy," Kapp argued. "It sure as hell looks like they're eating it."

I had no idea what they were arguing about.

"They need it for digestion," Earl cut in.

"Hah!" Kapp responded. "Where'd you learn about turkeys? In fire school?"

"It goes in their gullets, not their stomachs," Earl expanded.

"What's a gullet anyway?" Kapp demanded.

I looked around for Geneva. I couldn't believe that three grown men were sitting around arguing about turkeys. Actually, considering the day, I decided I could. It was as therapeutic as anything else.

But I didn't see my sister in the room.

"Where's Geneva?" I asked.

"In the kitchen," Kapp informed me. "She's probably taking gravel out of turkey gullets, according to these two."

"Kapp!" I warned him.

"What?" he asked innocently. "Are you going to beat me with your cane?"

I looked at Roy. He nodded before I even said I wanted to see Geneva alone, and he sat down to join the turkey club.

I stepped into the kitchen quietly. Geneva sat at the kitchen table, her back to me, her head in her hands. Was she crying?

"Geneva?" I whispered.

Her head popped up. I saw her neck straighten. Geneva was always strong. I wondered how hard that constant strength had to be on her system.

"I love you." The usually unspoken words tumbled out of my mouth.

"Oh, Cally," she murmured, but she didn't get up. She didn't even turn her head. I was sure she was crying then.

I left the kitchen as quietly as I'd entered. There was no one I could help in this house. There was no reason to stay.

"Roy," I whispered in my sweetie's ear. "Let's go now."

We had just said our good-byes to the living room contingents when we all heard the phone ring in the kitchen.

No one spoke as Geneva answered, her voice a low rumble.

A few breaths later, Geneva walked into the living room. She strode toward Pilar as the rest of us watched.

"Pilar," she pronounced. "You have to be calm." Victor put his arm around the girl as her face paled.

Geneva cleared her throat and continued.

"Aunt Daphne has passed away. She was gone by the time she reached the hospital."

SEVEN

"May Daphne find joy wherever she is," Victor intoned. "We loved her, and our love goes with her."

Roy grabbed me before my leg even had a chance to buckle. My eyes welled up instead, as if my whole body had turned to water looking for a way out.

"Amen," Earl added belatedly.

"Who called?" Kapp demanded, standing up stiffly with his cane. "Who was on the phone?"

"Bob," Geneva answered briefly. She looked pretty wobbly herself, except for her eyes.

"But what did they find?" Kapp pressed her. "Are they suspicious now?"

"I don't know," she stated for the record, keeping her eyes on Pilar.

I could barely hear them anymore. Would I truly never see my aunt Daphne again? I thought of the wizened woman she'd become, and the beautiful woman she'd been, both of them so full of light and grace on the inside. I thought—

Then Pilar began to scream. As she did, I wondered why it had taken her so long to react. Had Geneva's eyes held her in check?

"No!" Pilar wailed. The sound seemed to echo in the room, bouncing off the pale orchid walls and back.

"Oh, Pilar," I breathed and moved toward her.

But Geneva had already grabbed her by her shoulders.

"Pilar, listen to me—" she began.

"No, I won't!" Pilar shouted, shaking off her touch. "You said to be calm because Daphne would come back. But she didn't. She's never coming back! I'm not stupid. I see how this is going down. Everyone's going to lie and pretend to help me. But no one can help me."

I wanted to argue. But she was right. She wasn't stupid. And no one could really help her.

Linda rushed to the bathroom.

I searched for light inside of myself. Because Roy had been right, too. Daphne didn't mind the dying. It was us. And Pilar. I wondered once more what Daphne had been to Pilar. Pilar acted as if Daphne had been her mother. But she couldn't have been. Daphne was just too old. What was a teenager doing with such an elderly woman?

"Pilar," I tried, swallowing the bile that rose in my throat. "Daphne was happy at the end. She was with the people she loved, especially you, and she was joking, do you remember? I know it hurts, but Daphne had a good death."

"How do you know?" A mixture of anger and hope were in her voice.

I thought for a moment, trying to focus the wavering images in my mind. "Because she was enjoying herself till the moment she lost consciousness. You're the one that's hurting. I can see that. Can you bring some light into your hurt by knowing how much Daphne loved you?"

Pilar began to cry again then, more softly. Victor put his arm around her shoulders. She didn't seem to notice. But she didn't push him away either.

"I loved her!" she declared, her muffled voice still defiant.

"She knows that," Roy put in.

"Really?" Pilar asked, her head popping up.

"Really."

I grabbed Roy's hand. It was warm and bony and dry. It was solid.

Fern walked cautiously toward Pilar. It was hard to believe Fern was the same young woman who'd been laughing so recently. Her features were still, watchful.

"Pilar, we loved Aunt Daphne, too," she said carefully. "Maybe not the same way you did, but we did. I loved her because she was so cool. No matter what happens, you'll always remember her. Remember her jokes, her kindness, her willingness to fool around. She was a cool old lady."

"But what do I do *now*?" Pilar demanded.

Fern stopped moving. She didn't know the answer. None of us knew the answer.

"Who are you anyway?" Linda demanded of Pilar, coming back out of the bathroom, her sharp cheekbones cutting toward the surface of her face.

"Shush, honey," Victor admonished his daughter.

Fern looked over her mother's shoulder, and I saw the uncertainty in her eyes. "Granddad, do you have any of that valerian root?" she whispered.

"What's valerian root?" Pilar asked suspiciously.

"It calms you down," Victor explained and began searching in his backpack. I could smell herbs from where I stood.

"I don't want to calm down," Pilar announced, wiping the tears from her face. "I want to call the police."

There was a silence that felt like a repositioning. It was one thing to comfort a young teenager in need, the silence seemed to say. It was another to involve the police in a family gathering. And yet . . .

"Pilar," Linda tried, her voice strained with the attempt to be reasonable. "We would call the police if you told us something, anything that made sense of your theories. But nothing you've said yet does make sense. And what if you're wrong. Do you really want the police barging in here?"

"Yeah, I do," Pilar answered simply, her round, bland features impossible to read.

"I'm sure the police department of this town knows what it's doing," my uncle Earl put in. He raised his hands squarely, as if holding a box. "If there really is anything suspicious, they'll come on their own to ask questions."

"Hah!" Kapp snorted dismissively. "Not in this county."

"What do you mean?" Fern asked, and she wasn't just asking for curiosity's sake. I could almost hear her brain taking notes.

"The police hate to investigate anything that won't make it to a jury," Kapp replied. "They don't have the budget. They don't want to put in the hours or the money unless they've got a sure thing. A place like Estados doesn't want to hear about murder unless they've got the perp in handcuffs with a signed confession."

"So *we* should call *them,*" York concluded.

Uncle Earl shook his head. "With all due respect," he began, nodding Kapp's way. "Most police departments are filled with conscientious people doing their jobs. Mr. Kapp here may dislike the police for his own reasons, but that's not grounds to believe that they won't do their job—"

"Hooboy!" Kapp boomed and threw his arms in the air, practically knocking York over with his cane in the process. Luckily, York was fast on the back step. "I just explained why they won't do 'their job.' Besides, it's Thanksgiving. Do you know how many family squabbles there are on Thanksgiving? How many assaults? How many drunks? They have their plates full, and not with turkey either. Someone has to tell them that Daphne's death was suspicious. How are they going to notice otherwise? Who's gonna tell them? Holy Mother, think here, folks!"

"But *is* Daphne's death suspicious?" Fern asked, her voice sincere. "I don't understand why it's suspicious." She turned to Pilar. "Mom's right. You need to explain why you think so. Or else, what can we tell the police anyway?"

Pilar seemed to deflate. She looked down at the rug and mumbled. "It just looked like she was poisoned, you know. I mean, she ate and drank and then fell over. Duh! Poison. That's how it went down. End of story."

"But she *was* sick," Fern argued.

Pilar just crossed her arms and glared.

Kapp opened his mouth for another round.

"Shall we wait for Bob to decide?" Geneva suggested, her eyes still on Pilar. "Bob will be here soon. Would that be okay?"

"I guess so," Pilar agreed, her voice slow, as if searching for the trick in the question.

My mind was searching for a trick, too. Daphne's death shouldn't have been such a shock. We were all expecting it. But I was truly shaken. And I was pretty sure everyone in the room was as shaken as I was. And there was something else edging at my mind. How she died? Why she died? But my mind couldn't seem to hold whatever thought was prodding it.

"Could I make a suggestion?" Roy asked Pilar.

She nodded her permission. She seemed to trust Roy. But then, so did I.

"You folks are all grieving," he went on, his quiet voice as soothing as flannel sheets. "I think that you might want to say some words over your Daphne, some positive words. You all felt affection for her, some of you loved her dearly. Maybe you could share some of that now in memory. It might help the hurt. Pilar, would that help?"

Pilar nodded mutely again. But her face seemed to have a little color in it, finally. I squeezed Roy's hand.

"Aw, come on—" Kapp began.

Geneva spun around, pursed her mouth and eyes, and shook an elegant finger in his face as if he was an errant dog.

Kapp closed his mouth again and plopped back into his seat, sighing melodramatically. Actually, he was a lot like a dog in some ways. I was glad Geneva had learned to rein him in.

Everyone sat down again then. But we were no longer a healing circle. We were a good-bye-to-Daphne circle. Could we really do this?

Roy began. "I only met Daphne this very day, but I saw right off that she was a real lady. And I don't mean because of the way she dressed or because she read Miss Manners.

I mean her way of kindness. She made me feel welcome in an instant. She didn't feel the need to overshadow other people. In fact, I believe she put others before herself as often as not. She was a lady I feel graced to have met."

Roy turned to me then.

I took a deep breath before starting. "Aunt Daphne was kind," I agreed with Roy. "She was one of the kindest people I've ever known. Her heart was open to others. And with everything she was going through, she could still laugh. No matter the pressure, she was a picture of serenity. She noticed others. She cared. And she practiced joy despite her pain. I just hope that I'll be able to do as well . . ." I stopped. I couldn't finish for the tears.

I felt a silken hand on mine. It was Geneva's.

"My turn, little sister," she murmured. Then she withdrew her hand and spoke more loudly. "Aunt Daphne was one far-out woman. She was smart and not ashamed to show it in a generation that didn't appreciate uppity women. She was a feminist before her time. She didn't allow herself to be forced into marriage. She worked as a legal secretary, and she was a good one. She dressed elegantly every day of her life. I remember her clothes, professional but beautiful. She had an eye for beauty. I remember her apartment from when I was a kid, too. It was small but perfect. She did her own paint, picked her own furnishings, and made a home to be proud of." Geneva's voice was getting hoarse. "Aunt Daphne was everything a woman could hope to be." She turned to Pilar and asked softly, "Can you talk about what Daphne meant to you now?"

The girl nodded.

"Daphne loved me," she mumbled through a mouthful of sadness. "No one else did, you know. But she did. No lie. She wasn't ever mean to me. Even when I, like, made mistakes and stuff. She didn't yell. She just asked me what I thought. She didn't think I was stupid or a burden or any of that stuff. And she was fun. She was too cool." Pilar's eyes were bright as she remembered. "And she told me to be cool when she was gone. So, I guess I gotta do this thing. For her, you know." The light went from her eyes. "I just wish I'd thanked her more." Pilar put her head in her hands then.

"Thank her now," Roy suggested softly.

"Now?" Pilar's head came up again.

Roy nodded.

"Thank you, Daphne," she whispered and began sobbing.

Victor put his arm around the girl. "Don't forget, my dear, there may be others that love you," he reminded her. "You see, my sister Daphne didn't have bad taste. If she loved you, I love you, too. Daphne was smart. And she was funny. She always understood my bad puns, even when we were kids. And she was one of the only people who understood how I could be interested in George Sand one day and hydroponics the next. She *understood*. That meant a lot to me. She was sensitive. She could guess my feelings before I even knew I was having them. Cally gets that from her."

My head jerked. I'd never made that connection.

"That was my sister Daphne," Victor went on. "She cared about everyone. And she was truly interested, too. Cally, you wouldn't believe the perceptive questions she asked about your practice. And Geneva, she loved your clothes. And York, she thought your martial arts classes for the disabled were first rate. She noticed everyone, everything. I almost married another woman before Mary—"

"You didn't!" Linda broke in, her face reddening.

"Let him talk, Mom," Fern admonished.

Victor bent his head back and laughed, but his eyes were glossy beneath his glasses. "Her name was Beatrice. She was pretty, bright. I liked her a lot. Daphne said that 'liking' wasn't enough. That I should wait until I loved. She was correct. I knew it when I met Mary. I always wondered how Daphne knew. Daphne understood people. And she had a good heart." Victor stopped and pulled out a handkerchief. "I guess I've taken my share of time," he concluded and turned to his daughter.

Linda cleared her throat. "Aunt Daphne was a role model for me. Geneva said a lot of it. She was a feminist before there was such a thing. And she did well in a man's world. She may have been a secretary, but she worked hard and was a well-paid secretary. And she invested her money. She was shrewd. She never pushed herself in your face, but she was always thinking. Not very many single women her age did as well as she did, that's for sure. I don't know. I guess that's it for me." She turned to her daughter.

"Great-aunt Daphne was cool," Fern proclaimed. "It wasn't like she was some totally Goody Two-Shoes or anything. She *was* kind, and smart, and funny. But the really cool thing about her was her imagination. She was always thinking about people and their relationships. When I was little, she used to make up stories with me. We'd do it together. She could have been a famous writer. But maybe she didn't need that. She found whatever she needed just living exactly the way she did. I want to put her in a book. See, she was interesting. She was something different to each of us, but all of those things at once. I hope I can do her justice. That's all."

Earl was next on board. "I suppose I didn't really know Daphne as well as some of you, but I agree that she was a good woman," he said. He coughed, then continued. "She was loyal to her family. She even kept in touch with me, though I was just her brother-in-law's brother. She helped with the five of you Lazar kids. She was responsible and practical. She worked hard. And she kept her sense of humor. That's not always easy to do, but she did it."

There was a silence. It seemed that Earl was finished. Kapp waited a moment before diving into the silence.

"I only met Daphne today, the same as Roy," he led in. "But what a woman! Mother of God, what a prize. Smart, witty, beautiful—"

I smiled. Ah, Kapp. He'd seen Daphne's beauty beneath the ravages of her illness.

"If Bob hadn't been there, I would have asked to be first on her dance card, if you know what I mean. She played with words like nobody's business. And observant, sheesh! That woman would have made a fine lawyer. I'm ashamed to be part of the male establishment that made her a secretary instead. Her mind was top-notch and her people skills were even better." He shook his head. "I'm glad to have met her," he said to sum up.

York, my brother of few words, was next.

"Aunt Daphne was a woman of total integrity," he murmured. He squinted his eyes. "Once she chose a path, her mind was clear enough to follow it. That's not as simple as it sounds. She knew how to concentrate, how to focus, even in pain. She achieved clarity of mind in her life. She had courage. She was a warrior. She died a warrior."

Whoa. What York's voice lacked in volume, it made up for in intensity.

I looked around the circle. But there was no one left to speak who hadn't already spoken. I squeezed Roy's hand. He'd been right. Pilar had tears in her eyes, but her face was softer. Was she remembering Daphne? Was her mind absorbing all the different ways in which Daphne had been extraordinary to each of us?

"I think I'll go upstairs to wait for Bob," Pilar announced.

As she stood up from her chair, slowly, like someone many times her age, Victor stood with her. He walked with her to the stairway.

Pilar turned when she reached the stairway. "Thank you," she whispered. "I'm still stressing, but it's okay. I still think Daphne was poisoned, but I thank all of you for loving her. All of you who did, you know. Not the one who poisoned her. Still, all the stuff you said made me remember her even better. She was the coolest. No lie."

"Shall I come up with you, honey?" Victor asked.

"Nah," she replied, but she impulsively hugged the elderly man. "I gotta, like, think, you know?"

"I know," he answered.

And Pilar lumbered up the stairs.

Victor seemed to collapse then. He sat on his chair, pulled off his glasses, and wept, openly and freely.

I was glad for his ability to do that. With Daphne gone, he was the last of his generation of the Duprees. He had a right to weep.

"We should just leave," Linda rapped out. "This is too much for Dad. We should just get on a plane and go home."

"Linda's right," Earl agreed. "Something feels unhealthy here. And I'm worried for you kids."

I assumed he meant Geneva, York, Melinda, Arnot, and me. He usually did when he said "kids." But I was more worried for Earl than for us. His skin looked pasty, his face sadder than ever. At least Victor was having a good cry. I had no idea how my uncle Earl was coping.

"I have breakfast planned for you, Earl, and for Victor and Linda and Fern, tomorrow," Geneva reminded him.

I did, however, know how Geneva was coping. She was assuming control.

"And of course Pilar and Bob, and whoever else wants to come," she continued. "What time would you like to be here for breakfast?"

Earl looked at Linda, raising his brows, but Linda was looking at Geneva. When Geneva spoke, people usually listened. Even if the guests wanted to skip town, they wouldn't with Geneva in charge.

"How about nine o'clock?" Fern suggested diffidently.

"Good," Geneva told her, as if Fern was a student who'd come up with the right answer. "I'll count on it. And there's the family lunch at one. Everyone is coming to that. Melinda, Arnot, York, Roy, Cally. Am I correct?"

I knew that Geneva's last question was directed at me by her tone. I'd heard that tone of steel many times when I'd lived with her.

"One o'clock," I confirmed. "Yes, ma'am."

"Oh, Exalted Queen of the Kitchen?" Kapp said, wheedling in a falsetto. "May I come, too?"

"You can come to breakfast and lunch, and help clean up afterward," Geneva shot back.

Kapp saluted her. Geneva started to smile. The front doorbell rang.

The smile disappeared from Geneva's face with the sound. Geneva marched toward the door and flung it open.

Bob Ungerman was on the doorstep, looking very tired. His limbs trembled, and his dark skin had a gray cast.

"Oh, Bob—" Geneva began, the steel gone from her voice.

"Where's Pilar?" he interrupted her.

Geneva stepped back, shocked by the anger in his trembling voice.

"Upstairs in her room," she told him.

"Does she know?" he asked.

Geneva just nodded.

"Bob, what did the hospital say about the cause of death?" Kapp tried.

"Not now," Bob answered. "First Pilar, then we talk."

"But—" Kapp tried.

Bob strode past us all on shaking limbs and made his way up the staircase.

"So much for Bob settling this thing," Kapp muttered. "We need to call the police *now*."

"Listen, Dad's a wreck," Linda pointed out. "We've all had enough stress. Let Bob talk to Pilar. Maybe he can make sense of what she's saying."

"She's saying that your aunt Daphne was murdered!" Kapp bellowed. "What is so hard about that to understand? If you didn't do it, then let the police investigate."

"Are you implying that *I* had something to do with—"

"I'm not implying or accusing," Kapp explained in frustration, or possibly in feigned frustration. With Kapp, it was hard to tell the difference. "But we need to let the police know—"

"You're not even a member of this family," Earl threw in.

"Well, I am," York threw back. "And I agree with Kapp."

There was a short silence, then we heard the sound of footsteps on the staircase.

Pilar and Bob came down together, hand in hand.

"You can stop arguing," Bob informed us. "I called the police from the bedroom. They're coming right out."

EIGHT

"Yeah!" Pilar crowed. She looked stronger suddenly . . . and older. She slitted angry eyes under her red, plucked eyebrows and glared at us all, defying us to react.

Pilar wasn't a lone teenager anymore. She had Bob to back her up. And she was ready for action. It showed in her shoulders, no longer slumped but pulled back. It showed in the way her hands were balled into fists. And it showed in her wide gunslinger stance. She was fierce, a warrior like Daphne. A warrior *for* Daphne.

"Why'd you do that?" Linda shouted at Bob. "Jeez, can't you see what a mess this thing already is?"

"Linda—" her father, Victor, began.

"Daphne Dupree's death is not a 'thing' to be pushed aside," Bob cut him off quietly. For all the tics and shaking in his body and voice, he was a warrior, too. And his cause was the same as Pilar's. Together, they were formidable.

"Listen, I cared about Aunt Daphne myself," Linda argued, still not finished. Her face was red and sweating. "But Pilar still hasn't explained why she thinks Daphne was . . . was . . ."

"Murdered," Kapp offered helpfully.

"I hope no one uses that word when the police arrive," Earl advised. "I don't know much about this police business. But that's not a word to be bandied about."

"Oh, I wasn't bandying," Kapp informed him. "And I don't think Pilar is either."

Earl turned to say something to Kapp, but then turned back again, as if he'd thought better of it. I didn't blame him. Right or wrong, Kapp always got the last word.

"I need a cigarette," Earl mumbled. "Excuse me if you would." He pushed past the mob in Geneva's living room, through the dining room to the kitchen.

"You need to get your evidence together and coherent," Kapp advised Bob. We heard the kitchen door slam. "Linda's right in her own way. Nothing that Pilar has told us is really enough to light a firecracker under the police. Is there something you're not saying?"

Bob and Pilar looked at each other simultaneously. No one else spoke. Were we all trying to feel what they were saying with their eyes?

"There *is* something, isn't there?" Fern demanded, breaking the silence. "I knew it."

Pilar whipped her head back. "I know what I know," she replied sullenly. "You're not going to psyche me out. I'm not dumb. You think you're so smart—"

"What's done is done," Bob put in, giving Pilar's hand a squeeze. "The police are on their way. I don't believe Daphne's death was natural, and neither does Pilar."

"But *why?*" Fern asked, her voice high with frustration. "Why?"

"It doesn't matter," Bob answered before Pilar could. "Once the police are informed, then we'll each get to say our piece. Pilar can tell the police what she knows. I can tell them what I know."

"But why won't you tell us?" Fern kept on pressing. Maybe she would become an attorney instead of an author, I decided. She had the pit bull qualification.

Bob just sighed and shook his head.

"Oh, give it a break, Fern," Kapp cajoled, veering away from the get-the-evidence-together stance he'd espoused a few moments before. "Think a little here. If you believed someone in a group might be a murderer, would you give them the CliffsNotes on your theories so they could work on their defense?"

Fern opened her mouth again, and said, "But . . . ," then faltered. Finally, she just said, "Oh."

"We've got to do what's right for Daphne and what's right for Pilar," York put in. "It's certainly worth putting up with the police."

"Yes," Geneva agreed softly. "For Daphne. For Pilar."

I smelled Earl's smoky presence back in the room before I saw him.

"Listen, kids," Earl started, his eyes darting to me, to Geneva, and to York. "I hate to see you involved in this situation. I know that Pilar is upset, but it's always good practice to be clear and succinct with the police. Let's not fan the fires of hysteria by imagining the worst. It's so easy to look for someone to blame when someone you care about dies." I found myself nodding as he spoke. He was right on that score. "Death is sad. You remember when I lost your aunt Ingrid. I wanted to blame everyone. The doctors, the nurses, the pharmacists."

As he went on, I tried to remember Earl's reaction to my aunt's death, but I couldn't. For me, Aunt Ingrid's death had been totally eclipsed by my parents' deaths less than a year later. I felt ashamed. I hadn't ever really thought about Earl's grief. It hadn't even appeared on my mental radar.

"But your aunt Ingrid just died of leukemia," he reminded us. "There was nothing I could do about it. It's the same with your aunt Daphne. You want to do something. You want someone to blame. But she just died."

"No!" Pilar yelped. "You're not going to psyche everyone out." She softened her voice. "Maybe that's, like, what happened with your wife. But that's not the way it went down with Daphne. Somebody killed Daphne."

I looked over at Roy and saw him nodding in agreement with Pilar. The air felt funny, hard to breathe. Did Roy actually know something?

"Young lady," Earl said quietly. "You're certainly entitled

to your opinion. I'm just trying to help you calm down. When bad things happen—"

"Hel-lo!" Pilar cut in. "It isn't just an 'opinion.' Look, Daphne—"

"It's okay, Pilar," Bob interrupted his charge. "You don't have to explain yourself to these folks. The police are coming. That's what matters. We've set the wheels in motion."

"But nobody here gets it," Pilar complained. "No one knows what I'm talking about. They just want me to chill out. They think I'm nuts."

"I'd like to know what you're talking about," Kapp prodded.

Pilar looked at Kapp, appraising him slowly.

"Okay," she said finally. "First, ya gotta understand. Daphne was really sick, so—"

The doorbell rang before Pilar could finish her sentence. I wasn't the only one who jumped.

Geneva opened the door to two police officers in uniform.

The first one in was a dark-haired beauty of a woman. She looked more like a movie star playing a police officer than a real officer. A man with strong Middle Eastern features followed her.

"I'm Officer Rossetti, and this is Officer Khashoggi," she began. "We received a call—"

And everyone started talking at once.

"I made the call—"

"Someone killed Daphne—"

"Nonsense—"

"I'm an attorney—"

"Everyone calm down—"

"She was murdered—"

"Listen, this is my house—"

"Whoa!" Officer Rossetti shouted, her hand on her belt. Was that a gun near her hand?

She was a good shouter. Everyone stopped talking.

"Okay, who made the call?" she asked, pulling a notebook out of her pocket.

"I did," Bob admitted and crossed the room to face Officer Rossetti. "A woman died today. Daphne Dupree—"

"Is she here?" Officer Khashoggi asked. His voice was gentle, soothing. Maybe Rossetti was the designated shouter. "Is that why you called?"

"No, she died on the way to the hospital," Bob explained. "You can call them if you want. I believe that Ms. Dupree may have been poisoned—"

"Oh, come on—"

"Let him have his say—"

"But that's ridiculous—"

"She was too poisoned—"

The vocal races were on again.

"Quiet!" Officer Rossetti shouted. "Look, folks. I want to know why we were called, and I want to know it fast. Are you talking about an accident, a suicide, what?"

Pilar stepped forward. She spread out her arms.

"Daphne Dupree was poisoned by one of these people!" she accused.

"And why do you say that, young lady?" Officer Khashoggi asked gently.

"Okay, she was sick," Pilar dove in. "I, like, know that. And she was stressing. But, see, it was too soon. Daphne was really jazzed about this reunion. She wouldn't have offed herself if that's what you're thinking. She promised she'd let me know when it was time—"

"Time for what?" Rossetti broke in. "And what's your name and relationship to the deceased?"

These officers weren't going by the book, that was for sure. I was beginning to think Estados didn't have a "book." Maybe Kapp was right. Maybe they were overworked and hoping to leave as soon as possible. Had Bob's stand been for nothing?

"Time to . . . to . . . ," Pilar faltered.

"She knows something she's not telling," Fern put in helpfully.

"Who is 'she'?" Rossetti demanded. "And who are you?"

"I'm Fern Salcedo. And she's Pilar something-or-other.

She's with my great-aunt Daphne somehow, but she won't tell anyone exactly how. And she keeps screaming and accusing everyone of murdering Aunt Daphne."

"She's upset," Officer Khashoggi concluded.

"That's right, Officer," Victor agreed. "But she has reason to be upset."

"And you are?" Rossetti demanded.

Kapp rolled his eyes as Victor identified himself. I hoped Rossetti didn't see Kapp do it. Her organizational skills might have needed work, but she was the one with a gun on her belt.

"Perhaps, it would be easier if you took each one of us separately for questioning," Kapp suggested.

"Are you telling us how to do our jobs?" Rossetti replied. Her voice was quiet, but her glare wasn't. Ouch. She had seen him.

"Look, Officer," he tried. "I'm a trial attorney. I know a little bit about criminal law—"

"Fine," she cut him off. "You just save up your little speech for court. We answered the call, and you people are not telling us what we need to know. If you have something to say, say it. Or we're out of here."

"God forbid, you should treat citizens with respect," Kapp muttered. He flung up his hands. "God forbid you should listen to an old man who's been part of the legal system for decades before you were born. How rude of me to have intruded. Please, do go on."

Rossetti reached toward her belt again. Would she shoot Kapp? Criminy, I'd wanted to shoot Kapp a few times myself. But I'd never had a gun handy. Rossetti did.

Khashoggi stepped up to his fellow officer and whispered in her ear. She took a big breath in and sighed loudly.

"Okay, folks, where were we?"

Linda chose that moment to run toward the bathroom.

"That's just my mom, escaping the scene of the crime," Fern chimed in.

"Khashoggi, grab her!" Rossetti ordered.

Khashoggi began his run toward Linda, but she was

already in the bathroom with the door locked by the time he got there. He rapped on the door.

"I was just joking!" Fern cried before he could order Linda to come out.

Khashoggi turned, his face serious.

"My mom has a bladder infection," Fern explained, or at least she tried to explain.

"I thought your aunt was the one who was poisoned," Khashoggi said.

"She was, or maybe she was," Fern told him. "It's Pilar who thinks Aunt Daphne was poisoned. My mom's just going through menopause."

Khashoggi turned to look back at Rossetti. They both raised their eyebrows. I wasn't sure what the exchange meant.

"Well, people, this has been fun," Rossetti growled. Finally, I knew what the exchange meant. "But we have real work to do." She turned toward the still-open doorway.

"No!" Pilar shouted. "You don't get it. She really was poisoned."

"We'll log it in," Rossetti replied but didn't turn back.

"Wait!" Bob cried. Then he modulated his voice. "This isn't a prank. Please, just listen."

"Aren't you the one who called?" Rossetti asked, turning back.

"Yes, ma'am," Bob agreed, speaking slowly and carefully. "I need to tell you that Pilar is not the only one who believes Daphne was poisoned. I also believe she was poisoned."

"And why do you believe that, Mr . . ."

"Ungerman," Bob supplied politely. "If I may explain. Ms. Dupree was sick—"

"Cancer," Geneva interjected.

"Yes, cancer," Bob conceded, inclining his head Geneva's way. "And I had medical power of attorney. Daphne's health was failing but not that fast. She ate here and drank, and then she collapsed. I think she was having some trouble breathing before she collapsed. It wasn't anything to do with her cancer. I feel that she was poisoned."

"Are you a doctor, Mr. Ungerman?" Rossetti demanded.

"No, but—"

But Khashoggi had a different question for Bob.

"When you say 'poisoned,' do you mean an accident, a suicide, or are you making an accusation of murder?"

"I know it wasn't suicide," Bob answered diffidently. "I can't completely rule out an accident. So, yes, I believe it is possible that she was murdered."

"Didn't you say this woman went to the hospital, Mr. Ungerman?" Rossetti took over. "Don't you think the hospital would have noticed if this . . ." Rossetti stopped to look in her notebook. ". . . if this Daphne Dupree had been poisoned?"

"She was dead by the time she got there, Officer Rossetti," Bob answered with dignity in his trembling voice. "That's what they told me later. All that time I'd been waiting, she was already dead."

"And they didn't mention poison?" Officer Rossetti pressed. "Don't you think a doctor checked her over?"

"Yes, that may be true," Bob answered, the restraint telling on his strained features. "But if they heard she had cancer, they wouldn't have necessarily looked for poison."

"Did you ask them about the possibility of poison?" Kapp asked Bob. "I asked when I called, but they just told me she was dead. Case closed."

Rossetti glared his way, but it was an important question. She let Bob answer. And now I knew why Kapp had looked so old when he'd come back from calling the hospital.

"No, they rushed her away too quickly," Bob said. "They thought they still might be able to save her. I tried to talk to the nurses, but they weren't listening, short-staffed because of the holiday. Her MedicAlert bracelet says cancer. They just assumed—"

"And you assume she was poisoned?" Khashoggi asked.

"Yes," he answered. "It appears so to me."

Rossetti sighed and looked at Khashoggi. I felt a sudden sympathy for the two of them. I wondered how much ground they'd covered tonight. It was after eleven. Had they worked all day, too?

Linda came out of the bathroom, looking better than when she'd gone in.

"Perhaps you could call the hospital and ask what the cause of death was," Victor suggested. "I know you're tired. We're all tired. But Pilar and Bob really do need to know what happened."

"Excuse us for a moment," Khashoggi murmured and placed his hand on his partner's arm. He lead her into the dining room, where they whispered urgently. I thought I heard Rossetti cursing, then Khashoggi's voice soothing, cajoling.

"Okay," Rossetti muttered when they returned to the living room. "We'll make the call. What hospital did she go to?"

"Glasse County Memorial," Bob answered.

"I'm not promising anything," Rossetti told him, her voice softening for a moment. "Where's the phone?"

"There's a phone in the kitchen," Geneva answered.

The group of us standing in the living room were very, very quiet. We were all straining to hear what Rossetti had to say from the kitchen.

"This is Officer Rossetti from the Estados Police Department," she led in. "You got a DOA earlier today, name of Daphne Dupree. We'd like to know the cause of death."

We waited as something happened on the other end of the line. Were they transferring her? I rotated my head, trying to loosen my neck muscles.

"If you wanna check on me, call the Estados Police Department. You want my badge number?"

Another wait. I rotated my shoulders this time.

"Hey, I don't think this calls for a warrant," she snapped. "We just want a preliminary cause of death. Her relatives are here, and they need some answers."

In the next long silence, I surveyed auras casually. I saw a lot of frustration. And I saw darkness. Darkness? Dack. Was this what Roy saw? It floated around my uncle Victor, my uncle Earl, Linda, Geneva, and York. It was skipping those who weren't family members. And Fern was unaffected. My mind lost cohesion. Was I seeing my own fear? I could feel the dampness of my own sweat. I was certainly afraid. But was I afraid because of what I was seeing, or was what I was seeing making me afraid? Did it have to do with Daphne's—

"Well, fine!" Officer Rossetti barked, and the mist of darkness disappeared. "I'll just have the Chief call you!"

Finally, she slammed the phone down.

Officer Khashoggi murmured something then. But I couldn't make out his words. I blinked my eyes and looked around me. The darkness was still gone.

"Your sister?" Rossetti demanded. "I thought your sister was a teacher."

Officer Khashoggi murmured some more. I thought I caught "other sister."

"Of course you should call her," Rossetti argued. "If she's a desk nurse, she can find out, right? And she's working this evening, of all evenings. Come on, Khashoggi."

Khashoggi murmured a little more.

Then I thought I heard him pick up the phone and dial. Or maybe I just assumed it.

He asked someone for Aisha Khashoggi.

A few breaths later, I heard a rapid-fire exchange of words I couldn't understand.

"You, too," he said finally and hung up.

Rossetti and Khashoggi returned to the living room after another whispered interaction. No one spoke a word. My skin felt cold as well as damp by then.

"Respiratory failure," Khashoggi announced. "Daphne Dupree died of respiratory failure."

"Does cancer cause respiratory failure?" Linda asked.

"Could it be poison?" Bob asked a beat later.

"We're not doctors," Rossetti answered, shrugging her shoulders.

"You did your best," Victor offered.

"We'll log all this in," Khashoggi informed us gently.

He cleared his throat. "It's hard to accept death. It doesn't necessarily mean it's murder."

"But it—" Pilar began.

"You said she collapsed," Khashoggi cut in, looking at Bob. "Was she unconscious?"

"Yes," Bob answered.

"And she remained unconscious until the ambulance came?"

"Yes," Bob agreed.

Khashoggi frowned. I wondered why. Did it have to do with his leaning to or from the possibility of Daphne's murder? Or was it something about jurisdiction? Or—

"How about an autopsy?" Kapp demanded. "I know it costs the county money, but the situation seems to demand it. And respiratory failure could mean just about anything."

Rossetti sighed. "Look, there are a number of reasons that an autopsy can be called for," she began. She held up a finger. "No doctor to sign death certificate. That isn't the case." She held up another finger. "Doctor not sure of cause of death. It was respiratory failure, right?" A third finger went up. "The deceased was alone in a house—"

"Or the death was suspicious," Kapp finished for her. He didn't hold up any fingers.

We all looked at one another.

Roy began to open his mouth. But I beat him to it.

"Daphne Dupree's death was suspicious," I announced. "I'm a relative, and I'm requesting an autopsy."

NINE

"What the—"

"Yeah, tell them—"

"Everyone settle down—"

"But she's—"

"Be reasonable—"

"*Very* suspicious—"

"Quiet!" Officer Rossetti roared. And the voices came to a stop.

Rossetti turned to me. "Are you serious?" she asked.

"I am," I replied. My adrenaline was pumping. I felt like I'd gone back in time to become the attorney I had been in court, only worse. I used to get stomachaches in court. I had a full body ache as Rossetti stared at me.

She sighed and began writing in her notebook again. "Name?" she demanded.

"Cally Lazar."

"Relationship to the deceased?"

"Niece."

"You say you want to formally request an autopsy of Daphne Dupree?"

"I do."

No one said "kiss the bride," but I sensed the solemnity of my words.

"Okay, we'll log your request," Rossetti assured me.

She turned to Officer Khashoggi. They exchanged a glance, then turned and speeded out the front door before anyone could demand anything else of them.

It was only after they'd left that I stopped to ask myself if "logging" my request meant that it would necessarily be granted.

I turned to Kapp to ask him. He'd know. Kapp knew everything.

"Good job, Lazar," he whispered, an attempt at a grin on his too tired face. He leaned on his cane heavily. It was easy to forget that Kapp was more than eighty years old. Was this a good time to ask him legal questions? Maybe he was too frail.

I looked around the room and reconsidered my appraisal of my old friend. Maybe Kapp just looked tired, like everyone else there. Even Uncle Victor's usually enthusiastic shoulders were uncharacteristically stooped. Uncle Earl's skin was an unsettling yellowish white. Bob's skin was gray-toned. Geneva was staring out into the space above our heads, at a distant horizon that apparently only she could see through the wall. York's eyes were wild with movement. And Roy was staring at me, frowning, his freckles dark against his pale skin. I wondered what he saw.

"So much for the police," Linda commented. Contempt dripped from her tone. She rolled her blue eyes in her tight, bony face. "If you ask me, they could use a few management courses. Sheesh, talk about unprofessional! They wouldn't make it a day in my business—"

"Oh, I don't know," Fern broke in. "They almost arrested you for bladder impairment, Mom." Fern actually looked pretty good, her face alive with what looked like excitement. Or maybe she was just nervous.

"What?" Linda demanded, turning on her daughter, her tight face reddening.

Fern just laughed. But it wasn't a pleasant laugh. The sound was shrill and unaccompanied. Bob spoke before Linda could follow up.

"Mr. Kapp, Cally," he put in. "I want to thank you for

the autopsy request. I thought those officers were just going to turn around and leave without doing anything for us. I didn't even think of asking. You both did the right thing. Pilar and I appreciate it."

"Yeah, you were cool, Cally," Pilar added. She looked tired, too, but calmer than she had before. Her features were soft again. "It's, like, you take me seriously. Those cops didn't even let me talk, you know. It was, like, they thought I was stupid or something. But I know stuff—"

"Come on, Pilar," Bob suggested, cutting her off once again. Why did he always cut her off just when she was getting interesting? "Let's go upstairs. We could both use the rest."

"Are you okay, dude?" Pilar asked Bob, her voice concerned.

"I'm all right," he assured her, but his shaking voice belied his words. "Just a little fatigued."

His fatigue was the best prod he could have used to move Pilar. They went up the stairs together without any more to-ing and fro-ing.

We heard one door shut and then another.

"Who the hell is Pilar, anyway?" Linda demanded in a whisper once the second door shut.

"Linda, honey, leave it alone," Victor advised gently. "I'm sure she has her reasons for keeping quiet."

"But why is she accusing us of poisoning Aunt Daphne? It doesn't make any sense." Linda clenched her fists. "She must know something we don't."

"Maybe," Victor conceded. "But it's up to the police now."

"Do you think *she* did it?" Linda moved on like a freight train. "She's clearly not stable, and she's hiding something—"

"Hey, Mom, just 'cause Pilar's weird doesn't mean she's necessarily a murderer," Fern put in. "I mean, we don't know. . . . You just have to chill out on this thing."

Linda opened her mouth to argue with Fern, but Roy spoke before she could.

"I don't believe that Pilar is alone in her fears, ma'am,"

he pointed out softly. "Mr. Ungerman appears to be mighty concerned over your aunt's passing as well. I do believe they have their reasons." I leaned into Roy, glad for his physical as well as moral support.

"They're both nuts," Linda diagnosed brusquely.

"Let's talk about something else for a while," Earl proposed. "As Victor pointed out, it's up to the police to sort it out now. They understand what they're doing."

"But the girl isn't stable—" Linda started in again.

"She's upset!" York snapped. He was in full martial arts stance, ready to fight. But there was no one to fight except Linda. "Pilar's human. She's lost someone she cared for. Criminy, can't you stop dissecting her?"

"And what am I?" Linda demanded. "I'm human. I'm upset, too, but I don't go accusing people—"

"Honey, stop right this minute!" Victor commanded. I was surprised at the sudden steel in his voice. "Pilar is acting within reason. I know it's natural for a group in stress to pick on an apparent outsider. I read enough psychology to understand that. But merely because something feels natural doesn't mean it's necessarily right. You know what's right in your heart. And if you don't, you should. Your mother and I brought you up with kindness. Show some now."

Linda stuck her lower lip out in a pout. Had Victor's words stung that much?

"Mom, come sit down," Fern invited, seating herself on the magenta love seat and patting the cushion next to her.

Linda crossed her arms.

"Please?" Fern cajoled. "I love you, Mom."

Linda sighed and walked over to the love seat. Fern tugged on her mother's arm. Linda sat, her eyes tearing up as she settled onto the cushion. Her father's words *had* stung her that much.

"Well," Geneva burst in, false cheer brimming in her voice. "Who's hungry? We can fix a snack tray."

I looked at my sister. Had she suddenly become Beaver Cleaver's mother? Who was this woman?

"I wouldn't mind a little snack," Earl replied. By the look of him, he'd throw up that snack, but at least he was trying.

"Sure," Kapp added. He patted his tummy. "Always room for more."

I wondered how many people in the room were questioning the wisdom of eating in a house where poisoning accusations had been made. I certainly was. *She ate, she drank—*

"Cally?" Geneva interrupted my reverie. "It would be really far out if you'd help me in the kitchen."

I looked up at Roy, and wondered what I expected from him. Permission? I'd never asked Roy for permission to be with my sister before. What was I thinking?

Roy just kissed my forehead, as if to unscramble my mixed thoughts.

"Yeah, 'groovy,' " I mumbled. "I'll help." And I followed Geneva into the kitchen.

I'd forgotten the desserts. I'd forgotten Melinda and Arnot's kids. Half-eaten pieces of cake, pie, and pastries littered the room.

Geneva went into action, cleaning up the mess and rescuing what was left of the desserts before I even had a chance to ask her why she wanted me with her. I stood, leaning against the kitchen counter waiting, as she worked. Then she reached for the two biggest dishes she owned.

"One platter for sliced turkey, cheese, bread, crackers, and condiments," she thought aloud. "The other, an assortment of fruit and desserts?"

"I'll slice the turkey," I offered, straightening up and opening the refrigerator door to pull what remained of the bird out for further abuse.

"Geneva?" I tried as I set the turkey on the counter. "Do you think Aunt Daphne—"

"I don't know." Geneva cut me off. She took a breath and put a hand up to her face as if to shield herself. "I haven't had time to think."

I grabbed a cutting board angrily. Why had I imagined Geneva wanted to talk? We were Lazars, after all.

"It's good to see you here," Geneva said softly after I'd produced a good-sized mound of turkey pieces on the cutting board. I transferred the mound to the largest dish, trying to arrange the turkey attractively.

"Shall I do the cheese?" I asked her. Dack, now I was the one who wasn't communicating.

My sister teased me gently: "Maybe you'd rather do cheese than turkey after meeting the Turkey Sisters." I recognized the teasing as an effort at bonding, even if it wasn't exactly the one I'd been trying for.

"I saw a different turkey this evening," I told her, softening my voice and my spine as I reached for the cheese. "Roy said this one was a male."

"Oh!" Geneva clapped her hands together over the dessert tray, looking truly happy for the first time since Daphne had collapsed. "Cally, it's so funny. I think the Turkey Sisters are hiding out from him. They always come around together. They are *très* cool, pecking all the time, enjoying themselves. And after they're gone, I see the male one arrive, but he's always alone. They disappear before I see him."

"Do you think he's looking for them?"

"I think maybe the sisters are in a witness protection program or something. He looks Mafia-connected to me."

I laughed and started cutting cheese.

"Maybe you could make them a couple of little disguises," I said with a straight face. Cheering up Geneva was cheering me up. "Perfect, comfortable jackets and pants. They'd be so elegant, he'd never recognize them."

"Hee-hee!" Finally, Geneva was giggling, something she rarely did. The sound relaxed places on my body that I hadn't even realized were stiff.

"Earth tones, I think," she answered as her fingers arranged pastries. "I hate all that orange and brown, but the Turkey Sisters have just *got* to wear autumn colors."

We continued to talk turkey fashion as we finished our platters. Mine didn't look nearly as pretty as Geneva's, but then I wasn't a clothing designer. Geneva took a stack of dessert-sized plates and napkins to the living room and came back so we could make our grand entrance together.

"Thanks, Cally," Geneva whispered, and we carried our food-laden dishes into the living room.

"Any time," I whispered back. And I meant it. So what if Lazars kept secrets? Geneva would always be my big sister.

"Well, don't those look nice," Earl commented as we set the huge dishes down next to the plates and napkins on the coffee table. He took a short trip to the table, speared some turkey, and put it on a plate before returning to the couch he shared with Roy.

Roy and Earl had settled onto one of the couches while Geneva and I had been in the kitchen. They were talking science fiction. Victor was in an easy chair next to them, commenting from the sidelines. They'd been discussing Isaac Asimov when Geneva and I had made our grand entrance. I was glad they had something to talk about. York and Kapp sat on another couch, whispering conspiratorially. I didn't think they'd even noticed the food yet. And Fern and her mother were still on the love seat.

"Shall I fix coffee and tea?" Victor asked.

"Thank you, Uncle Victor," Geneva replied, smiling.

I took a plate and piled it with fruit and cheese, finding that I actually was hungry. That was a surprise. I'd thought my eating days at Geneva's might have been over. But I'd prepared the turkey and cheese platter myself. And it would be hard to poison grapes and apples . . . I hoped. I took my plate and sat down next to Roy. Fern fixed her mother and herself a little pastry feast and returned to the love seat.

It almost felt like Thanksgiving again.

"Your young man is giving me an education about some science fiction writers I didn't know about," Earl told me. "We both agree about Brunner, of course, but I hadn't heard of Sheri Tepper."

"That's because she's a woman," Linda pointed out from across the room. She bit into an éclair, squishing custard out the other end. "You probably don't read women."

It was a good call, but mean-spirited, so I kept my laughter inward.

"Earl's read Tiptree!" Victor shouted over his shoulder as he headed toward the kitchen.

"Only because Tiptree wrote under a man's name," Linda shot back. "James Tiptree, Jr. I'll bet Earl never knew she was a woman."

"Now, now. I'm not that sexist," Earl objected earnestly. "It's true that I didn't know that Tiptree was a woman at first, but I would have read her anyway. She's a wonderful writer."

"Hah! You're a man," Linda corrected him. "Men read other men. Women read men and women."

"Oh, Mom, cut him a break," Fern weighed in. "Granddad's a man, and he's not a sexist. He's out there making coffee. And he reads all kinds of women writers."

"Try being raised by him," Linda snapped. "Then you can tell me he isn't sexist. Girls should be all sweetness and light. La-di-da. Well, I'm not, and that's the way it is."

Yep. It was beginning to feel like Thanksgiving all right.

I shoved a piece of cheese into my mouth, and offered the plate to Roy. He shook his head. Did he know something I didn't? I chewed slowly and swallowed cautiously, as if slowing down might be an antidote to poison. Earl reached over my "young man" to pat my hand. Then he turned to the couch where Kapp and York were seated.

"So, York!" he boomed. "How's your martial arts studio doing?"

York mumbled something I couldn't make out in answer.

"You're too modest," Earl kept on. "Even an old guy like me has heard of your studio. All the way in Los Angeles. People say good things about your work. And Melinda sent me a copy of that newspaper article about you. Martial arts for the disabled. I'm proud of you."

Roy tapped my arm as York replied with more mumbling.

"How're you doing, darlin?" he whispered in my ear.

"Okay?" I whispered back.

He raised his brows.

"Not so okay," I admitted.

"Let's find a little space where we can talk," he suggested quietly.

"And canoodle?" I countered hopefully.

"And canoodle."

Our little space turned out to be very little—the corner of the dining room table farthest from the entrance to the living room and the door to the kitchen. Earl hadn't said anything when Roy and I left the couch. He'd been too busy trying to elicit an audible response from York. And I could hear Victor in the kitchen, clanking cups over the whistle of the teapot.

"Cally, I just don't rightly know what to think about this day," Roy began when we were seated. "But I do believe we need to share our thoughts on this."

I pulled my chair closer to his and kissed him. His mouth was soft on mine, then more insistent. I closed my eyes and gave into the rush of feelings. Roy. His hand stroked my hair—

I smelled coffee.

I opened one eye. Victor stood at the other end of the dining room table holding a tray loaded with cups, a teapot, and a coffeepot. I opened the other eye and drew back from Roy. Victor smiled at us benignly.

"Tea?" he asked, winking.

"Um, no thanks," I chirped. I lowered my voice. "We're just fine," I assured him.

"You certainly are," he agreed, a mischievous smile on his wrinkled face. He turned to take the hot drinks into the living room, then turned back. "The kitchen is empty now," he offered with another wink.

So Roy and I ended up in the kitchen. Once we were there, we didn't even risk a kiss. We just held each other in an embrace that might have been romantic or might have just been two people comforting each other. It didn't matter. It felt good and warm and safe.

Finally, we sat at the kitchen table to talk seriously.

"Did Geneva get around to speaking to you about your aunt Daphne's passing?" he asked me.

I shook my head.

"That's not why she asked you into the kitchen?"

"No," I told him. I kept my sigh internal. "I don't think she's ready to talk."

"But—" he began and then stopped himself.

"But, what?" I asked.

"I expect I still just don't understand why you aren't talking to your relatives about all that's happened," he began slowly. Then he speeded up. "I do understand that they're hurting, Cally. But I thought you were having a heart-to-heart with your sister in this very room. Shouldn't you and York and Geneva all be supporting each other now, darlin'? Shouldn't you at least be working on figuring out what's happened here? Your aunt's passed on. And to my way of thinking, someone here may well have poisoned her. I know you guys don't much like to talk, but this situation is truly serious."

"I tried to talk to Geneva," I said defensively. "I'm not sure why she didn't answer me."

"Because you're her baby sister?" he guessed after a moment.

I rolled that one around in my mind for a while. Geneva was protective. But I didn't think that was the real reason she wouldn't talk to me. Geneva was a private person. And she was afraid. I shivered in the warm kitchen. I was afraid, too. And hurt. Hurt by the loss of Aunt Daphne. Hurt by the dysfunctionality of my family. Hurt by old memories.

I took a deep breath in before trying to explain the Lazar family dynamic to Roy for the second time that night.

I dove in. "I guess we just loved our aunt too much to talk about her death. Even now that it looks like she might have been killed, it's too hard. You know, we used to call her 'Aunt Daffy' when we were kids. She was all we really had left of my mother. She was so much like her. I don't know. It's just too painful to even think about her dying, much less talk about it—"

"Like your parents' deaths?" Roy interrupted.

It was lucky I was sitting down. His question felt like a blow to the chest, maybe to the heart. But it was a good question. I took another deep breath and answered it.

"Yeah, like my parents," I admitted. "I told you before. We almost never talk about our parents. We don't talk about their deaths. Once, York talked to me a little, but he stopped. It's as if there's a rule that if we don't talk about them, the bad stuff doesn't exist."

"But it does exist, doesn't it, darlin'?"

"I know it does, Roy!" I blurted out in frustration. "But what am I supposed to do? I can't *make* them talk. You said it before. 'They just can't speak for the hurt.' And I don't even know what happened here *today,* much less what happened twenty years ago. Even Pilar doesn't know what happened to Aunt Daphne for sure. But it's not good. It's just too scary."

"Is that why you requested an autopsy?"

"Yeah, I suppose so," I murmured, only understanding the truth as I spoke it. "I'm so tired of sticking my head in the sand. And Roy, you see darkness here—"

"You believe I'm truly seeing something?" Roy's eyes rounded in surprise.

"Yes, Roy," I told him. I reached up and touched his face. "I never disbelieved you. And Roy, I see it, too. It's all around us, swirling. It's around each of the family members but the younger ones. Geneva, York, Linda, Earl, Victor. Roy, I'm afraid. Maybe we're all in danger."

"Do you see the darkness around one person in particular?" he asked.

"No."

"Still, do you suspect one individual more than the others of poisoning your aunt Daphne?"

"I don't know." I whispered. I wanted to cry. "I just don't know."

"It's okay, darlin'" Roy told me and got up to put his arms around me.

"No, no." I shook my head. "It isn't okay. It's not okay at all!"

As Roy stretched his arms around the back of my chair to hold me, we heard twelve chimes. I felt Roy jump at the same time I did.

The clock in the living room had struck midnight.

TEN

But Geneva's grandfather clock didn't strike the time. At least it hadn't struck in as many years as I could remember it sitting in her living room. Pop had rigged it up so that you could turn the chimes off by pulling the cord. Geneva had never pulled the cord back the other way. And the last time I'd looked, the red flag that indicated that the chimes were turned off had still been showing. Had someone pulled the other end of the cord? Or had Pop—

I shook my head, trying to shake away the thought. Pop couldn't have had anything to do with this. Whoever had pulled that cord was alive and probably in Geneva's house. But why touch the clock?

I rose from my chair quickly, fueled by the tingling that prickled at my fingertips and toes. Roy and I speeded into the living room together.

Geneva stood there in the center of the room, erect but pale. She had adopted the clock along with me when our parents died. It was her responsibility. And Geneva took her responsibilities seriously.

"Who did this?" she demanded. Her voice deepened. "Tell me, right now. This isn't funny."

But no one admitted anything.

Kapp stepped up to the clock. "The blue tag's showing,"

he announced, tapping it with his cane. "Someone pulled this cord."

Still, no one admitted to the act.

"Not one of us is leaving until we find out who did this," York announced. He went to the door and stood, ready to fight any deserters. I had the feeling that he was hoping that someone would try to bolt.

But nobody moved toward the door. York glared at the crowd in general. I glared, too, though not so effectively.

"Who reset this?" York asked once more, as if *his* asking would force an answer.

There was a long silence.

"It could have been anyone." Fern finally broke the silence. "Melinda's kids or Arnot's kid or something—"

"Yeah, the kids," Linda agreed, with relief in her voice. "They get into everything. They were probably fooling around."

Geneva frowned, considering the idea. "I didn't see any of them near the clock," she muttered. "They went straight to the kitchen."

"You weren't watching them every second," Linda reminded her.

"No, I wasn't," Geneva conceded. Her erect posture seemed to give a little.

But I wasn't buying the explanation. Those kids hadn't been interested in the clock. They'd only been interested in dessert. There was something spooky about the clock chiming, something malicious, something—

"I hate to cause you folks any more worry," Roy put in. "But it seems to me as if the clock must have been reset during the last hour. I don't believe it chimed at eleven. And those children were all bundled up and gone by then."

There was a short period of quiet while we all absorbed the information. He was right. And his being right didn't make him any more popular in some quarters.

"What do you know about it?" Linda challenged Roy.

She turned and pointed a finger at him. "You're not even part of the family."

"Yes, indeed," Uncle Earl added. "Young man—"

"Hooboy!" Kapp cut in. "Are you guys trying to say that logic is limited to members of the family here? Because Roy is the only one who actually thought this out logically. Look at the evidence he's presented. The clock didn't chime at eleven. It chimed at twelve. So someone reset it between eleven and twelve. One of us in this house. We've all been moving around: going to the bathroom, getting snacks, smoking. I couldn't tell you who's been near the clock and who hasn't. Any of us could have reset it."

"Well, I didn't do it!" Linda announced.

"I didn't say you did." Kapp told her. "I'm merely pointing out that you could have. Any of us could have."

"This is family business," Earl declared, scowling at Kapp. "And you're not family. And if anyone looks suspicious, it's you. You were the one that was fooling with the clock earlier."

"Is that an accusation?" Kapp asked amiably, his eyebrows raised above the rims of his glasses.

"I'm not making any accusations—" Earl went on.

"Well, that's a good thing," Kapp countered. "Have you ever heard of slander?"

"Lawyers!" Earl spat out.

" 'Lawyers,' " Kapp mimicked, throwing one hand into the air melodramatically. "Send them all to hell. They only stand for justice and truth. . . ."

Geneva crossed her arms and watched as the two men sparred. I could see the anger in her face. Her space had been violated by Daphne's death and by the uncertainty as to its cause. This new, smaller violation had brought that truth home to her.

"Come on, someone did this!" she shouted finally, startling both of the arguing men. "And I want to know why."

"Did what?" a voice from the stairway asked. Pilar stood three stairs from the landing, her eyes coolly surveying us.

"Nothing to worry about, my dear," Victor assured her.

But I wasn't assured. Whoever had reset the clock must have also killed Aunt Daphne, I decided. I couldn't have explained how the two actions were connected, but at that moment, I was sure they were. "Someone just reset the grandfather clock," Victor went on. "It doesn't usually chime—"

"And it chimed at midnight," she finished for him quietly.

The hair went up on my neck. Had Pilar reset the clock before going back upstairs? I couldn't even remember what time it had been when she'd left the living room with Bob.

"Yeah, at midnight," York growled from the door where he was still stationed.

Pilar spread her arms as if ready to embrace a ghost.

"Hel-lo!" she cried. "It's telling us Daphne was murdered."

Was she right? My fingers and toes started to tingle again. What if I was wrong in assuming a living, breathing human had reset the clock? What about Pop? Or Daphne? Or Mom?

Bob appeared, walking slowly down the stairs behind Pilar. He didn't look as if he'd slept at all.

"What?" he asked simply.

"The clock rang at midnight," Pilar explained. "It's not supposed to do that. It's, like, a message from Daphne. She's telling us to do something. She's telling us not to get psyched by whoever killed her—"

"Stop that!" Linda screamed. She had her arms wrapped around herself, and her eyes were tearing up.

"Don't shout at Pilar," Geneva ordered evenly. "You will not shout at anyone in my home. Do you hear me?"

"Oh, right!" Linda snapped. "I'm just a guest here. What's Pilar to you?"

"Listen, you girls—" Earl began.

"You'll just take Geneva's side!" Linda yelped. "I know you. The Lazars can do no wrong. It's been this way since I was a kid. Just because their parents died. Boo-hoo, big tragedy. Well, my mother died, and nobody cares about me. Nobody, do you hear. Nobody!"

Then Linda collapsed in a heap on the floor and began sobbing.

Fern and Victor ran to her as one.

Whoa! I checked Linda's aura automatically and saw that she was truly in pain. She felt so sad, so sorry for herself that no other emotion could make it past her self-pity. Linda had been a teenager when I was born, already ill-tempered according to family lore. By the time I could speak, she was nearing adulthood. I'd never questioned her unpleasantness. That was just Linda. But why was that Linda? Victor was such a good-hearted man. At least I thought he was. And my aunt Mary had been his equal. Where did Linda's hurt come from? I thought of her older sister, Natalie. Was that the source?

I found myself exploring her energetically. She hadn't agreed to the intrusion, but I couldn't seem to stop myself. Jealousy? Had Victor's and Mary's love for each other left no room for Linda? Or—

"Nobody!" she screamed. Then, over and over again, "Nobody! Nobody!"

"I love you, Mom," Fern whispered, stroking her mother's back where she lay curled up on the mauve rug. "I always love you."

"Honey, I've got some Relax," Victor tried, reaching into his ever-ready backpack. "It's a great herbal complex. I'll get some water and you can take a couple of capsules."

"No!" Linda shouted. "I don't need your phony-baloney capsules. Or your pop psychology. It's way too late for that."

I looked at this women, my cousin, on the floor. I asked myself why I wasn't assisting her. And I thought of a friend of a friend who had acted very much like Linda was acting now. A psychologist had called that woman a borderline personality. Did borderline personalities kill other people? I didn't have an answer. And there wasn't a therapist in the room. Unless it was supposed to be me.

"Linda?" I tried. "Is there anything I can—"

"Just stay away from me," she sobbed.

I felt relief in my chest, and I swallowed guiltily. I didn't want to help Linda. And I didn't feel good about not wanting to help her. I almost wished I had the temperament to curl up in a fetal ball and sob myself.

"What the heck is wrong with her?" Earl whispered to the room in general.

No one answered him.

"The clock was a warning," Pilar cut in, reminding us where we'd started.

"Shush," Bob whispered gently. "Linda's having her own trouble."

"I won't shush," Pilar declared, but she kept her volume low. "Just 'cause she's stressing doesn't mean we stop thinking about Daphne. Maybe she's, like, faking it or something. Maybe she killed Daphne."

Great minds think alike. I jerked my head up. York and Geneva and I all looked at one another at the same time. Maybe Linda had crossed the borderline into full-fledged psychosis.

"Please, Mom, sit in a chair," Fern cajoled.

Amazingly, Linda did as asked. She was still crying, but she let her daughter lead her to an easy chair and plopped into it, covering her face with her hands.

"She's really okay," Fern assured us, turning around after her mother was seated. "This happens sometimes. Her therapist says it's good to let her feelings out, you know. So she does. It's cool, really."

I wondered when Fern let her feelings out, if ever. Always the good daughter, her first instinct was to protect her mother. I wondered if there was a murder motive there.

"Maybe we should all go back to our hotels for the night," Earl suggested.

"But the clock," Pilar reminded us. "What about the clock?"

"It's just a clock," Earl told us, as if that would settle the matter. He rolled his shoulders and clasped his hands together. "Edgar Allan Poe couldn't have timed the chime better, but there is nothing we can do about it—"

"I suppose you want us to leave this mystery to our ever efficient police force, too," Kapp muttered.

Earl straightened his posture. "I don't believe that Daphne was murdered, and I don't believe that there is any great mystery about the clock. So what if someone set it to chime? I think it's about time for those of us who aren't staying the night here to go back to our homes and motels. Geneva needs some sleep. It's after twelve."

"Someone reset the clock," York insisted. "We don't know yet if Aunt Daphne was murdered, but someone *did* reset the clock. We need to find out why."

"Why?" Fern repeated.

"Whoever set that clock did it for a reason," Kapp explained.

"To scare us?" I guessed.

"But what would that do?" Victor asked.

"Make everyone go home?" York tried. His tone firmed. "Maybe the person who reset the clock thought that it would freak everyone out so that everyone would leave this place rather than question Daphne's death."

"Hah!" Kapp snorted. He looked around the room. "If that was the purpose, then this person failed miserably."

"Because whoever set the clock showed us that they were afraid," I whispered. "Whoever set the clock wanted us to leave because they really did kill Aunt Daphne."

I almost wished I hadn't said it aloud.

Even Linda brought her head out of her hands to stare at me in the hush that followed.

"Now, Cally, don't you make assumptions." Uncle Earl chided me. "I can think of a number of other explanations. Maybe whoever set the clock wanted us to *think* your aunt was killed." He looked pointedly at the staircase, where Pilar and Bob still stood.

"Hey!" Pilar objected. "That's not the way it went down. You're not laying this on us—"

"Or perhaps," Earl went on, "the clock merely malfunctioned."

"Do you really think so?" Fern asked hopefully.

"Of course," Earl soothed her. "It makes more sense than all this murder hogwash—"

"And did the clock pull its own cord?" Kapp inquired. He tapped his cane and sneered.

"I'm just setting out some other possibilities," Earl shot back. "I'm not in court. And even if I was, how about 'reasonable doubt'? I have quite a bit more than a reasonable doubt that there's only one explanation for the clock's chime."

York left his place at the door and went to check the clock himself. He tugged on the cord. When he turned back to us, it was clear that he didn't think the cord had slipped.

"In any case," Earl reminded us before York could verbalize his doubts, "it's time to go home and leave Geneva in peace. She worked very hard today and prepared a lovely feast. I'm sure she's tired."

"Let's just go and not come back," Linda muttered as she rose from her chair. "We're not wanted here anyway." She sighed and looked at the floor. "Especially me, after I made such a fool of myself."

"We understand you're distressed," Roy offered. "No one's going to judge you unkindly for being a tad upset."

I looked at Roy. Roy wasn't judging Linda unkindly, but I had. And I was pretty sure that Geneva and York had, too. And I was supposed to be the one who believed in goodness and light.

"Linda," Geneva offered. "You're always welcome here. You've done nothing to be ashamed of."

Unless she'd murdered Aunt Daphne, I added in my own mind.

"Linda, will you please listen to what everyone is saying?" Victor put in. "No one here thinks you made a fool of yourself. They understand. It's been an upsetting day. We're all family, remember? And we have to stick together. Daphne was your aunt, too. The Lazars and Duprees are one family now. When Hugh and Simone married, they forged that bond. The three of us came all the way from Colorado, and Earl came from Los Angeles. We're here to be together. We were here to be with Daphne." Tears misted his eyes. "Daphne is gone, and we won't leave until we figure out what happened to her. I don't know yet. What Earl said about reasonable doubt was important. I don't know what happened to the clock. I don't know why your aunt Daphne died. But it's up to us to reason it out."

"That's just the way it should be," Roy added solemnly. "You folks care about each other. None of the shouting—"

"Dad, can we go home now?" Linda asked her father. Maybe she didn't want to think about the shouting.

Victor nodded.

"We'll have a good night's sleep and come back tomorrow just as we planned," he declared. "Will that work for you, Earl?"

"Perfect," Earl agreed.

Then the Colorado and Los Angeles contingents started gathering up their belongings to make their exit.

I looked at York. He shrugged. He couldn't guard the doorway all night. And no one was going to admit to resetting the clock. Kapp tapped York on the shoulder and whispered something in his ear. Then they were huddled. What were they discussing?

Uncle Earl was first out the door, with a tired good-bye over his shoulder. Then Uncle Victor, Linda, and Fern followed with more tired good-byes.

And finally, Kapp and York left together. They didn't say anything, but Kapp grunted as he pulled the front door closed behind them. I supposed that counted.

I looked around. Pilar and Bob were trudging up the staircase. I took Roy's hand in mine. Once we left, Geneva would be alone. Or would she?

Bob and Pilar had nowhere else to go. They had been staying with Geneva along with Daphne. And they would continue to stay with Geneva even though Daphne had gone. Geneva would never ask them to leave. They probably couldn't even find a motel this late if they wanted to.

Geneva! Suddenly, I was afraid for Geneva. Were Pilar

or Bob a threat to her? Could Bob or Pilar protect her if someone else was a threat?

"Roy," I whispered urgently. "We've got to stay here with Geneva tonight."

"But, Cally, darlin' " Roy whispered back. "Isn't it time to be going home? This has been a truly difficult day all around, and—"

"Geneva's not safe."

Roy looked at Geneva and frowned, considering my words.

"Geneva," I announced, still holding Roy's hand. "Roy's going to drive home to pack a bag. Then he'll be back, and we'll both spend the night here."

"Why would you do that?" Geneva asked.

I was trying to think of an answer that would satisfy my big sister when Roy blundered in with the truth.

"She's afraid for your safety," he said.

Geneva threw her head back and laughed. "*My* safety? Cally, you're not the only one who's taken martial arts classes from your brother."

"I know, but—"

"And I've been taking them longer than you," she finished up. "I'm perfectly safe."

"Geneva, we still don't even know who reset the clock," I pointed out. "And we certainly don't know who, if anyone, poisoned Aunt Daphne. And it all happened here, in this house. I don't want you alone here."

"Cally, I'm safe in my own home," Geneva insisted. Her voice had taken on that big-sisterly tone that brooked no argument.

"Then how about if you come home with us?" I tried.

"No sale," she answered, a smile on her face. "But thanks for caring."

Fifteen minutes later, the answer was still the same.

"Cally," she ordered. "You need to go home and sleep now. You can't sleep here."

"But—"

"No 'buts,'" she answered and put her arms around me and hugged.

"Geneva—" My words were cut off by her embrace. But she kept on talking.

"Cally, I take care of myself," she proclaimed. "If I'm not able to do that, I might as well be dead anyway. So you go home and come back tomorrow. I have lunch planned for one o'clock, remember? Earl and Victor and the others may come earlier for breakfast, but I think you should sleep in if you can." She let me go from her hug, and held me out at arm's length for inspection. "This has been a long day, a long night. But Cally, everything is very groovy now. Trust me on this."

I sighed and gave up.

Roy and I got our things and left through the front door, waving good-bye to Geneva as we went.

"Cally," Roy whispered, once we were outside, walking down the gravel driveway. "Are Kapp and Geneva sweethearts? Or are they just friends?"

"I don't know," I answered him angrily. "And do you think either of them would tell me? I'm just the little sister. She wants to take care of me, but will she let me take care of her? Huh?" I took in a breath for the rest of my rant. "The Lazars! Arnot wouldn't have even told us about Huey if it hadn't been for Barbara. If I ask one single question—"

We heard a rustle in the bushes. I stopped mid-rant and turned.

I saw a dark shadow, two dark shadows. My heart thumped double-time. Were those human forms? I told myself to calm my imagination. Maybe they were just turkeys? Yeah, turkeys. What would humans be doing in the bushes?

"Psst!" a turkey hissed.

Only it wasn't a turkey.

ELEVEN

A familiar smell wafted through the cool night air. I sniffed, and my body went limp in relief. I knew the shadow that had hissed at me wasn't a turkey because turkeys didn't wear aftershave. And it wasn't somebody scary either. It had to be Kapp, or someone who was unfortunate enough to wear the same aftershave as Kapp. I reached out with my cane and touched his automatically. A truce. And as my eyes adjusted, I saw York standing just behind Kapp.

Not turkeys, then. Not murderers. Only my friend and my brother.

"Come here!" Kapp ordered, his whisper urgent.

I looked at Roy, and we both followed Kapp and York into a thicket of scratchy bushes. Were we supposed to be hiding? Even if we might have been invisible in the thicket, I doubted that we were inaudible.

"We were waiting for you," Kapp explained. "We knew you'd be worried—"

"So, now *you're* psychic?" I teased.

He wasn't in the mood. "Yuk-yuk. Very funny, Lazar," he growled.

"We're not leaving Geneva alone with Pilar and Bob," York cut in. "We'll protect her against whoever's doing these things. We're spending the night."

"But how are you going to get into her house?" I demanded. "I just tried to get her to let me stay, and she wouldn't."

York stretched his fist out in answer. Was he going to use his martial arts training to bust down the door? Then he opened his hand. In the glint of moonlight, I saw a key resting on his palm.

"Did you steal that from Geneva?" I asked in awe. Whoa. York was braver than I was.

"Your brother 'borrowed' the key from your sister's drawer." Kapp, ever the defense attorney, already had the right word thought up. "It's a spare. She'll never notice."

"But won't she see you in the house?" I pressed him.

"Not until tomorrow morning," York assured me.

Kapp grinned. "Here's the beauty of it, Lazar. We're going to wait until she goes to bed."

He jerked his head up toward Geneva's window. The light filled the window as if on cue.

"See, she's already in her room." He gloated. "Once the lights go out, we'll tiptoe on in. I've got a bag packed—"

"Why the bag?" I asked suspiciously. Had he known beforehand what horrors were going to happen?

"To go to the hospital," Kapp specified gruffly. "I always keep it in my car, just in case."

My heart clenched. Of course, Kapp hadn't known beforehand. But the hospital . . . I didn't like to think of my friend in the hospital.

"Oh, Kapp—" I began.

"Never mind," he commanded. "The point is that I have everything I need to spend the night here in my bag. And York says he has a clean shirt in his car. We can share my toothbrush."

York flinched.

Kapp laughed. We were definitely not inaudible by then. "Just kidding," he told my brother. "No one shares my toothbrush."

"I'm going to sleep on the top landing of the stairway," York cut in impatiently.

"And I'm on the couch in the living room," Kapp told us. "A man my age deserves his comforts. If anyone comes in the front door or the kitchen door, they'll probably wake me up. And if they don't, they'll trip over your brother on the stairway. We've got it covered, Lazar."

I looked at Roy. I was too tired to know if there was a flaw in their plan.

"I do believe these two have it well thought out, Cally," he proclaimed.

That was good enough for me. I closed my eyes and breathed in the night air. Aftershave, greenery, fireplace smoke. It was heaven. I felt the warmth of Roy's body behind mine. Kapp and York would protect Geneva. The anxiety twisting in my head began to untangle.

"Thank you both," I whispered.

Then I quickly kissed Kapp's cheek and York's.

I was surprised York didn't cut me in half with a martial move. Kapp just grumbled, but I thought he was smiling beneath the grumble.

York and Kapp moved toward the edge of the bushes.

"Wait!" I ordered. "Do you really think that Daphne was murdered?"

"Holy Mother, Lazar!" Kapp shot back. "Is the Dalai Lama a Buddhist?"

I took that as a yes. I turned to York.

"How about you?" I tried.

"Well . . ." York paused. He looked past me at Roy. "Did you see that darkness stuff in Geneva's house?" he asked.

"As much as it pains me to say it, the darkness appears to be centered here," Roy answered quietly.

"A family heirloom," I added. "Like the clock."

"Then, yeah, I say it's quite possible that Aunt Daphne was murdered," York finally answered me.

"It's more than possible," Kapp put in his two cents.

"But who would—"

"Oh, come on," Kapp chided me. "Just look at these jokers. We don't know who inherits, for starters. And they don't either. Your uncle Victor isn't doing so well in his

bookstore, and Fern needs the money if she's going to be a
writer. And her mother would probably kill just for spite.
And your unctuous uncle Earl's just gotta have a motive. I
can't stand the guy. And he smokes at his age! Holy Mother!
Motives? There's money to begin with. Remember, Bob's a
tax attorney. And you know how *evil* attorneys are. Then
there's blackmail. There's fear. There's hatred. Who knows
what your aunt Daphne meant to these people?"

"How about Pilar?" I prodded. Why hadn't he mentioned Pilar? "Where did she come from? What was she to
Daphne?"

Kapp didn't answer me. I squinted in the moonlight.
Kapp's face was unaccountably blank. Did Kapp know
something about Pilar? Kapp's face was rarely blank. He
was hiding something. I was sure of it.

"Kapp, what is it?" I began. "What do you know—"

The light in Geneva's window went off.

"Duty calls," Kapp announced cheerfully.

He was right. I'd find out what he knew about Pilar later.
Or maybe not. Kapp was a good friend, but he was also a
formidable opponent.

"Thanks, you guys," I whispered again.

Kapp hobbled stealthily from the bushes up the gravel
driveway to the house.

York lingered for a moment, looking at me and Roy.
"Take care of each other," he ordered gruffly. "I mean it."

Roy and I both saluted simultaneously.

Then York exited the thicket and sprinted gracefully,
catching up with Kapp just in time to open the front door.

The two men walked inside, the door shut, and the night
was quiet again except for a few cars in the distance and
the wind.

"Home?" Roy asked hopefully, holding back a scratchy
branch gallantly.

"Home," I agreed, stepping back out onto the gravel.

And finally, Roy and I climbed into my old Honda, and
I drove home. Roy was quiet on the drive. And so was I. It

was a relief not to have to talk. If and when I married Roy, it would be as much for his ability to entertain silence as for his conversational skills.

Then we were home at my house. Dack, I love my little house. As we walked in the doorway, I breathed in the scent of aromatic oils, wood, books, and cat. Leona meowed reprovingly at my feet, and I picked her up by feel, burying my face in her silken fur. Roy turned on the light. I looked around at my bookshelves, the massage table, the stuffed chairs, and the eclectic artwork. Beautiful. At least to me.

"We're home, darlin' " Roy murmured.

I turned to hug him. Leona jumped out of my arms in disgust. Group hugs were not for her, no matter how gentle. But Roy was another matter. His familiar form felt so good here in my own room. We sunk into each other, holding tight and swaying almost as if we were dancing. I don't know how long we held each other before the phone rang. But it wasn't long enough.

Roy let go of me carefully and picked up the receiver. Who was calling us this late? My stomach tightened. Had something else happened?

"Hello," Roy answered pleasantly. "Uh-huh," he went on. "I believe so. But let me check."

He put his hand over the receiver. "Cally, are you up to speaking to your brother Arnot?"

I kissed Roy before taking the receiver into my hand.

"Arnot, do you know what time it is?" I began.

"I've been calling all night," he shot back. "You just got home, didn't you?"

"Yeah," I admitted with a sigh.

"Cally, I know this late night call, or early morning call, or whatever it is, lacks my usual style, but I'm concerned. People talked about Aunt Daphne being poisoned. Is it true?"

"I'm not sure," I told him slowly.

"Cally, talk to me, kiddo," he cajoled. "I know nobody in our family communicates, but try."

"Like you not telling us about Huey," I accused. The words were out of my mouth before I could stop them.

"Absolutely," he agreed. "Guilty as charged. That's just the kind of thing I mean. I know I should talk more. In fact, I think I probably need to *feel* more. That's what Barbara tells me. Somewhere along the line, I learned how to keep a lid on my feelings. And I learned never to talk about the important stuff. Barbara wants to go to family therapy."

"That sounds like a good idea," I offered gently. He was already talking more to me than he had in the last twenty years. Barbara was right about a lot of things. She was probably right about this.

"You want to come with us, Cally?" he asked. I could feel the whimsy in his tone, almost see the laughter in his eyes. "You're family."

"Arnot!" I squeaked, playing up to his teasing.

"Oh, but it would be absolutely perfect," he insisted. "Can you see Geneva and York in family therapy?"

Then I was laughing. I couldn't help it. Because I could see it. York with his arms crossed. Melinda rambling and knocking things over. And Geneva, bossy and pointing her elegant finger.

"But seriously, Cally," Arnot said, the mischief gone from his voice. "What about Aunt Daphne?"

"Listen, I wasn't trying to shine you on when I said I didn't know," I explained. "I don't *know* if she was poisoned." I took a deep breath and dove into the truth. "But I think she might have been. Kapp's almost sure of it. And York thinks it's possible that someone killed her."

"Criminy," he whispered. "But why would anyone do that?"

"We don't know, but I've asked for an autopsy. The police are involved."

There was silence from his end of the line. Then he murmured, "Thank you."

"For what?" I asked.

"For telling me the truth," he answered seriously. "Night-night, Cally. See you in family therapy."

"Night-night, Arnot," I repeated, and we hung up the phone together.

I turned to Roy.

"Now, where were we?" I inquired, opening my arms.

The phone rang again. This time it was my sister, Melinda.

"Acuto from Pluto calling," she greeted me cheerily, naming the cartoon character she'd created for her comic strip. Or maybe she really thought she was Acuto. With Melinda, it was hard to tell. She'd been doing the strip so long, she'd almost become Acuto, the accident-prone alien from Pluto.

"What's up, Acuto?" I tried.

"Cally, I feel really weirded out," she began.

I didn't say anything. I knew she'd keep talking. She always did. And I was tired.

"I get spooked every once in a while, I mean, really spooked," she told me. "I mean, I'm happy with Zack and the kids and Acuto and everything, but sometimes it's like a ghost steps in." She took a breath. "I shouldn't be talking about this," she finished.

"Yes, you should," I challenged her.

"Nah, I'm sorry." Her voice was so quiet that I pressed my ear to the receiver.

"What were you trying to tell me?" I demanded.

"Oh, I always goof up," she replied. She laughed abruptly, but it wasn't a happy laugh. "Just like Acuto—"

"Melinda, tell me!"

"No. I just got spooked. But it's fine. The kids didn't get sick or anything. I gotta go. Bye, Cally."

Then she hung up. But not before something had seeped over the phone line. I tried to figure out what that something was. Maybe it was the auditory version of the darkness Roy saw. The darkness I had seen. Because whatever Melinda had or hadn't said to me seemed to slow my brain. Or maybe it was just the late hour.

Who were my brothers and sisters, really? For a moment, a chill descended. I felt that I didn't know them, any of them. Not Geneva. Not York. Not Arnot. Not Melinda. It was like being suddenly struck blind. If I didn't know them, who was I? I shivered, not seeing my beautiful room anymore.

"Cally?" Roy breathed.

I turned to him slowly.

"Everyone is acting weird," I explained. "Maybe they're just on alert or something."

"And—" Roy prodded.

"They're all afraid," I whispered. There, I'd said it aloud. "Including me," I added.

"Of what?"

"I don't know," I told him. How many times had I used that phrase in the last hour? Maybe that was what I was afraid of, the not knowing.

"Cally, let me tuck you into bed now," Roy suggested. "I'll be here with you. We'll make it on through. I promise."

So I let Roy tuck me into bed. I felt like an invalid as he escorted me into the bedroom, helped me off with my clothes and into my pajamas. Once I was in bed, he pulled the covers up under my chin and kissed me on the forehead.

"What about you, Roy?" I murmured sleepily.

"Don't you worry one little bit over me, darlin'," he whispered softly. "Sweet dreams."

Then I was asleep, dreaming of a cool, rushing river.

I woke a little later. I wasn't sure how long it had been. An hour, two hours?

Roy was seated in a low chair, staring at me, concern in his eyes.

I knew he was seeing the darkness.

And yet, I knew he was watching over me.

I wondered how I could ever sleep again, even as I slipped into the cold rush of my river dream once more.

Geneva had been right. I slept in until eleven on Friday morning. I was sure breakfast at her house had been eaten a long time ago. And Roy was still watching me, but this time he was watching from his side of the bed in his own pajamas. And this time, he was smiling.

"Feeling better, darlin'?" he asked.

I was feeling better.

I kissed him to prove it.

By the time I'd finished with Roy, eaten a bowl of oatmeal and fruit, showered, and meditated, we had just enough time to make Geneva's day-after-Thanksgiving one o'clock lunch date.

We rushed out of my little house toward my car. I looked back at my home with a lurch of longing. Then we got in my car, and I drove to Geneva's.

We didn't see the Turkey Sisters as we walked up Geneva's gravel driveway, only Geneva's flower beds on the sides of the drive. Maybe the sisters had moved to a safer neighborhood.

The front door was open an inch or so when we got there, so Roy and I just walked on in, shutting the door behind us. Earl was settled into the easy chair. Linda and Fern shared the magenta love seat. And Victor sat alone on the plum-colored couch, his face troubled. I didn't see Geneva or York anywhere in sight. Or Pilar, Bob, or Kapp, for that matter.

"Mom, it's okay," Fern murmured.

"No, it's not," Linda replied. "Dad is so stubborn. I just want to go home."

"She has a point," Earl put in. "Maybe we should all leave and let everyone get back to their lives after lunch. Geneva looked really tired this morning."

"So, you suggest we just abandon them?" Victor demanded.

"No, I just—"

Earl cut off his own sentence as he noticed that Roy and I had arrived.

"Cally," he said and rose to give me a hug. He seemed to be ignoring Roy, my "young man" of the night before.

"Look, if she was poisoned, it's not safe here," Linda went on, as if she hadn't noticed our entrance.

I gave in to Earl's smoky embrace.

"Hi, everyone!" I tried

"Cally, I'm glad you're here," Victor pronounced. "This morning has had some sadness—"

"Sadness!" Linda interrupted. "This place is a loony bin."

"Calm down, Mom," Fern ordered.

"All right, fine," Linda muttered. "No one ever listens to me, anyway."

"Where's Geneva?" I asked, keeping my voice calmer than I felt.

"In the kitchen," Victor told us. "With your brother York and their friend."

Roy and I walked through the dining room into the kitchen.

Geneva, York, and Kapp were there as promised. But they didn't smile as we entered.

My leg shook under me as we stopped in front of them.

"What happened?" I demanded.

"Pilar went to the hospital," Geneva answered, her voice raw as if she'd been crying.

"What happened to Pilar?" I pressed her. But even as I spoke, I felt the center of my mind drifting away, deserting me, as if I'd taken a narcotic.

"Oh, Cally," Geneva said, her tone rising. "Pilar came down late this morning. York was fixing one of his super shakes, and she asked if she could have one. So York gave her his."

Yuck. York's super shakes were a concoction of bee pollen, blue-green algae, wheatgrass, and a whole lot of other things that only bees, cows, and fish should ingest.

"I set it down on the kitchen counter," York continued for Geneva. "Then I went back to make myself another one. I think it was on the counter for a long time before she drank it." York looked down at the floor. "Then a while later . . . we don't really know. She just fell over like Aunt Daphne."

"Someone put something into Pilar's drink," Kapp accused. "Those things taste so awful, you could put gasoline in and no one would notice."

"Have you ever had one?" I asked him.

"A sip, Lazar," he shot back. "A sip is enough for a lifetime."

But this wasn't about the flavor of York's super shakes. This was about poison. I'd thought Linda had been talking about Aunt Daphne when she'd mentioned poisoning, but I realized she'd been talking about Pilar. That was what Victor had been talking about, too. My drifting mind tried to absorb this new event. My body absorbed it instead, cooling as if the temperature had been turned down in the room.

"Is the poor girl all right?" Roy asked.

"She's in the hospital," Geneva told us. "We're waiting to hear."

"Who put something in her shake?" I asked, angry suddenly. How could this have happened?

Three sets of shoulders shrugged.

"It could have been anyone," Kapp explained. "Everyone and their dog was in here, talking and fixing plates of food, going in the refrigerator, pouring drinks. There were the three of us here. And there were Linda, Fern, Victor, Earl, Bob, and Pilar, too. Hooboy, just take your pick."

"And Pilar was arguing with everyone, especially Linda, while her shake sat on the counter," Geneva added. "They were arguing so hot and heavy that no one really noticed anything else."

"But—" I began, wanting to argue away the fear I felt cooling my body.

The doorbell rang.

The five of us from the kitchen all hurried into the living room. Earl was opening the front door as we got there.

"Chief Kaifu," a stocky man with tight, Asian features introduced himself. He nodded toward the man next to him. "And this is Sergeant Quantrill." Quantrill was a lanky redhead with a sad face.

Geneva pushed past Earl to announce herself.

"I'm Geneva Lazar," she told the chief. "How's Pilar?"

"Pilar Vaughn is suffering from a morphine overdose, ma'am," Kaifu explained. "Mr. Ungerman has told us that Daphne Dupree carried her own supply of liquid morphine for pain. We think that must be where the girl got the morphine. Mr. Ungerman was upset, something about this Daphne Dupree's death being related."

So that was the source of poison that Pilar had been hinting about. Morphine, of course.

"But is she okay?" Victor asked again.

"A nurse spotted it right off, especially since Mr. Ungerman was insisting that she'd been poisoned. They gave her the antidote. She'll pull through, they say."

I felt the whole room sigh with relief. No, not the whole room. Someone was frightened by Pilar's recovery. I looked around. Who?

"We need to talk to you folks." Sergeant Quantrill took over. "It looks like a suicide attempt, but Mr. Ungerman said it was attempted murder. He wasn't real coherent. Said this Daphne Dupree had been murdered as well."

"But Aunt Daphne died of cancer," Linda told them diffidently.

"No," Victor objected. "That is not necessarily true. We don't know how Daphne died."

"Now, Victor," Earl cut in.

"Daphne died in very similar circumstances to Pilar's collapse," Kapp overrode him. "Mr. Ungerman called it in to your office last night. Two officers came and took our statements. Mr. Ungerman assumes you know all that—"

"Wait a minute," Kaifu ordered, holding up his hand. "Are you saying that this woman, Daphne Dupree, died here, last night?" His voice was incredulous.

"Chief Kaifu," Roy broke in, his voice respectful but clearly audible. "You must understand something for a certainty. Mr. Ungerman was right. We just weren't listening well enough to hear him. Daphne Dupree was murdered yesterday. And now someone has tried to kill that poor girl, Pilar, as well."

TWELVE

Chief Kaifu just stared at Roy for one long moment. Then he snapped, "Quantrill, take this all down."

Roy stood a little straighter as Quantrill brought a tiny computer out of one of the pouches on his belt and began to tap the keys.

"What's your name?" Kaifu began.

"Roy Beaumont."

"And what is your relationship to these people?"

"He's my fiancé," I put in. This situation was too serious for "boyfriend."

"And you are?" Kaifu looked at me as if he wished I'd disappear.

"Cally Lazar." I looked him in the eye. "Daphne Dupree was my aunt."

He turned his attention back to Roy.

"And you're alleging a murder and an attempted murder?"

"Yes, sir, I'm afraid I am."

"Listen," Kapp interrupted. "The murder was already 'alleged' last night to your officers, at least by Mr. Ungerman and Ms. Vaughn—"

"Well, no one bothered to tell me—" Kaifu began and then stopped himself. Was he thinking of possible suits that might be brought against his own police department?

"I requested an autopsy on Daphne Dupree, too," I threw in.

Kaifu's face tightened a notch more. That was scary. I had a feeling Khashoggi and Rossetti were going to be in trouble. It was obvious that they hadn't reported their visit to their chief. Had they even logged it in?

"You're sure the police were called?" Kaifu asked Kapp. His tone begged for a negative response. "The *Estados* Police Department?"

"Bob Ungerman called the Estados Police Department," Kapp replied. "Two officers paid us a visit. Officers Rossetti and Khashoggi."

Kaifu did something with his face that looked like he might be grinding his teeth . . . or possibly imploding. Then he took a deep breath.

"You'll have to excuse my ignorance of last night's events," he offered. I guessed he was trying for a pleasant tone, but he wasn't succeeding. His clenched fists made more of a statement than his words. "Thanksgiving is always very busy. We're still processing yesterday's calls."

"Look, Chief Kaifu," Kapp fired back, not even trying for a pleasant tone. "No one cares if there was a failure of communication last night. We just want to know if we'll be taken seriously today."

"Oh, you'll be taken seriously," the chief told him, clasping his hands behind his back, military style. "Very seriously. Who wants to tell me what's been happening here?"

York, Geneva, Roy, and I all looked at Kapp.

"I think I can sum up the events for you," Kapp purred.

"Your name?" Kaifu asked.

"Warren Kapp, friend of the family."

Kapp might as well have said, "friend of the court." Chief Kaifu blanched. He knew who Kapp was. And more important, he knew what Kapp was, a respected trial attorney, the "Melvin Belli of Glasse County." If the officers of the night before had been negligent, Kapp knew just how to litigate the matter.

Kapp grinned briefly at the chief's discomfort, but only briefly.

Then he got serious. "There were thirteen of us present at Thanksgiving dinner yesterday," Kapp began. He ticked off the family members on his fingers first, then the others, himself included. As he spoke, I found myself drawn into his story, as if I hadn't been there. I'd forgotten Geneva's assistant, Zoe. I'd forgotten who'd arrived when and where. Kapp remembered it all, down to what had been consumed and at what times. He spoke calmly of Daphne's collapse, and Pilar's repeated accusations, and Bob's apparent agreement with Pilar's belief that one of us had killed Aunt Daphne, while Sergeant Quantrill was tapping his keys faster and faster. The only thing Kapp left out was the incident with the clock. He proceeded to the current events of the day. He was succinct, clear, and frightening in his assurance that Daphne had been purposely killed, and that someone had made an attempt on Pilar's life, too.

"Daphne Dupree drank crème de menthe," he finally summed up. "No one else did. It seems the family members knew that was Daphne's drink. It might have been tampered with in her glass or in the bottle itself. Pilar drank a separate 'super shake.' It sat on the kitchen counter long enough to be tampered with. The killer had to know about Daphne's morphine supply. And I'm sure many of us present did know."

The room was silent except for the sound of Quantrill's belated key-tapping when Kapp finished speaking. Kapp bowed slightly, as if to throw the ball back into Chief Kaifu's court.

"Does anyone else have anything to add?" the chief asked.

"Daphne and Pilar both acted the same way," Geneva put in quietly. "They both got spacier and spacier until they fell over."

"And they were both having trouble breathing," York added.

"Do you really think they were poisoned?" Chief Kaifu asked my siblings.

They both nodded.

Kaifu turned to me. "Why did you ask for an autopsy?"

"Because I thought that Pilar's accusations might be true," I told him. "The hospital apparently assumed that Aunt Daphne died of respiratory failure caused by complications of her cancer. Pilar said she was poisoned. It seemed to me that an autopsy would settle the question."

"And now Pilar's been poisoned," Fern whispered.

"We don't know that!" Linda objected. Her face reddened. "At least we don't know that anyone purposely poisoned Pilar. For all we know, she was experimenting. Teenagers do, as you well know."

"Mo-om!" Fern objected. The strength of her objection hinted at a little drug problem closer to home.

"Is that possible?" Victor asked the chief. "Is it possible that Pilar took the drug herself?"

"Quite possible," Kaifu answered quickly. "We don't know yet. We'll look into the possibility that someone poisoned Daphne Dupree and then tried to poison Pilar Vaughn, but the simplest explanation is probably the truth."

"And what would that simple explanation be?" Kapp asked. I hoped Kaifu couldn't hear the sarcasm in Kapp's voice.

"Most likely, the older woman died from complications of cancer, and the girl, who seems to be some sort of ward of the older woman, got depressed and took the morphine herself. These things happen. It wouldn't be a first." Kaifu sounded reasonable enough. It was the content of his words that made my stomach roil.

"Pilar wasn't depressed," York stated for the record. "She was angry. She believed Daphne had been murdered. She wasn't the type to attempt suicide." He turned toward Linda. "And she wasn't the type to 'experiment' with morphine after her best friend in the world died. I still don't know what Daphne was to Pilar, but Pilar cared for her."

"And Pilar said she 'knew stuff,' " I remembered aloud. "Maybe the killer believed her. Maybe that would explain the attempt on her life."

"Or maybe Chief Kaifu is correct," Uncle Earl reminded us gently. "Remember, he's the expert. When someone you care for that much dies, it's only natural to be upset, even suicidal."

"Thank you," Chief Kaifu said to Earl. "So I take it that not everyone in this room believes the murder scenario?"

"I sure don't!" Linda exclaimed.

"Well, I do believe the 'murder scenario,'" Kapp put in. "It may or may not prove to be true, but it's certainly worth checking the evidence."

"Rest assured, Mr. Kapp," Kaifu pronounced. "We will do everything to check it out. I just want you people to remember that there are other possibilities than murder."

"Will an autopsy be done on Daphne Dupree?" Roy asked softly.

Kaifu sighed. "Yes, an autopsy will be done. I'll order it. But it'll take time."

He looked around the room, as if memorizing our faces, then jerked his head back toward Roy. "In the meantime, since you're so eager to be helpful, you can be first in line with your identification. I want all of you people to show Sergeant Quantrill your driver's licenses and give him your home phone numbers."

I got in line after Roy. Linda went to the bathroom.

"Wait a minute, ma'am!" Quantrill shouted as the bathroom door banged shut. My heart jumped at the shout.

"She'll be out in a minute," I told him. I hoped I was telling the truth. I hoped she wasn't flushing any evidence down the toilet.

"May I get my purse?" Geneva asked.

"Me, too," Fern chimed in. "And my mom's?"

"Fine," Kaifu snarled. "Let the women get their purses." His tone reminded me of Linda's in that moment. Petulance in a police chief wasn't a pretty thing. I was glad I wore a fanny pack.

Midway through the processing, Quantrill told the chief that some of us were out-of-towners.

"I hope you understand that you'll need to stay in the

area until we make some preliminary findings," he told us.

"I want to go home!" Linda yelped predictably, having returned from the bathroom in time to join the identification line.

"We'll stay," Victor assured him.

I wondered how long preliminary findings were going to take.

And finally, everyone's name and information had been processed. Quantrill and Kaifu turned to leave the house. They were just to the door when Quantrill whispered something into the chief's ear.

Chief Kaifu whipped around. "Where is the crème de menthe bottle?" he demanded.

Kapp's brows shot up. Hah! He hadn't thought of that question.

I'll show you," Geneva offered and took the chief to the liquor cabinet at the end of the dining room. She opened the doors and looked in.

"But the bottle's gone," she whispered after a moment. "I put it back myself. It should be right there."

My body jerked as if I'd been lassoed. I had almost bought Chief Kaifu's proposition of natural death followed by suicide attempt. But if his ever-so-reasonable proposition was right, where was the crème de menthe bottle?

I could smell fear in the room. There is a certain smell that the perspiration of fear produces, and the room was filled with it.

Kaifu must have smelled it, too.

He looked at us angrily. I didn't blame him. This was going to cost the city time and money. Or maybe he'd just realized for the first time that there really might have been a murder committed.

"We'll be back," Kaifu promised. He turned stiffly and left the house through the front door, with Sergeant Quantrill in his wake.

There was a short time of silence before Geneva suggested that we eat lunch.

"Are you kidding?" Linda demanded, crossing her arms.

"You're the one who thinks no one was poisoned, Mom," Fern pointed out.

"I think *probably* no one was poisoned," Linda corrected her daughter. "I'm not eating or drinking a thing—"

"Mother of God, folks," Kapp cut in. "Didn't you hear the chief? Pilar is going to pull through. We should be celebrating, not arguing."

"Yeah," I whispered, feeling warmth flowing through my body. Pilar was going to be all right.

"I do believe you're correct again, Mr. Kapp," Roy agreed with a gentle smile.

"*And* there's an antidote," Kapp finished up, grinning at his own joke. "So eat, drink, and be merry, because I have the hospital phone number."

"Hee-hee!" I turned and saw that it was Linda who was laughing. Linda! Then Fern joined in along with Geneva. Even Roy was chuckling. I smiled. Kapp could convince cats to take swimming lessons.

"Let's eat," I announced.

Geneva took my hand and led me into the kitchen, where she started unloading the refrigerator. Whoa! She'd been working. There were three kinds of breads and spreads, quiches for everyone (tofu for the strict vegetarians, cheese for those of us who were ambivalent, and ham for the rest), bowls of salads (potato, green, coleslaw, and three bean), pickles, baked pears, and fresh fruit.

"Nice job," I told her.

"Look," she whispered. "I went out after Pilar left for the hospital. I got all this stuff down at Choice Foods. I threw out the leftovers. Do you think it's safe?"

"Has anyone else touched this food?" I asked. "Does anyone else even know that it's here?"

"Kapp and York," she answered. "And we were taking turns watching the refrigerator until the police came. I don't think anyone could have tampered with it. Tell me it's groovy, Cally."

"It's groovy," I assured her. I patted my stomach. "I'm

ready to eat." Still, it was nice to know there was an antidote. But I didn't say that.

"Thanks, kid," she murmured and hugged me tight. She smelled of soap and nerves, an unusual scent for my elegant sister.

The dining room table was already set. We carried in the food, and everyone took a place at the table. I began the action. I cut a piece from the cheese quiche and passed the rest of it to Roy. He took a piece and passed what remained along to Fern. Then I started the coleslaw going. Kapp was already slicing bread and handing it to his left. The dishes made the rounds. Linda took a tiny scoop of potato salad when it reached her. Victor accepted some tofu quiche. Fern scooped three bean salad onto her plate. Pretty soon, all the food had been passed from hand to hand. Then we all waited for someone to take a bite. It was like a game of Russian roulette. But I knew the bullets were all blanks.

I took a big bite of quiche, chewed, and swallowed. "Yummy," I commented. It wasn't really that great, but someone had to be the first.

York and Kapp dove in next. York tasted the three bean salad and declared it "good," and Kapp had the same word for the bread and herbed butter.

Then Geneva spilled the beans. "It's takeout," she said. "It's safe."

With that, everyone started eating. And they started talking.

Earl gobbled a bite of ham quiche, cleared his throat, and took the floor. "That Kaifu's a good man. He has a quick mind. Sensible. You know, there are all kinds of possible explanations for the events that have happened here besides murder. I'm beginning to wonder if Daphne committed suicide herself. Maybe that was the point of seeing us all one last time. And maybe young Pilar felt betrayed."

I considered his words, trying the coleslaw. It was crunchy and sweet. The images his words brought were not so sweet. Would Daphne do that?

"It's possible," Victor agreed hesitantly. "Feelings of betrayal can be a reaction to a loved one's death. But still, Daphne wouldn't have left us in so much confusion and pain purposely. It's just not like her."

"But if it was Daphne herself, what happened to the bottle of crème de menthe?" Fern asked, frowning. "That's what I don't understand. 'Cause Aunt Daphne died, and then the bottle disappeared—"

"I'm sure there's a reasonable explanation for the bottle," Earl pontificated. "We have to think reasonably, not hysterically. In fact, we don't know when the bottle disappeared."

"How about the clock?" Kapp put in just for fun.

"Have it your way, Mr. Kapp," Earl murmured. He speared a lettuce leaf. "I'm sure Kaifu and his men will reach the proper conclusion."

"Okay," York tried. "Let's just pretend that we don't know the cause of the death or the morphine overdose. Let's keep our minds open. Are the two events necessarily related?"

"I find it hard to believe that they aren't," Roy answered.

"I think Zoe did it," Linda declared. She pointed her fork across the table at York. "If we're going to consider all the possibilities, how come were not talking about Zoe?"

"Zoe?" Geneva questioned. She pursed her lips and glared.

But her expression didn't stop Linda. "That woman was rude to Aunt Daphne," Linda added. "I saw it. She was the only person at dinner who didn't like Aunt Daphne. If anyone killed her, it was that Zoe."

"Wait a minute," York objected. "If Zoe killed Aunt Daphne, then who poisoned Pilar? Zoe hasn't been here all day."

"Pilar poisoned herself," Linda shot back, bending across the table. "Zoe poisoned Daphne, and Pilar tried to off herself. Case closed."

"But, honey," Victor put in. "Why would Zoe want to kill Daphne?"

Linda turned to Geneva with a smug smile on her face.

"Why don't you explain to my dad why Zoe was so mean to Aunt Daphne?"

Geneva sighed. "I don't believe that Zoe had anything to do with this. She was sorry that she was rude to Aunt Daphne. Years ago, Zoe was an object of charity. It's a time she doesn't like to remember. That's all."

"Come on," Linda challenged. "You're the one that thinks there was a murder. Be more specific."

"Aunt Daphne was a volunteer—" Geneva began. Then she stopped and shook her head. "No, this is private. It's up to Zoe to tell you herself."

"Uh-uh," Linda pressed. "You say this is serious. You have to tell us what went on between those two."

The table was quiet. No one was eating anymore. We were all watching the battle between Linda and Geneva. The two of them glared at each other angrily. They could have been ten years old, or thirteen, or the women in their fifties that they were.

"So much for truth!" Linda crowed. "I figure it out, but do I get any support? No. I—"

"Give it up, Mom," Fern interrupted.

"What?" Linda yelped, outraged.

"I said, give it up. Your cell phone is out of batteries. Zoe wasn't here for the clock. She wasn't here for Pilar. Your theory doesn't make any sense."

"You give it up," Linda shot back. "I'm the mother here. I'll say what I want to—"

"Fern's right, honey," Victor interjected.

"And he's the grandfather here," Fern mimicked in a low whisper.

"How about Bob?" Earl threw in. "What hold did he have over Daphne? He's an attorney."

"Oh, hang him then," Kapp muttered.

"And he's, he's . . ." Earl faltered.

"Black?" Geneva offered helpfully. Her face still looked angry. But she was angry at Earl now.

"Well, yes," Earl conceded. "Why was Daphne with

him? I don't have anything against his race. A lot of good firefighters are black. But why would Daphne . . . I just don't understand."

"Because he's a kind, good man," I explained through gritted teeth.

"And he's an attorney in good standing," Kapp added.

"How do you know that?" Earl demanded.

"Contacts," Kapp explained succinctly.

"Look, Mr. Kapp," Earl tried. "I don't believe any murder was done here. But if there was a murder, it wasn't any member of this family who did it. And who else does that leave?"

"Zoe?" Linda guessed. "Pilar?"

"Not Pilar," Victor objected.

"Why not, Dad?" Linda demanded in frustration. "Why not Pilar? You keep saying Pilar can do no wrong. I mean, do you even know her?"

In the silence, I looked at Victor's face. And I looked at Kapp's face. They both knew something about Pilar. Why weren't they sharing their information?

"I want to know who Pilar—" I began.

But Uncle Earl was on a roll.

"Just who are you, Mr. Warren Kapp?" he demanded. "I know that Roy is Cally's fiancé. But who are you to this family?"

"He's my friend," Geneva and I replied at the same time.

"But, Geneva, is he more than a friend to you?" Earl pressed on. "I know it's none of my business, but under the circumstances . . ."

Geneva's face flushed. This was getting interesting.

"No, he's my friend, that's all," she answered evenly. "We go out together. We do all the groovy things friends do together."

I looked at Kapp. But he was exercising his right to remain silent.

"I know it's not my place," Earl started up again. "But this man seems to be at the middle of all of—"

"Look!" Geneva finally snapped. "Kapp isn't my

lover, if that's what you're asking. My lover is someone else."

"But you never talk about him," Earl accused. And he was right.

"My lover is a married man!" Geneva blurted out. "Is that enough for you? My lover is a married man, and neither he nor Kapp had anything to do with Aunt Daphne's death!"

THIRTEEN

No one spoke immediately after Geneva's announcement. The stillness felt as if it might go on forever. Then Fern dropped her fork on her plate. The twang jarred the silence.

"What?" Earl gasped belatedly, staring at Geneva as though he'd never seen her before.

"A married man?" I whispered. No, it couldn't be true. My sister was an ethical person. She wouldn't be involved with a married man. Would she? I'd often wondered at the absence of a relationship in her life, but this . . . this just couldn't be true.

"Yes, a married man," Geneva answered, her voice softer. She looked out over all our heads at something we couldn't see. "He's been married for a very long time to a wife who has very good reasons to abhor sex. And no, I won't tell you what her reasons are. They have a grown re-tarded child and a younger adopted child. And he has a po-litical career. They need to stay together. The wife knows and approves of our affair. Criminy, I don't even know why I'm telling you this. There's no reason for you to know. I don't have to excuse myself to anyone."

I was feeling blind again. I thought I knew Geneva, and I didn't. How many more secrets were there in my family?

"How long?" I demanded, my angry tone unrecognizable, even to myself. I could feel Roy's body recoil next to me.

"Over twenty years," Geneva answered. I heard the thickening of tears in her voice. "Twenty-five in December. Till death."

My mind calculated rapidly. Had Geneva already been involved in this affair when I'd lived with her? I'd moved in with her when I was fifteen years old. I counted back carefully. She had been involved, even then. How could she have hidden it so well?

I looked at Kapp. He looked back at me, his face asking me to reserve judgment. Did Kapp know about this affair? Of course he did.

Then why hadn't Geneva told *me*? Some sane voice in my head informed me that she'd never told me exactly because of the way I was reacting in that moment. I wasn't hearing her words, her pain, her reasons. I wanted Geneva to be the perfect role model, the perfect sister. "Till death," she'd said. She really loved this man. And she'd raised me through my teenage years without ever putting him first.

"It's okay," I said. I didn't say it very loudly, but I said it. I needed her to know.

"It certainly isn't okay," Uncle Earl started in. I turned toward him slowly, remembering why we were all there, coming back to earth with a *whumph*.

"I only spoke about my private business because of your insinuations about me and Kapp," Geneva proclaimed. She steepled her hands in front of her and pursed her lips. "That's the end of it. No more discussion."

Earl sighed and shook his head, but he didn't say anything more. He recognized the steepled hands and pursed lips of the queen stance. Once Geneva was in that stance, she couldn't be moved.

"Why?" York asked. I whipped my head around to look at him. How could he ask such a thing when Geneva had just closed the discussion? But he wasn't speaking to Geneva. He was speaking to Earl. And he was asking about something else. My brain stumbled to catch up. "Why do you think the murderer couldn't be a member of this family?" York expanded.

"Well, it just couldn't be," Uncle Earl sputtered. His volume went up. "We all loved Daphne. She was a member of our family."

"Oh, come on," Kapp objected, his hands in the air. "People are more likely to be killed by family members than strangers. Just look at the statistics."

"Well, not in our family," Earl replied, as if his words settled it.

"So who do you think it was, Earl?" Fern asked.

"I still don't believe there was even a murder committed," Earl reminded her. "And if there was a murder committed, I wouldn't be so irresponsible as to accuse anyone."

"Earl is right," Victor put in. "This might be interesting if we weren't talking about real people. But we are talking about real people. We don't want to end up with hurt feelings that can't be repaired. This subject is far too serious for speculation."

"Maybe Pilar killed Daphne," Linda offered brightly. So much for listening to her father. Or maybe that was her point. "Pilar is the one person we don't know anything about. Why was she even with Daphne? It's all really weird if you ask me."

"But Pilar was a *victim*!" I objected in frustration. "She was poisoned herself."

"Maybe she just pretended that someone else poisoned her," Linda hazarded. She screwed up her eyes to think. "She probably had a pretty good idea of how much morphine would really kill her. So she takes a little bit, then does a big song and dance so she goes to the hospital and gets the antidote."

"But why?" Fern asked.

"That's where it gets interesting," Linda told her. "We don't know anything about Pilar. We don't know anything about her motives. For all we know, she's some street kid Aunt Daphne picked up. So she does this big act of being *so* fond of Daphne, and then she kills her."

"But *why*?" Fern pressed her mother, her voice getting louder as she repeated herself.

"Maybe she stole from Daphne," Linda suggested. "Or maybe Daphne had the power to send her back to her real family. Or maybe she inherits money when Daphne dies. There could be all kinds of reasons. Because the point is, we don't know anything about her. She could be putting us all on."

"I don't think so," York argued.

"What, are you some kind of psychologist?" Linda demanded. "The girl has a crush on you, so you like her. You think I didn't see the way she was looking at you?"

York blushed. Maybe Linda had noticed Pilar's crush, but York probably hadn't.

Linda took a bite of baked pear and savored her victory. She swallowed and went on.

"And there's Bob." She looked around the table. "Do any of you know anything about Bob besides his being an 'attorney in good standing,' whatever that means? Huh? You have no idea what the deal was between him and Daphne. Maybe they had a lover's quarrel. Or maybe it's about money. He's a tax attorney. Maybe he was embezzling or something. Or maybe he's one of those angel-of-death guys, you know, helping Daphne out of her pain. You think I don't notice stuff, but I do. He was suffering for her. Maybe he wanted the suffering to stop. Maybe he and Pilar were in it together. We all know each other. We don't know Bob and Pilar. And they were the ones who were closest to Daphne. If there was any poisoning done, they probably had the best reasons."

"I just can't find it in my heart to believe that either Bob or Pilar would harm Daphne," Roy offered softly. "I could certainly be wrong, but it seems to me that they wanted to help her live."

"Well, fine," Linda stated. Then she smiled. "You guys are the ones who think she was poisoned, but you don't want it to be anybody you know. Would you rather it was your girlfriend, Cally? Or her brother or sister?"

Roy's face went a shade whiter under his freckles. "Ma'am," he announced. "I know Cally as well as one person can know another. And I can tell you for a certainty that she is not capable of hurting another human being purposely. She is a healer, and you'd best not be forgetting that. She is not mean-spirited in any way."

"It's okay," I told him in a whisper, patting his wrist. "She's just trying to rile you." And succeeding. Anger was pouring off of my sweet Roy in sheets of colored light.

"See, no one has even ever suspected Cally's boyfriend because he speaks so softly," Linda pressed on. "But look at him now. He could be a murderer. What do we know about him?"

My muscles tightened. I grabbed my cane without thinking. My body wanted to lash out.

"How about yourself, Linda?" Kapp asked genially. I let myself exhale. If I'd tried to speak to Linda, I don't know what I would have said . . . or done. "If there's been one person at this gathering who's been consistently angry, it's been you. I don't know you well enough to know what you're angry about, but if anger was the deciding factor in picking a murderer . . ." He paused and smirked. "Well, let the evidence speak for itself."

"How dare you!" Linda shouted, slapping her palms on the table.

"As I said, the evidence speaks for itself," Kapp added. "Or in this case, shouts." He was clearly goading her. Did he really believe that Linda was our murderer?

Kapp did have a point. Linda was the angriest person here, as far as superficial signs went. I could imagine her hitting someone, even throttling someone, someone like Kapp, for instance. But a careful poisoning?

"Linda," Uncle Victor tried again. "I told you there would be hurt feelings if you began with your accusations. You can't expect to air your own theories and not receive any feedback."

"Are you siding with them, Dad?" Linda demanded, her eyes widening with hurt.

"No, honey," he said to soothe her. He looked so old.

Poor Victor. "I'm trying to guide you in the right direction. I know your divorce has left you bitter, but your bitterness is spilling everywhere. It's corrosive. It's hurting you; it's hurting your daughter; it's hurting me. Don't let it burn your bridges with the rest of your family."

I wondered if she'd start crying again. Despite her accusations, I felt pity for her when I saw the hurt on her face. She wasn't pleasant, but she was clearly in pain.

"Linda—" I began.

The doorbell rang, and I jumped in my seat.

Geneva rose from the table. I'd almost forgotten she was there. I'd almost forgotten her confession. She hadn't spoken since she'd closed her sex life to discussion.

She made her way to the front door. I stood and followed her. I'd never had a chance to touch her, to assure her I still loved her. As she opened the door, I put my hand on her back and gave her a quick stroke.

She turned and smiled wistfully at me. "Cally, I—"

I mouthed the words "I love you" her way and saw light enter her face. She understood.

Then she opened the door.

Bob was on the doorstep. His body tremor was more pronounced, and his dark skin had a gray cast that worried me.

"How is Pilar?" I asked.

Bob looked down at his feet before replying. I didn't blame him. He didn't know who in this house might have tried to harm Pilar, who might have killed Daphne.

"She'll be okay," he answered finally. "They have a police guard on her room. I thank whoever alerted the police to what was going on."

"The chief of police was here," I told him. "I think Kapp bullied him into taking our accusations seriously."

Bob smiled a little then.

"Pilar wanted me to get her things," he explained. "I won't take much of your time."

"Take all the time you need," Geneva told him. "We want to help. We want to know who did these things."

Bob looked at her, his dark, intense eyes appraising her. "Yes," he commented briefly. It was hard to know what he meant.

"Has she said who she thinks did these things?" Geneva asked in a whisper.

"No," Bob replied. He sighed. "She didn't see who got near her drink any better than anyone else. I didn't see either. I wish I could point a finger, but I can't."

I heard footsteps behind us, then Earl's voice.

"Did Pilar take the morphine herself?" he demanded.

Bob looked at my uncle with clear distaste on his face. But he answered him. "No, Pilar did not take the morphine herself. She was very sick. Do you think she'd make herself that sick on purpose? I know it would make you all very happy to think that this was all Pilar's doing, or mine, but it wasn't. I don't know which of you killed Daphne. I could almost forgive that. She was so close to her own death. But to poison Pilar . . ." Bob shook his head. "If any of you really cared about Daphne, you'll not shield the murderer. I know it's too much to think any of you cared about Pilar. But you folks were related to Daphne. Don't you care about the truth? Don't you want to do the right thing?"

"Bob," Geneva answered gently. "I care. I think most of us care. I know you can't tell who to trust right now. Nor can I. But I know that Kapp, Cally, York, and Roy pushed the police into taking Pilar's accusations seriously. We want to know who killed Daphne. And I, for one, am very concerned about Pilar."

Bob stared at Geneva, his dark eyes moistening. "You're right. I don't know who to trust. I would love to thank you for helping me find Daphne's murderer. But I don't know if I'm talking to a murderer. That goes for everyone in this house. I don't know how to do the right thing. I should probably be apologizing to most of you. But there is one person who I can't be polite to, and I don't know who that person is. So, I'll just go upstairs and get Daphne's things now. And when all of this is cleared up, I'll make my apologies. And I hope I'll be able to spit on the person who killed my Daphne."

With that, he turned and made his way to the staircase.

As my eyes followed his dignified ascent, I saw that almost everyone had drifted into the living room. I just hoped the murderer had heard Bob speak. As I looked around, I understood a little of what Bob had felt. Uncle Victor, Fern, Uncle Earl, my own brother and sister—what if one of them was a murderer? I couldn't believe anyone was a murderer, and yet Bob was right. How could I trust anyone either? Not even Bob. Not even Pilar.

"Do you think Pilar really knows something?" York whispered in my ear.

I whirled around, startled.

"What?" I asked, confused.

"Pilar. You were right. She said she 'knew stuff.' What do you think she knows?"

"Bob said she didn't know who the murderer was," I murmured slowly.

"Then what did she mean?"

I looked at York. It was an important question. Did I have the nerve to ask Bob, assuming he knew himself what Pilar meant?

"Cally?" a new voice addressed me. It was Fern, standing next to me with an unhappy face. "I know Mom makes a bad impression. But she wouldn't kill anyone. She's all upset these days. But she's not . . ." She faltered. "She's not organized. She couldn't plan a murder. I don't think she even considers what she says until it comes out of her mouth. She's all messed up from the divorce. My dad left her for this woman who was her friend. It really weirded her out. Now she doesn't know who to trust. She's alienated all her old friends. And she works so hard all the time, she hasn't had time to deal with her feelings. Even with her therapist's help, she's still confused. So she says all these angry things. We're used to it. It doesn't mean anything—"

"It's okay," I assured her. "I know people in pain say things they don't mean."

"But your friend Kapp thinks she killed Aunt Daphne!"

"I don't think Kapp has any more idea who killed Aunt Daphne than the rest of us. He was just trying to get your mom to stop accusing other people."

"Are you sure?" She pressed me.

I hesitated. Was I sure?

"It's just that he's an attorney and all," Fern went on. "He could get Mom into trouble if he wanted. I'm just scared for her—"

"Don't be," I tried again. "Kapp is scary sometimes, but he's a fair man. He wouldn't make unfounded accusations." At least I was sure of that. But if Linda was guilty—

Bob came back downstairs with two suitcases and a duffel bag in hand.

"Hey, let me help you with those," Uncle Earl offered.

Bob shook his head. "I'll just take these out to the car," he muttered. "Then I'll get the rest of our stuff. I'm taking mine and Daphne's things as well."

Earl shrugged, his face red with the rebuff.

Bob went out the front door, lugging the bags.

Kapp and Roy came into the living room with Linda trailing behind as Bob left. Linda marched up behind her father.

"Maybe Bob would like some privacy," Kapp suggested. "It looks like a circus out here. And we're the clowns."

But Bob returned before any of us could act upon Kapp's suggestion. Bob headed back upstairs.

"Ask him who Pilar is," Linda ordered her father in a carrying whisper.

"Honey, stop," Uncle Victor told her. "It's none of our business."

"Everyone's talking about murder, and it's none of our business?" Linda shot back incredulously. "This Pilar could be the key to the whole thing."

"Granddad," Fern put in. "Maybe Mom's right on this. We all want to know who killed Aunt Daphne. We need information. Who was Pilar to Aunt Daphne? That police guy said she was some kind of ward of Aunt Daphne's. How could that be?"

"Yeah, who is she?" Linda pressed. "Pilar Vaughn? Has anybody ever heard of—"

Bob came back down the stairs carrying another suitcase, a purse, a backpack, and a makeup tote bag.

All eyes turned to him.

"Sir," Roy tried. "We are all mighty concerned about your Daphne's death, and we are in a lot of confusion on many points. We'd like to help figure these things out. Could you help us by telling us a little about young Pilar?"

Bob's face stiffened. He stared at Roy, and Roy stared back, matching Bob's anger with his own mildness. This was Roy's style of martial art. Finally, Bob seemed to relax.

"First, let me say that Pilar had nothing to do with Daphne's death," Bob began, setting down the bags he carried. "I know you're all curious about her, but her relationship to Daphne was a matter of confidence. It's hard to know how much is right to tell you."

"Just tell us what feels right, if you could," Roy prodded. And I thought Kapp was good at manipulation. Of course, Roy was just doing what came naturally.

"Well, I will tell you this," Bob offered. "Pilar has been living with Daphne for about six years now. Let's just assume that Pilar was related to Daphne in some way." Bob lowered his eyes. "Daphne always did the right thing. And she was doing the right thing with Pilar."

When it appeared that Bob had finished speaking, Roy said, "Thank you kindly, sir."

Bob bent over to pick up the bags again.

"Who inherits?" Kapp asked. "I know I'm not as diplomatic as Roy. But it's an important question."

Bob straightened back up.

"Well," he muttered, looking everywhere but into anyone's eyes. "I don't know if that's important here."

"You're a tax attorney," Kapp reminded him. "Money is always important. Even if only for the sake of ruling it out as a motive."

Bob finally raised his eyes to Kapp's. I think he knew that Kapp of all people had nothing to do with Daphne's death. Or at least he hoped so. "I wasn't their wills and trust attorney—" he began.

"But you know how the money was to be distributed," Kapp stated.

Bob put his hand into his short hair and pulled, as if he might find the right thing to do there.

"All right," he conceded. "I wasn't their attorney, but Daphne had talked to me. I think Pilar gets the bulk of the estate. But that means nothing as far as motive goes. Daphne never told Pilar anything about finances. She just told her she'd be taken care of.

"And Pilar's too young to be greedy," Kapp added.

"Yes," Bob answered seriously.

"And the rest?" Kapp led Bob on.

"To Victor, Fern, Linda," he answered. "And some charities. I don't know the details. This was just what Daphne told me. I don't do wills. And since Daphne and I had a relationship, it would have been improper for me to draw up her will anyway."

Somehow, I felt comforted that we Lazar siblings hadn't been included in Daphne's will.

"Attorneys," Earl muttered. "Always *talking* about what's proper and improper—"

"Terrible thing," Kapp parried. "Attorneys with ethics. A crying shame."

Bob gave Kapp a wan smile, and bent over to grab his bags again.

But he'd only bent a couple of inches when York asked, "What did Pilar mean by saying she 'knew stuff'?"

Bob looked up at the roof this time. Maybe he was tired of looking at the floor.

"Please, sir," Roy threw in. "We're all of us fretting over the possibility that Pilar might have known something important, something that could identify the murderer. Was that what she meant?"

Bob shook his head. But I could see his eyes misting up.

What could Pilar have meant?

"What?" York pressed.

"Bob," I tried, in my best healer tone. "I know there is one person here that you can't trust. I understand that. But there are a bunch of us here that you *can* trust. So maybe you could trust us as a group. I can see that what Pilar said had an emotional meaning for you. I can see it in your eyes. And we're asking you for information so that we can get to the bottom of this thing. So—"

Bob began to cry then. The tears streamed out of his eyes, but he did nothing to stop their flow. He just stood alone, crying in a group of strangers.

I stepped up to him and put my arms around him. I had to. I could feel the tremors in his body. And I could feel his illness and his sadness. I closed my eyes and invited light in, light that could help him through this terrible time.

"Daphne," he whispered through his tears. "Daphne was hoarding morphine so she could commit suicide when the pain got too great. Pilar knew. But Daphne was going to tell us both when she was ready. She never did. Someone stole her morphine and poisoned her before she was ready."

FOURTEEN

I could hear the clock ticking, my own heart beating, and Bob's quiet sobs. But no one spoke right away.

"You knew about Daphne's hoard?" Fern ventured finally, her voice filled with puzzlement.

"Did Pilar know?" Linda followed up, her agenda more obvious.

Bob gently removed himself from my embrace. It's hard to be formidable when crying on the shoulder of a small woman. And Bob needed to be formidable.

"Yes," Bob answered. "Pilar knew about the hoard. That's why she immediately thought of poison when Daphne passed away. She was sure someone had found Daphne's hoard and poisoned her with it."

"But—" Linda began.

"Honey," Victor warned.

Linda opened her mouth, shut it again, and went to the bathroom, slamming the door behind her.

"You let Daphne do this hoarding?" York asked. There was no judgment in his voice, only the question.

"Yes. It wasn't a matter of 'letting' her. She'd made up her mind. If I'd objected, she just would have gone ahead and kept it from me. Even her doctor knew. A tacit agreement. Daphne didn't want the pain. She didn't deserve the pain. You can't imagine what it's been like for her. And she didn't want it getting worse. She called her hoard her 'insurance policy.' I couldn't let her suffer unnecessarily."

"But—" Fern tried.

"This happens more often than people know," Kapp lectured. "Doctors can't give public agreement, but they make it easy for their patients with terminal conditions. The good doctors who care, that is. They allow the hoarding, knowing how difficult it is for the patient." He paused. "I think those doctors with ethics understand that their interference extends life unnecessarily sometimes. So they try to make amends."

"Oh, but that can't be right," Uncle Earl began.

"I read a lot about this while Mary was dying," Victor put in quickly. His voice shook a little. "There is some controversy of course. But compassion can call for extreme measures. Often cancer treatments don't really extend a patient's life. But doctors do heroics for the family's sake. The family wants to believe that every effort has been made to keep the patient alive. But the patient—" He drew in a sharp breath. "The patient just suffers. Mary chose to live with the suffering. It was her decision. She thought that the universe might have more meaning if she passed through her final stages without intervention. But she didn't ask for treatment either."

"Oh, Granddad," Fern whispered and stroked the old man's cheek. "Grandma was so brave."

Victor just jerked his head in a nod.

"My Ingrid had more time on this earth with treatment than she would have had without," Earl interjected stiffly. "That's what matters. That's what she wanted."

"That's what *she* wanted," I reminded him gently. "It clearly wasn't what Aunt Daphne wanted. Each woman made her own decision."

"Quality of life or quantity of life," Kapp muttered. I looked at my elderly friend. How much had he thought about this? I was fairly sure I knew what he would choose if he came to the point that Aunt Daphne had. Dack, I didn't want to think about it.

"Daphne was her own woman," Geneva pronounced. "She had a right to do what she thought best. And Bob and Pilar respected her right."

No one argued with her. Maybe everyone agreed with her. But it was more likely that no one actually had the nerve to argue with Geneva just then.

Linda made her way out of the bathroom and back to the group of people massed around Bob. She smelled of hand soap and perspiration.

"Did Pilar know where Daphne kept the morphine?" she asked Bob. "Did you?"

"Daphne kept it in her makeup tote bag. I knew. Pilar may have. It wasn't really a secret. Her friends knew." His eyes blurred in memory. "She liked to tell people. She liked to see their reactions. Especially uptight people. You know how she was. She was a rabble-rouser, a truth-teller. If the emperor was wearing no clothes, she'd be the one to point it out."

"Is the morphine still there in the bag?" Kapp asked quietly. His uncharacteristic stillness told me he was tense.

"No," Bob replied. "It was one of the first things I checked. Her supply is gone. Someone took it."

As a group, we all surged toward the tote bag. Victor reached down, almost touching it.

"Whoa!" Kapp warned sharply. "Fingerprints."

Victor jerked his hand back.

Bob looked up, his eyes rounding. "I didn't think of that," he murmured. "Damn, I didn't even think of it."

"That's okay," Kapp assured him. "We'll take care of it now." He looked around and found Geneva with his eyes. "Got a plastic bag?" he asked.

"I'll find one," she promised and rushed up the stairs.

"But what good—" Linda objected.

"Let them do what they need to," Victor told her.

Kapp took Victor aside and whispered in his ear. Victor

headed toward the kitchen. I didn't have time to really wonder what that was all about before Uncle Earl started in again.

"I'm not sure about this decision-making process," Earl objected. He turned to Kapp. "You may be an attorney, but you're not a member of the police department. What right do you have to handle evidence?"

"He's doing the right thing," Bob shot back. "No one else thought of fingerprints. He knows what to do. Do you know what to do?"

Earl bent over as if to grab the tote bag. I supposed that was his answer to Bob. But York was in front of him before he could even get close.

"Kapp is a disinterested party," York articulated. "I trust him. The majority of us trust him. He *is* the right person to be making these decisions. He knows more than the rest of us about legal matters."

"Maybe we should call the police," Fern suggested in a whisper.

"That's right where this evidence is going," Kapp assured her. "We've all witnessed its presence. And Bob will deliver it, or—"

"How's this?" Geneva asked, coming back down the stairs. She held a plastic zipped bag that might have once enclosed a blanket or a duvet.

"Perfect," Kapp breathed.

Geneva set the plastic bag on the floor, said, "Wait a minute," and sprinted to the kitchen. She returned with a set of kitchen tongs. Uncle Victor followed her, his face somber.

"Holy Mother, you're good," Kapp told Geneva, smiling. "Have you ever thought of a career in law enforcement?"

"Oh, stop it, you old fraud," she threw back affectionately.

Kapp took over then, gripping the strap of the tote bag with the tongs, and gently lowering it into the plastic bag. My mind told me that Fern might be right. Maybe the police should be handling the tote bag, not Kapp. But Kapp was here, and they weren't. It would get there faster if Kapp and Bob dealt with it. Once the tote bag was inside the bag, Kapp zipped it up and ceremonially handed it to Bob.

"I could take this to the police station," Bob suggested diffidently. "I could take it on the way back to the hospital."

"Now, wait a minute," Linda objected. "Are you sure Bob should be the one to take it to the police?"

"Hooboy," Kapp commented mildly. "Bob already has his fingerprints all over the tote bag. Who better? Anyway, maybe the police will show up to retrieve it before he goes."

"What do you—" Linda tried.

"Do you know where the local police station is?" Kapp asked Bob.

"Ninth and Ash?" Bob replied, his head tilted.

Kapp nodded. "But a couple of things before you go—" he began.

"Are Pilar's prints on that bag?" Linda asked.

"That's up to the police to find out, isn't it?" Kapp declared. "What are you afraid of? Do you really think Bob's going to find a way to erase Pilar's prints without erasing his own and Daphne's? What's important is who else's prints might be on it. Bob is the only person who *is* safe to take it to the police. He's the only one who's already admitted to touching it. He's the only person with no reason to conveniently lose it or mess with it."

But Linda wasn't finished. She might not have had Miss Marple's wisdom or finesse, but she had the spinster's nosy curiosity.

"Did Pilar have access to the morphine?" she demanded.

"I don't know," Bob answered evenly. "I just know she loved Daphne with absolute devotion. Accuse me if you want to, but don't accuse a sixteen-year-old child who's lying sick in the hospital."

"Here, here!" Kapp agreed.

"Attorneys stick together, of course," Earl put in. I was beginning to wonder what attorney had made Earl's life so miserable. He certainly seemed to hate the breed. He hadn't even been divorced. Had he been sued?

"Attorneys challenged our policies at the fire department," he muttered as if having heard my question. "There was nothing wrong with our policies. We hired qualified women and minorities. Qualified! There was no discrimination. But the attorneys couldn't accept that. They tied us up in knots for years. Cost the fire department enough to have hired more people, improved services. And those attorneys put the money of the people in their pockets. Houses burned down. But the attorneys didn't care. They were too busy lining their own pockets. Sharks, all of them! And then—"

"If one firefighter embezzled from your department, would you have blamed all the firefighters?" Kapp asked gently.

"What?" Earl said. He frowned, unhappy to be off track.

"There are attorneys, and there are attorneys," Kapp explained. "Some of us try to do the right thing. And every client deserves a defense. That *is* the right thing. If you were ever on the wrong side of the law, you might appreciate that."

"But I wouldn't be on the wrong side of the law," Earl stated.

"You'd be surprised," Kapp told him evenly. "If someone sues you because they tripped on the way up your driveway, you might be looking for one of us sharks. Or maybe you get hit in the parking lot by a drunk. Who's going to make sure your rights are protected?"

"But—"

"Holy Mary, you've been attorney-bashing for two days," Kapp broke back in. "We're a convenient target for everyone, aren't we? But without attorneys, people's rights would be trampled. For every story of a frivolous lawsuit, there're another hundred of people's lives saved by attorneys. And not just for money either. Do you read the papers? Did you read about the guy who they were going to convict of murder, only his attorney found out that he was in jail in another state at the time of the murder? The guy could have been put to death. And the attorney was defending him pro bono. Without pay, you understand? Did you hear about the attorney who helped those people next to the toxic dump? It took years of her life, but that attorney did what it took. No one else was lining up to help those people. They were too poor—"

"But—"

"So, enough of the attorney-bashing, okay?" Kapp finished. "I promise not to say anything about firefighters who start fires if you let up about evil attorneys. How's that for a deal?"

"Now, that's just not fair," Earl objected. "Just because there're some nuts who go into firefighting doesn't mean that all firefighters are bad."

"Thank you, Mr. Lazar!" Kapp boomed. "You have just made my case." He reached out his hand. "Shake?" he offered.

Earl rolled his shoulders, thinking.

"Uncle Earl?" Geneva prodded.

Hesitantly, Earl stuck out his hand and shook Kapp's. I still didn't think it was a marriage made in heaven.

"Mr. Ungerman, sir?" Roy put in, turning back toward Bob. "I don't think we've thanked you properly for telling us what you knew about Daphne and Pilar. That was a brave and kind thing to do. We need the truth right now, and you told us the truth. It just might help us solve our puzzlement. Thank you."

Bob looked stunned, as if this unexpected kindness was a harder blow than hostility. Then he muttered something that might have been "you're welcome," and bent over his bags one more time.

He was going to have a hard time carrying them while holding the precious tote bag carefully. He straightened back up.

"Kapp—" he began.

The doorbell rang.

Kapp answered the door this time. There was some muttering, and Officers Rossetti and Khashoggi entered.

"Hi, folks," Officer Rossetti greeted us. "I hear you have some evidence to hand over."

"But how . . ." Linda didn't even finish her sentence.

Had Kapp arranged this? He'd acted as if he wanted Bob to take the tote bag in, but hadn't he whispered something to Victor? Or had Geneva called them? I looked at Kapp. He was smiling smugly. Had he just been taking up time while he argued with Uncle Earl about attorneys? Had Bob understood that? Bob certainly looked relieved that the officers had arrived.

Bob carried the plastic-wrapped tote bag over to Officer Rossetti. "This is it," he told her. "This is where Ms. Dupree kept her morphine. There's no morphine in the bag now. And my fingerprints are all over it. I looked for the morphine without thinking about fingerprints."

"That's okay, sir," Khashoggi allowed. "We all make mistakes. Who put it in plastic?"

At least five fingers pointed at Kapp.

Kapp bowed. It was no wonder he drove Uncle Earl crazy.

"Good job, Mr. Kapp," Rossetti praised, and took the bag from Bob. I was surprised that she remembered Kapp's name. But perhaps Chief Kaifu had impressed it on her mind the hard way.

Rossetti cleared her throat. "We're also here to apologize. See, we really did write down your comments last night. We weren't shining you on. And we noted your request for an autopsy. We just hadn't logged in our notes to the computer yet. It gets a little crazy at the police station around the holidays." She gave us a forced smile before going on. "But Chief Kaifu and Khashoggi and I have all conferenced over this matter now. We're putting our attention on your concerns."

"What do you mean by that?" Linda asked.

It wasn't a bad question. I had a feeling someone else had prepared Rossetti's apology speech for her.

"We believe you," Khashoggi translated. "We're taking the possibility that Daphne Dupree may have been murdered seriously."

"Now, there're still a number of other possibilities to explore," Rossetti added. "But the murder scenario is no longer out of the question."

"Because of Pilar?" Fern asked.

"You mean Ms. Vaughn?" Rossetti countered. So much for being on top of the case.

"Yeah, her," Fern said.

"Ms. Vaughn's ingestion of morphine is under investigation, too," Rossetti agreed. "And the two incidents happening so close together might have some sort of relationship. Of course, with that kind of drug around, there's always the possibility of multiple accidents."

"Aunt Daphne's death was no accident," York insisted.

Rossetti put up the hand that wasn't holding the tote bag. "You may be right, sir," she conceded. "We're investigating all possible avenues. The case is in good hands."

"We all trust the police force," Uncle Earl put in.

Kapp muffled a quick snort.

Rossetti turned to Kapp. "Thank you for your confidence," she said tightly.

"Does anyone else have any more comments to add?" Officer Khashoggi asked quickly.

"Yeah," Linda jumped in, her voice excited. "There was this woman, Zoe something-or-other, here yesterday before Daphne died—"

"Zoe Jackson," Geneva put in. "She works for me. She was here for Thanksgiving dinner. But she wasn't here this morning when Pilar was poisoned. And Mr. Kapp has already given Chief Kaifu that information."

"Can you give me her name, phone number, and address, ma'am?" Rossetti asked. She was being a lot more careful this time around.

Geneva obliged, but not without a cutting glance at Linda.

"Chief Kaifu will come back for more extensive interviews," Rossetti informed us after she'd written down Geneva's information on Zoe. "But if anything occurs to you, please call us at the station. We're just starting to sort out the facts." She held up the tote bag. "And the evidence."

I thought they would leave then, but they weren't through.

"Now, I'd like you to all line up please," Khashoggi ordered. "I will take each of your fingerprints. A full set."

"But why?" Linda challenged.

"Get in line, Mom," Fern whispered. "Don't be a jerk."

So we lined up. Victor was first. Roy was next. And then me. I was tired. My muscles ached as if I'd been exercising for hours. And my mind was floating from thought to thought like a disengaged balloon. But even so, I realized that the fingerprinting routine was a good sign. The original indifference to Aunt Daphne's death had been replaced by what looked like an active investigation. But still, what if the murderer had left no fingerprints on the tote bag? I had a feeling he or she had been careful. How would we ever know what had really happened? My thoughts continued to float.

The printing didn't take long. Khashoggi had some sort of high-tech scanner. No black ink. At least that was one less thing for Linda to complain about.

Once Khashoggi had scanned all of our digits, he and Rossetti took their leave. Both of them apologized again on the way out the door.

The door slammed behind the officers, and Geneva turned toward Linda in a flat second. I flinched instinctively. Scary movie music played in my head.

"Why did you have to start in on Zoe again?" Geneva demanded. She shook her finger in Linda's face. "What is with you? Zoe wasn't even here today—"

Linda cut her off. "Hey, you're the one who won't come

clean about Zoe. If you won't tell us how Zoe knew Daphne, how are we supposed to figure out what went on between the two? And you can't fool me, something was going on."

"It has nothing to do with Aunt Daphne's murder!" Geneva shouted.

"How do we know that? Huh? Are we just supposed to take your word for everything because everyone's afraid of you?"

"Afraid of me?" Geneva asked, her head jerking back. She looked confused. Was it possible she didn't know what an intimidating woman she was?

"How come you can just shake your finger and say a discussion is closed, and everyone just shuts their yaps?" Linda pressed. "No one would do that if I was the one closing the discussion."

"Linda, I'm not trying to scare you," Geneva began. "It's just that some things are private."

"Not anymore, they're not," Linda announced. "When you called in the police, you gave up your right to privacy. You gave up all of our rights to privacy. So I suggest we all start talking honestly about what's going on here."

For once, I was with her.

"Like Bob, here," Linda kept on. "He's hiding something he knows. I can tell."

Bob's head snapped up when he heard his name.

Linda turned on him.

"How do we know Daphne didn't really leave you her money?" she pushed. "Are we just supposed to believe you? You're lying about something."

"Linda, you can't—" Victor began.

"No, she's right," Bob conceded, his voice trembling. "I haven't been lying. But I haven't told you the full truth either."

"Go ahead," Kapp encouraged him. "They need to know."

"All right, all right," Bob said, his voice getting stronger. "Perhaps you do need to know. You'll all know soon enough anyway. The only role I have in Daphne's money is as a trustee. Daphne left most of her money to Pilar because she was Pilar's grandmother."

FIFTEEN

"What?!" Uncle Earl exploded.

"Daphne gave birth to an illegitimate daughter over fifty years ago and gave her up for adoption," Bob explained patiently. "That daughter, in turn, had her own daughter, Pilar. Daphne's daughter tried to raise Pilar, but . . . well . . ." Bob frowned.

"Aunt Daphne had a daughter?" Fern repeated incredulously. She crooked her head and closed one eye, as if that might help her understand. Or maybe she had a migraine. "But she wasn't married, was she?"

"No," Bob acknowledged.

"But she was so old—" Fern began.

"She wasn't always old," Victor contributed. "Your great-aunt Daphne was an exceptionally beautiful woman back then."

"She is . . . was still beautiful to me," Bob muttered.

"Of course she was," I told Bob. "Her beauty shone through—"

"I don't believe it!" Earl interrupted. "This must be some kind of scam. Daphne couldn't have had a child without us knowing. Where's this daughter?"

"The daughter has problems," Bob answered, looking at the ground again. "That's why she gave up on raising Pilar. She just felt she couldn't do it. So Daphne stepped in and took Pilar. Then Daphne moved to a new community, one where no one knew she'd never been married. And she continued to raise her granddaughter. She did the right thing. She always did the right thing. And she wanted to introduce Pilar to her family gradually. But she wasn't sure how much time she had left. She was trying to figure out how to tell you—"

"Were you the father?" Fern asked Bob.

"Me?" Bob replied, visibly caught off guard, head back, eyebrows up.

"The father of Daphne's daughter?" Fern pressed. "Was it you? I mean, did you chill out 'cause of the racial thing? I could understand that—"

"No, no," Bob stopped her, trembling palms up. "I met Daphne just after she moved up to Oregon. Oregon was her new community. We met at a county board meeting. I didn't even know about Pilar's history until a year into our relationship."

"Well, if it wasn't you, who was it?" Fern kept at him.

Journalism, I thought. The girl might have a career in journalism. For all her apparent passivity, she was pulling the story right out of Bob.

"Was it you, Earl?" Fern asked, turning away from Bob for a moment. "Were you the father of Aunt Daphne's baby?"

"What?!" Uncle Earl roared. "I can't believe—"

"The father was a career soldier," Bob interrupted. "Daphne never even told me his name. She didn't like to talk about him. He left and never turned back once she got pregnant."

"Well, it certainly wasn't me," Uncle Earl fumed. "And I just can't believe that Daphne was capable of such behavior."

"Oh, she was," Uncle Victor assured him quietly. "It's all true. Simone knew. And later, Daphne told me. But my two sisters, Simone and Daphne, they shared everything. Daphne told Simone first."

Bob cleared his throat. "Daphne was a wonderful

woman, a good woman, and a practical woman," he pronounced. "There was no shame in what she did."

"Yes," Victor agreed quietly. "My sister was a person to be proud of."

"But what about Pilar's *father*?" Fern questioned, not to be derailed. "Her mother left her with Daphne, but how about the father?"

"The father was long gone by the time Pilar was born. The daughter doesn't speak to him."

"Why do you keep saying 'the daughter'?" Linda put in. "Is this daughter someone we know?"

"Honey, stop it," Victor ordered sharply.

"Why?" Linda smiled suddenly. She pointed at my sister, triumph on her face. "Is it Geneva?"

"No, it isn't Geneva," Bob said wearily. Linda quit smiling. Bob bent over, grabbed a handful of straps, and hefted the suitcase, backpack, and purse. "I'll be going now."

"Can I help?" York offered.

"No, but thank you," Bob replied. "Geneva was right. I can thank all of you but the murderer. I feel better having told you people about Daphne. Maybe it will help you in your 'puzzlement.'" He directed a wan smile toward Roy.

"Thank you, too, sir," Roy put in. "Your Daphne was as gracious a human being as I've ever had the honor to meet. I'm glad to have met her and glad to have met you."

Bob tipped his head toward Roy and quietly turned to take his load out to his car.

But when Bob opened the front door, his way was blocked. A stocky, smiling Asian man stood in front of Bob, his hand raised up to knock on the door. He wore a black T-shirt and jeans much like York's.

The Asian man stepped back at the same moment that Bob stepped back. Then they each stepped forward again.

The Asian man laughed. "Shall we dance?" he asked.

Bob shook his head, unable to smile.

"Well, let me help you with those bags," the newcomer offered, reaching forward. "I'm Tom Weng."

"No, but thank you," Bob replied. "I'm just going."

Tom Weng stood back once more. And this time, Bob passed him on the way out the front door.

Tom stepped through the doorway cautiously. I gave him a quick once-over. Although I'd seen his work and talked to York about him at length, I'd never actually met Tom Weng before.

"York?" Tom inquired. York was at the door in an instant, motioning Tom in.

"Who's this?" Linda asked, her eyes widening.

"York's friend, Tom," I answered automatically. I wasn't sure how York wanted to handle introductions. And I wanted to give him a chance to think.

"Oh, great," Linda said, rolling her eyes. "Someone else to play with the Lazars."

"He was invited," Geneva snapped, then smiled at Tom, striding forward with her hand held out to be shaken.

"I thought this was just for family," Linda complained before Geneva could even reach Tom. "And now with Daphne and everything, don't you think—"

"This is my partner," York asserted. "He was invited before we knew about Daphne and Pilar."

"You mean your partner in your martial arts studio?" Uncle Earl asked, his voice confused.

"No," York answered brusquely. "My partner in life."

Uncle Earl squinted at Tom as if trying to figure him out.

Tom just laughed easily. I smiled with him. I had a feeling I was going to like this man.

"Is that enough information for you?" York demanded of Earl. I stopped smiling in surprise. York was usually cool. But Uncle Earl was getting to him. Or maybe it was the poisonings. I felt a little light-headed myself. I tightened my grasp on my cane instinctively.

Tom grabbed Geneva's hand and shook it. Then he shook my hand, Kapp's, Roy's, Fern's, Linda's, Victor's, and finally, Earl's. He seemed completely at ease . . . much more at ease than York was.

"So what's going on?" he finally asked York. His spoken question implied another unspoken one. *Is your family always so weird?*

"I should have called you last night, Tom," York answered tightly. "Family secrets are going on. Always family secrets." I felt a chill across my shoulders as my brother spoke.

"Where's your aunt Daphne?" Tom asked to follow up. "She was good to me. She bought a picture at my last show in Oregon. I wanted to say an obsequious 'hello and bless you' to her."

"She's dead," Linda announced.

Tom's easy smile left his face slowly. "Are you joking or something?" he asked. "What—"

"You knew her?" Earl demanded of Tom. Then his eyes darted to York and back to Tom again. A conspiracy? Is that what he thought?

But Tom Weng was still absorbing the idea of Daphne's death. "Was it the cancer?" he asked gently.

A silence came over the room.

Finally, Kapp answered him. "The jury's still out on the cause of death," he told Tom. It occurred to me that I hadn't heard Kapp's voice the whole time Bob had been telling us about Daphne. Had Kapp already known what Bob had told us? I looked at Kapp. But not fast enough.

"But how come you both knew her?" Earl demanded of York.

"Oh, come on, Uncle Earl," Geneva scolded. "Tom met Daphne at one of his shows. What are you trying to say?"

"May I translate?" Kapp offered with a little bow. "Earl is saying that it is way too suspicious that three people might know each other independently. Unheard of. They ought to be sent to jail."

Earl ignored Kapp, turning back to York. "Son," he tried. "If you'll just explain—"

"Listen, Uncle Earl," York said evenly. "I just told you. Tom's my partner. Don't you understand?"

"No," Earl answered, shaking his head. "I don't. Do you mean that he's a partner in your martial arts studio? I didn't know you had another business. I thought—"

"No, Uncle Earl." York took a breath and loosened the tension in his body. "Tom is a painter. Aunt Daphne knew him from the exhibit he had in Oregon. Tom and I are 'life partners.' "

"But what do you *mean* by that?"

"Think about it, Earl," Linda suggested scornfully. "If two men aren't allowed to marry, then . . ."

York smiled and reached out to grasp Tom's hand. I'd never seen York publicly touch a man like that before. And I thought how odd we all were, we Lazars. Secrets. York was right. But at least he was exposing one secret.

Earl's sad eyes widened with sudden understanding. Then he looked away. But all he said was "Well then, let's just sit down and enjoy some civilized conversation."

Linda took that opportunity to rush to the bathroom.

"So what do you paint, Mr. Weng?" Earl asked, lowering himself onto a chair. I smiled. Good old Uncle Earl. He was biting the bullet. He may not have liked the idea, but if York was to have a male lover, Earl was going to vet him. He was still our godfather.

"I paint still lifes with real lives," Tom answered enigmatically, sitting down across from Earl. I couldn't blame him for his enigmatic answer. His paintings were hard to classify. Tom had rated a mention in *The New Yorker* recently. They'd called his work "transcendent."

"Oh," Earl said, obviously mystified.

"I suppose it would be more useful if I painted houses," Tom tried, his tone verging on flirtatious.

"Tom does Art, Uncle Earl," Geneva put in. "The stuff people hang on their walls. Tom is a wonderful visual artist."

Tom bowed toward Geneva. "You are too kind," he teased. But then his tone turned serious again. "What happened to your aunt Daphne?"

Linda was talking as she came back from the bathroom.

"Aunt Daphne had a baby," she told him, her eyes blinking with excitement. "Do you believe it?"

Now Tom really was confused. "Are you trying to say that Daphne Dupree died in childbirth?" he demanded. Then he shook his own head. "She must have been at least sixty, seventy—"

"She was murdered," York blurted out.

Tom frowned and tilted his head. He didn't ask York if he was serious. York was always serious in his statements.

"We *think* she might have been murdered," Uncle Victor corrected York mildly. "The police are looking into it."

"Not here?" Tom pressed, his hand raised to his chest.

"Yes, here," Geneva told him grimly. "She collapsed here. She may have been poisoned here."

"But why?" Tom whispered. He might have been talking to himself.

"That is something Cally and her family are attempting to ascertain," Roy tried. "The police have been notified—"

Then everyone tried to explain, their voices flying through the air like caged birds.

"She might have committed suicide."

"Then what about Pilar?"

"Maybe she tried to commit suicide, too."

"We don't even know that Daphne was poisoned yet. We only know that Pilar was poisoned."

"And she may have been trying to fake us out."

"Oh, come on. Pilar didn't poison herself just to make trouble for us—"

"Maybe she was trying to get high."

"Look, we've been through this before. Someone poisoned Pilar's super shake."

"Not necessarily. She might have taken it herself."

"Or maybe an accident."

"Pilar isn't stupid—"

"Who is Pilar?" Tom interrupted. I was glad for the interruption. I was tired of listening to the free-for-all.

"Pilar is Daphne's granddaughter," Geneva stated for the record.

"Daphne had a granddaughter?" Tom asked. "What was going on—"

"Tom," York muttered, a warning in his tone.

"Don't worry," Tom answered, smiling York's way. "You're the strong silent type. I'm the nosy talkative one. Right? That's why we get along."

York shrugged his strong silent shoulders.

"It's like a story," Fern cut in. "Daphne had this secret love child. No one knew. She was so cool—"

"Having an illegitimate child is not 'cool,'" Uncle Earl pronounced. "And it seems entirely out of character for the Daphne I knew. She and Simone were good—"

"What I don't understand is how she actually got away with it," Linda questioned. "These days, single mothers are no big deal—"

"Not to everyone—" Earl began.

Linda just kept going. "But in Aunt Daphne's day, an illegitimate kid must have been a really big deal. Wasn't she a legal secretary? How'd she hide having a baby?"

"A trip abroad, perhaps," Kapp ventured. "There were a lot more illegitimate kids born than people knew in 'Daphne's day,' in my day. People made arrangements. Families stuck together to hide these things. Society agreed to look away."

Victor nodded. "Daphne was going out with this young man. He was in the service. And suddenly, he was gone. And Daphne was pregnant. She went to our parents. They took her on a trip to France. They said they'd been called there by relatives. At the end of five months, they came back. Daphne returned on an earlier flight. Then our parents came home with a baby, a distant relative, they claimed. A needy orphan. No one questioned the story."

"And they raised her?" Linda challenged. "I don't remember any little girl at Grandmere and Grandpere's. How old was she?"

"She was a little older than you, honey," Victor told his daughter.

Linda crossed her arms. "How come I don't remember

her? She must have been just about Natalie's age. Natalie never said anything about her."

"So did they raise her, Granddad?" Fern pressed, back to the point.

"No," Victor answered. "They tried for a while, but it was just too hard at their age. Especially after your great-grandmother had a stroke."

"So what happened to her?" Linda pushed.

Victor looked sad. "Daphne wanted to raise the daughter, but it just wasn't possible. Not then."

"Aunt Daphne was really brave, wasn't she?" Fern murmured. "Having her baby like that?"

"It would make a great story," Kapp put in. "Maybe you can write it, young lady."

"Wow," Fern whispered. Her eyes flicked back and forth as if she was reading the story she was writing in her head.

"But first we have to figure out who killed Daphne," York insisted.

"We don't know that anyone killed Daphne," Earl reminded him.

York glared at Earl.

Geneva raised her arms. "Don't you two start in again!" she commanded. "And nobody is writing a story about Aunt Daphne. Don't you think she suffered enough protecting her privacy? Don't you think—"

"But she was so cool," Fern insisted. "It's really romantic. I wonder if that's why she never married. Maybe her heart was broken until Bob came into her life. Or maybe she was watching her daughter from afar."

"It wasn't romantic," Geneva put in. "And she probably never remarried because of the way that pig of a man treated her in the first place."

"Did you know about this daughter, Geneva?" Linda demanded.

"No," Geneva sighed. "I'm just guessing. And I'm imagining how hard this all must have been for Aunt Daphne."

I nodded. Even now, it wasn't so easy for unwed mothers.

Daphne must have been torn in two, not being able to raise her own child. No wonder she'd taken Pilar in.

"Who was this man in the service?" Earl demanded of Victor. He sounded as if he wanted to hunt him down and challenge him to a duel.

Victor shrugged. "Just a GI. I don't even remember his name now. I just remember how sad Daphne was when he deserted her. She hadn't expected that. She thought well of people. She never got over his abandoning her. I'm surprised that Bob was able to enter her life. But I'm glad. At least she got a little of the happiness that she deserved."

"All I remember of Aunt Daphne is how fun she could be," I said. "I never thought of her as sad."

"She kept it a secret," Victor clarified. "She kept so many secrets."

"And you helped her keep her secrets," Linda accused.

"Of course I did," Victor answered. "She was my sister."

"So what happened to the daughter after Daphne's parents couldn't take care of her?" Fern asked.

"She was taken in," Victor muttered. "She wasn't told until she was out of high school that she was adopted and who her birth mother was. But she saw Daphne on holidays. I think the right things were done. It's hard to know."

"Why would you doubt that the right things were done?" I asked. Victor was very troubled right then. I didn't have to look at his aura to know that he felt guilty. But guilty of what?

"The daughter turned out, well . . . difficult," Victor tried. "She was cruel. She hurt animals—"

"Like Natalie?" Linda asked. I hadn't realized that Linda's sister, Natalie, had hurt animals, but it made sense.

Victor nodded and continued. "As she got older, she ran with a tough crowd. Not just high-spirited hippies, but cruel people. People who vandalized and fought and took drugs, hard drugs. I try to think that the root cause was in her father's genetics, but I don't know. She left home and lived on her own. She had Pilar in her thirties, but she treated her own daughter as if she was a pet. She'd leave

Pilar at home alone. Daphne found out that she was leaving Pilar alone without adequate food for weeks on end. Pilar struggled with school. She dressed herself, got herself there. Can you imagine? Pilar tried to pretend her mother was like other mothers, but she wasn't. When Pilar turned ten, Daphne stepped in and asked if she could raise Pilar. Pilar's mother didn't care. She said 'fine,' and let Daphne take the girl. She never even asked about her."

"Poor Pilar," Fern whispered.

Poor Pilar indeed. And she was in the hospital, alone except for Bob.

"Pilar was with Daphne for the last six years," Victor finished up, his eyes bleary with tears. "I don't know how she'll survive without her. I really don't."

"But who was her mother?" Linda demanded. "Who was Daphne's child? How could you let her go to someone outside of the family?"

"I didn't," Victor said.

There was a silence. I tried to digest his meaning, but couldn't. Nor could Linda.

"What do you mean, you didn't?" she asked.

Victor was crying. He just shook his head.

"Dad?" Linda asked, her voice a whisper. She walked up to her father and put her arm gently around his bent shoulders.

"Honey," he forced out. "Daphne's daughter was your sister, Natalie."

SIXTEEN

"Natalie?" Linda demanded, dropping her arm from her father's shoulders and taking a step backward. "But if Natalie was Daphne's daughter, how could she be my sister? I mean—"

"We adopted her," Victor elucidated.

"Oh," Linda said quietly. Linda seemed to be turning inside out in front of our eyes. Her shoulders were slumped, her aggression receding. The tension in her face had given way to a softer, almost childlike, expression of confusion.

"We were the only ones who could, honey," Victor said to defend himself. He looked guiltily at the floor. Kapp turned his head away. Kapp had known the story all along. I was sure of it. I just didn't know if he'd wheedled it out of Bob or Victor.

"You see, Simone and Hugh took her for a brief time," Victor went on sadly. "But Simone was pregnant with Geneva, and Natalie kept kicking her stomach."

"Yeah, I can imagine that," Linda conceded. But her voice was emotionless.

"Natalie was a difficult child," Victor expanded. "Mary and I had our doubts, but what could we do?"

Linda didn't answer her father. She had her own question.

"Is that why she was so mean to me?" Linda asked. There was no whine in her voice, just simple curiosity. "Was it because she was adopted? Do you think she always realized it?"

"I don't know, honey," Victor admitted. "I've struggled with my feeling over the way that Natalie treated you. We did our best with her. I don't think she knew she was adopted until we told her. She was just . . . wired badly, I suppose. She had no real empathy. It was as if she didn't know that other people were important, too. The doctor we went to said she was a nearly a sociopath. I know she was abusive. Your mother and I had promised Daphne we'd raise her. But we did our best to protect you—"

"It's all right, Dad," Linda murmured. "I know you did. I remember. You stood up for me."

Fern walked up to her mother and laid her hand on the small of her mother's back.

"It'll be okay, Mom," she soothed. "I wouldn't let anyone hurt you."

"Thanks, sweetie," Linda said, trying to smile. But I saw old fear dancing in her aura. And I remembered her speaking of Natalie's pranks with admiration before. Maybe she'd conditioned herself to see Natalie as charmingly troublesome instead of severely troubled, and tried to like her. Denial had its uses.

All these years, I'd disliked Linda. My mouth tasted sour with guilt. I'd never asked myself why Linda was so defensive, so whining, so aggressive. I'd just decided I wouldn't like her. But if she'd grown up under attack—

"You shouldn't have exposed your daughter to a sadist!" Earl shouted at Victor.

Whoa! I jumped in place.

"What do you—" Victor began, his head jerking back.

"Grandpa Lazar," York muttered. "He's talking about—"

"Children and women have to be protected from sadists at all costs!" Uncle Earl bulldozed on. He pounded his fist into his hand. "And you let this Natalie prey on your own daughter? How could you?"

"But I—" Victor tried again.

"Dad, it's really all right," Linda assured him. "You did

protect me. I know you did. I was afraid of Natalie, but you and Mom protected me once you realized what she was doing to me. It's not your fault."

"Of course it's his fault," Earl insisted.

Victor looked at Earl, his tired face broken.

"Uncle Earl isn't really talking about you, Uncle Victor," I put in. "Uncle Earl's upset about his own father."

"We know about Grandpa Lazar, Uncle Earl," Geneva added. "Pop told us how he hurt you boys, how he hurt your mother. We knew he was cruel. Pop didn't keep it a secret." She rubbed her own arms as if she were cold. "He even told us the details. Grandpa Lazar went beyond anything that could have been considered normal discipline."

Earl put his head into his hands and mumbled through them. "I always tried to protect you kids and Simone. I worried all the time. I tried—"

"I know." Geneva tried to soothe him. "You were like Pop. You never left any of us alone with Grandpa Lazar. We knew why."

"But—" Earl started, then stopped.

"But what?" I asked. I wanted to know. I didn't want any more secrets.

"Never mind," he told me. Then he straightened his back. "I'm sorry I flew off the handle, Victor."

"No problem," Victor absolved him, waving his hands in the air. "You have a right to your opinions."

"But he doesn't, Dad," Linda insisted. Some of her old aggression was coming back as she turned toward Earl. "You lay off my father. He hasn't done anything to you."

Earl just nodded miserably.

"Where is this girl, Pilar?" Tom Weng asked.

"In the hospital," Geneva answered. She looked almost as guilty as Victor then. "She was poisoned here, too."

This time, no one argued with her assessment of poisoning. And if Tom Weng was shocked, he covered it well. But then, he didn't know Pilar. And he had clearly gotten a measure of the strangeness of our family gathering. One more poisoning was probably looking normal to him.

"What are we going to do about Pilar?" York asked into the silence. "Natalie isn't here. Grandpa Lazar's dead. But Pilar's here. And she's alone in the world without Daphne."

Victor looked up. "I'm supposed to take custody of her," he replied. He shook his head. "But I'm just too old. What if I die before she grows up? Bob is her financial trustee, but I'm supposed to be her custodial trustee. I just don't know what's right."

"Oh, Dad," Linda said with tears in her own voice. "I'm sorry."

"I could take care of Pilar," York offered. Tom leaned back and looked at his new life partner beneath tightened eyelids. Was he imagining helping York raise a trauma-tized teenager? Or was he wondering about our whole family, York included? I wouldn't blame him.

"No, that's ridiculous," Geneva told York. She shook her hands in the air, jangling bracelets. "I know how to raise a teenager. I'm an expert." She winked my way. "I should take her."

"Or I could," I put in. I saw Pilar in my mind. Roy, Pilar, and I were eating breakfast at my kitchen table. She was smiling. "It would be like paying you back for what you did for me, Geneva."

I turned to Roy, hoping he wasn't giving me the look Tom was giving York. He wasn't. He just squeezed my hand. Maybe he saw the same vision that I did. Or maybe he was humoring me.

"I think I should take her," Linda proposed. All the heads in the room seemed to turn toward her. Was Pilar's accuser suddenly Pilar's protector? "Mom took Natalie in, and she wasn't even related. But I am related to Pilar. No wonder the poor kid's such a mess. I didn't know—"

"But Mom," Fern objected. "Don't you think you're al-ready under enough stress? The therapist said—"

"I know what the therapist said." Linda cut her off. I wished she hadn't. Another secret nipped in the bud. "But do you really think Dad can take care of her? I'm Natalie's sister. I understand what Pilar's been through."

"Oh, honey," Victor interceded. "You don't need more worry in your life. We'll find a way to help Pilar. Don't you even think about it now."

"I take it that Natalie signed off on the adoption papers," Kapp put in. "She can't make trouble for whoever ends up taking the kid in."

Victor nodded. "It's all in the adoption agreement. I'm Pilar's guardian now. And I can choose another guardian if I want to. Daphne made sure that Natalie couldn't renege on the agreement. It was hard, but she was too afraid for Pilar to be soft with Natalie."

"Then why is that Bob fellow down at the hospital with Pilar?" Uncle Earl asked. "Shouldn't you be with her if you have custody?"

Victor scrunched up his face. Was he trying not to cry? "Pilar wanted Bob," he muttered. "Pilar is afraid of the rest of us. I told Bob to take care of her until this is resolved. And this absolutely *has* to be resolved. I'm not leaving until it is. Not just for Daphne's sake, but for Pilar's. How will she ever feel safe again if we don't find out who killed her grandmother and tried to kill her."

"If that's what happened," Linda put in quietly.

"Exactly," Victor agreed. "We need to know if any or all of this poisoning story is true. Pilar has to know. How can I trust myself to place Pilar in anyone's care until I know?"

"Poor Dad," Linda murmured. Her eyes looked vague.

"Granddad?" Fern began inquisitorially. "Why didn't you ever tell Mom that Natalie had a child? You didn't have to say who, but couldn't you have told her, told us?"

Victor rolled his shoulders before speaking. He looked like a puppet suspended by invisible wires, tired wires.

"Do you want to sit down, Dad?" Linda asked.

"No," he answered. Then he spoke to Fern. "I didn't even know at first. I'd lost contact with Natalie. So had Daphne. We both worried about her. But we didn't know where she was, much less what she was doing. Then one day, Natalie called me. She told me she had a child. I offered to take the child, but Natalie just wanted money—"

"Money?" Fern interrupted. "Why money?"

"She said she couldn't raise Pilar without money," Victor expanded. "She said she was working as a waitress, but that she didn't have enough money to really take care of her child, Daphne's grandchild. I talked to Daphne. We knew Natalie might just be asking for herself, that she might just be making up the existence of her daughter out of whole cloth. But still, for all of Natalie's problems, Daphne and I still cared about her. So did your grandmother. So the three of us agreed that Mary and I would send her a little money each month and so would Daphne. Not enough for her to quit working, but hopefully enough to give her and her daughter a better life. She even visited once. But without Pilar. I think she was afraid we'd try to take Pilar away if she allowed us to meet her. And Natalie liked keeping us in suspense. Fern, that's why I never told your mother. I didn't want Natalie contacting either of you. I didn't want to give her any chance to con or harm you."

"I understand," Linda murmured. Her voice sounded spacey.

"Then Natalie finally went into a drug rehab program," Victor went on. "That's when she allowed Daphne to meet Pilar. Pilar stayed with Daphne while Natalie was in the program. When Natalie got out, she told Daphne that Daphne could keep Pilar, that she hadn't been a good mother. I was proud of Natalie then. She was facing her reality. Maybe it was part of the program, but she gave Daphne enough detail to prove she was an unfit mother." Victor rolled his shoulders again. "And she told Daphne that she could take over with Pilar. I think Natalie was truly thinking of Pilar's best interests then. We still send her money. Or at least I do, I guess. Daphne won't be able to anymore."

"Does Natalie know she wasn't in the will?" Kapp asked.

Fern butted in before Victor could answer. "Why didn't Aunt Daphne put Natalie in her will?" she demanded of her grandfather. "Natalie was her own daughter."

"It's a bad idea to give people with drug problems large sums of money," Kapp answered for Victor. "And I think Daphne knew that Victor would continue to support Natalie a little at a time. Maybe that's why she left your grandfather money in the first place."

"I don't think Natalie knew anything about the will," Victor murmured. "Daphne was never unkind to Natalie, but she was firm that Natalie couldn't contact Pilar unless Pilar wanted to see her. And Pilar never asked to see Natalie."

I stood in Geneva's brightly colored living room wondering if there was a murder motive buried in here somewhere. Had Pilar been secretly angry over the way she'd been shunted around? And what if Linda had really known the whole time about Natalie's adoption? Could Linda be under Natalie's influence even now? Had Natalie somehow slipped in unseen—

The doorbell rang before I could travel any further into paranoia.

Geneva approached the door cautiously. But when she opened it, only Melinda and Arnot were on the doorstep.

"Happy day after Thanksgiving!" Melinda greeted the room at large. She held out a terra-cotta turkey to Geneva. The turkey had a flowering cabbage growing out of its spine. That was my sister Melinda, always inappropriate in all things.

Geneva smiled, accepted the turkey and gave Melinda a one-armed hug.

"We just wanted to check in with you guys," Arnot explained. "Things seemed pretty dicey last night. Barbara said it would help if we came over to check out what really happened."

"It would help if we *knew* what really happened," I told Arnot.

He laughed tentatively.

"You're welcome to stay and help us figure it out," Geneva offered.

"Aliens landed?" Melinda tried.

"Just Lazars," Linda muttered.

"Well, it's good to see you all, anyway," Arnot said. "We can't miss a gathering of the most superb clan in the universe."

"This is Tom Weng," York introduced. "My brother Arnot and sister Melinda."

Tom held out a hand enthusiastically. But as he shook Melinda's hand, Melinda looked over his shoulder.

"Where's Pilar?" she asked, her eyes searching the room.

"Pilar's in the hospital," Tom told her.

Both Melinda and Arnot stopped smiling.

"Why?" Arnot demanded.

"Morphine overdose," York provided brusquely.

"It wasn't a poisoning attempt, was it?" Arnot hazarded.

"Not necessarily—" Earl began.

"Poisoning," York confirmed.

Melinda's tiny body seemed to shrink a little more. "Too much death," she muttered. "Too much death. It's this family. All the secrets."

Arnot put his arm around her. He wasn't playing the grinning fool he usually did. His face was solemn, older. "This isn't good," he agreed.

"Pilar's alive," Tom offered.

"No need to worry," Earl put in. "Pilar's going to pull through. She was very upset over Daphne's death, confused. She might have taken the morphine for a hundred reasons. Poor girl. I can't say that I blame her."

"Especially if *someone else* poisoned her," Kapp added, sarcasm floating on his words like garlic on pizza. "Not much blame there, eh?"

"And Daphne was her grandmother," Tom Weng went on.

"What?" Melinda asked, her eyes popping open.

"Grandmother?" Arnot said simultaneously. "That can't be right. Daphne was never married."

"Pilar was Daphne's illegitimate granddaughter," Tom expounded. "Didn't you know?"

"Are you Pilar's doctor?" Melinda asked Tom in confusion.

"No, I'm—"

"Are you Pilar's father?" Arnot demanded, looking stern.

"God, no!" Tom objected. "I'm just—"

"What do you have to do with Pilar?" Melinda challenged him. Her voice was high. "What's this about Daphne being her grandmother?"

"Tom is York's 'life partner,'" Earl announced. He looked smug as he drew out the description.

"What does that mean—" Melinda began. Then her face opened up. "Oh, whoops! I know what that means. Congratulations, York. But how come he's the expert on Pilar?"

"He doesn't have anything to do with Pilar," York grumbled. "He just heard us all talking. He thought you guys already knew—"

"But—"

As everyone tried to explain, untangle, and confuse, I took the opportunity to take Kapp aside. I tapped him on his elbow with my cane and jerked my head toward the kitchen. He sighed but followed me in, along with Roy.

"You knew all about Pilar, didn't you?" I accused Kapp once the three of us were alone.

"Well, not all—"

"I want a straight answer," I hissed. "How'd you find out?"

Kapp grinned. "I called some friends in government and they found Pilar's adoption papers—"

"How do you get people to tell you these things?" I demanded in exasperation.

"Just natural charm," Kapp told me. I narrowed my eyes and raised my cane. "And connections," he added. "Heh-heh."

"Okay," I went over it again. "So you called these friends. What did they tell you?"

"They told me that Daphne Dupree had legally adopted Pilar Vaughn," Kapp admitted. "It sounded like there was some kind of tie there, so I asked Bob."

"And Bob crumbled," I guessed.

"Look, Bob trusts me," Kapp argued. "Holy Mary, I'm one of the few people here that didn't know your aunt previously. He told me the whole story. I wanted it out on the table, but Bob wasn't sure. And he told me about Pilar in confidentiality."

"So you prodded him until he spilled the beans, himself," I accused.

"Hey!" Kapp defended himself. "He knew it was the right thing to do. He's very big on doing the right thing."

"But why did you want it out on the table?" I asked. "Do you think that Pilar and Daphne's relationship is a motive for murder?"

"I'm not sure," Kapp muttered, his grin fading. "I can't figure it out. Your family is weird, Lazar, really weird. And they get weirder all the time. But I still can't find a reasonable motive for murder."

"What if Pilar is really in touch with her mama?" Roy questioned. "It worries me. That little girl is still young. Could her mama convince her to do something wrong?"

"It worries me, too, Roy-boy," Kapp conceded. "This Natalie sounds like the very kind of person who might have the temperament for murder—"

"But she's not here, is she?" I asked. Somehow, it didn't feel like a stupid question anymore.

"She isn't here, but who would she have influence over?" Kapp muttered, rubbing his face. "Linda seems to be surprised, but what if it's an act? What if she and Natalie are in cahoots?"

"That's why you asked if Natalie knew she wasn't in the will," Roy guessed.

"And we really don't have an answer to that question," Kapp shot back. "If I were Natalie, I'd expect my birth mother to put me in the will."

"But Daphne put in Pilar," I argued, feeling suddenly defensive of my aunt Daphne. "In a way that was for Natalie. You're the one who said that giving Natalie a big lump of money might backfire. And Uncle Victor will take care of her."

"And Pilar might have known she inherited," Kapp rumbled on, ignoring me. "I don't think Pilar had anything to do with all of this except to be a victim. But she is the financial beneficiary."

We were all silent for a while. The Pilar-Daphne connection kept leading back to Pilar.

"Pilar wouldn't have killed Daphne," I announced finally. "She was crying over Daphne's condition. She was afraid Daphne might die. She wasn't looking forward to it."

"I don't want it to be Pilar either," Kapp said.

I wanted to open my mouth and tell him he misunderstood me, but I realized he didn't. I just wanted it not to be Pilar. I had no proof.

"There is one thing, though," Kapp offered provocatively.

"What?" Roy and I asked together.

"We know that your mother and your aunt shared secrets," Kapp said thoughtfully.

My body froze.

"What does that mean?" I asked slowly.

"I'm not sure," Kapp admitted. "But it seemed to me that Daphne wanted to clear up some secrets. She came here partly to tell you about Pilar. Maybe there was more."

"More?"

"Look, I just said maybe," Kapp told me, holding up a hand as if to stave off objections. "I haven't figured out what. I just have a feeling. That's all."

"Do you mean something about my mother?"

"Not necessarily." Kapp shook his head. "Hell. I don't know what I mean. I don't want to upset you. I was just thinking out loud."

Upset? It took me a moment to take in the word. But both Kapp and Roy were eyeing me intently. Upset? I *was* holding my breath, I realized. And the room seemed unnaturally bright. I grasped my cane more tightly and let my breath out slowly. I tried to pin down just what was upsetting me.

"It's all right, darlin' " Roy told me. "It'll be better once you find out the truth."

"The truth?"

"The truth of what happened here," he explained slowly.

Roy kissed my forehead. It felt good. I remembered my mother pressing a wet washcloth to my forehead when I was sick. Had she kissed me then, too?

"Lazar?" Kapp questioned. "Are you going to be okay?"

His voice was too soft, too gentle. I wanted to cry.

But I just nodded.

The three of us walked back into the living room together.

I was still thinking about my mother when I saw Linda. My mind cleared. Linda was lying on the floor in the fetal position with Fern at her side.

SEVENTEEN

Had Linda been poisoned, too?

I ran toward her, shouting out questions. "When did she collapse? Is she acting like Daphne and Pilar? Have you called the hospital?"

"It's okay," Victor assured me, his voice very quiet.

I jerked my head toward Linda's father, wondering if he was in complete denial. His daughter was lying on the floor, her eyes closed shut. My heart pounded out another question.

"What do you mean she's okay?" I demanded. "She's not okay. Criminy, she's—"

Fern piped up then. "Mom's cool." She looked at me over her shoulder. "She just does this when she's upset. She feels overwhelmed, and she withdraws, that's all. She chills." Fern stroked her mother's hair gently.

"Has anyone checked her for symptoms of poison?" Kapp asked from behind me.

"I checked," York muttered. "Her heartbeat is fine. She's conscious. She's just . . . resting. I thought she'd been poisoned, too. But she hasn't been."

"Are you absolutely sure?" Kapp pushed. His usually playful face was stern.

York frowned. He looked back at Linda. What if her usual withdrawal routine *was* something worse? I could almost hear his brain cells clicking. York was unsure. That in itself was frightening.

I put out my feelers to Linda then. This was not a time to ask permission to do healing work. And I felt her life force. It was strong and healthy, physically. But emotionally—

"I'm fine," Linda mumbled. Still, she didn't open her eyes.

"But—"

Victor pulled out a bottle from his backpack and poured a couple of tiny white pills into his hand.

He knelt down by Linda and Fern and held out the pills in his palm.

"Linda, honey," he cajoled. "Put these under your tongue. They're sublinguals. Just let them melt. It'll make you feel better."

"Please, Mom," Fern whispered.

Linda reached out her hand, not even bothering to open her eyes, and popped the pills into her mouth. I just hoped Victor wasn't feeding his own daughter morphine. Then I wanted to slap myself. Victor wouldn't harm his daughter. He was helping her. And he probably knew what he was doing. He'd probably had a lot of practice. Poor Linda. Poor Victor. Poor Fern.

I tried to breathe in positivism. But even the perfect colors of the living room looked wrong to me, as if they had been dulled by a thick, gray mist. I told myself to snap out of it. I closed my eyes for a moment, trying to regroup.

When I opened my eyes again, I surveyed the people in the living room. I wasn't the only one who needed to snap out of it. Earl's bland face was stretched so tight his cheekbones actually showed. Geneva's impeccable posture was drooping. Melinda and Arnot were huddled together, their eyes identically round with horror. Tom Weng wasn't even trying to smile anymore. He stared at York, who was staring at Linda.

And no one was saying anything. Roy laid his hand on mine. I felt the kindness of his gentle touch and tried to extend it to the whole group.

"Melinda," I began conversationally. "Did you tell Tom that you were an artist, too?"

But Melinda just jumped at the sound of her name, bumping into the coffee table next to her. A glass fell over and rolled onto the floor. At least Melinda was still clumsy. That was some kind of normalcy.

"Whoa!" Melinda protested, bending over to get the glass and knocking her elbow into the table for her effort.

Arnot put his hand out in front of her and picked up the glass himself.

Melinda giggled then. But the sound wasn't right. The giggle was too high, too loud, even for Melinda. And no one was laughing with her.

So much for conversation.

Abruptly, Linda stretched out from her fetal position and sat up on the floor as if she had merely been doing yoga. Finally, I believed she hadn't been poisoned. I wondered what was in those little white pills her father was handing out. I wondered if Victor would give me some.

"I think we should go back home now," Linda announced. "We aren't doing any good staying here. We aren't detectives. Maybe we're all in danger. Aunt Daphne actually died." A whine insinuated itself into her tone. "I don't want to die like Aunt Daphne. It's all too much for me. I mean, where's the leverage in staying? We're just driving each other crazy. . . ."

As Linda droned on, I decided I didn't really want any of those little white pills after all. I had to remind myself again that Linda had a reason for being unlovable, her sister/cousin Natalie. On the other hand, maybe everyone who was unlovable had their reasons.

"We're staying." Uncle Victor finally interrupted her. "At least I am. You and Fern can take the car and go back to the motel if you want to. But I need to see this thing through."

"But why, Dad?" Linda objected. "Do you think that you can figure out what happened here? Or are you just feeling guilty because of Natalie?"

"Honey," Victor said gently. "I know you're upset. I know my first duty is to you. But I don't feel that any of us will be safe until we figure out whether Daphne was poisoned. And if she was poisoned, who did it? And who poisoned Pilar? I can't just walk away from this—"

"But—"

"We know more than the police detectives, not less," Victor insisted. "We know this family. We know the ins and outs of the Lazars and the Duprees. We know the secrets. If each of us speaks of what we know, we'll have the whole picture. Do you think a detective can do that?" He shook his head. "I don't. Between the whole group of us, we know the answers. The police would be looking in from the outside. They don't always solve their cases."

"But I'm scared, Dad," Linda whispered. "I'm really scared."

"So am I, honey," Victor told her. "That's why I need to stay. So I won't be scared anymore. Can you walk away, never knowing the truth? Can you?"

"Mom, if we find out the truth—" Fern began.

"How about the clock?" Linda demanded, ignoring her daughter momentarily. "What if it was some kind of sign or something? What if we're just supposed to go away?"

"Somebody tampered with the clock," Kapp interjected. "Your father's right. The police don't know the things your family knows. If anyone is going to figure out who's doing these things, it will be with the help of your family, all of your family. Everyone needs to be honest, even if it's painful."

"Now, now," Uncle Earl put in. "Maybe Linda's right. Maybe we should leave. I'm just an old fuddy-duddy. I don't want to believe anything bad happened. But if there's a chance, the safest thing would be for everyone to go home. I don't want you kids in danger. Maybe the best plan would be to just all go our separate ways now. We don't want any more incidents."

"I can't just go home," Geneva put in. "I already am home. And I wouldn't leave if I could. Uncle Victor's right on this. No one is going to feel safe until we find out the what, who, and why of this."

"We're going to have to talk," York put in, his voice pained.

"About what?" Linda yelped. "We don't have anything to talk about! All we've done since we got here is talk. What good does it do?"

"How about a time-out?" Victor suggested. "Everyone is upset now. But let's just spend some time together as family for a while. Everyone can calm down. Then we can pool our knowledge."

"Everyone" was obviously Linda. But Victor's idea didn't seem to be a bad one to me. I could certainly use a little time to calm down.

"Dad, please," Linda kept trying. "Come back to the motel with me and Fern."

"No," Victor muttered. "No." He shook his head. "Pilar is still at risk. *I'm* certainly not at risk. And at my age, it doesn't much matter anyway."

"Listen," York · directed. "If you're worried about safety, we can reduce the risk. Arnot and I will stand guard—"

"But against what?" Linda shrieked. She threw her hands in the air. "How can you stand guard against poisoning? How can you—"

"Don't eat anything," York advised. "Don't drink anything. If you're really afraid, go down to the corner store for provisions. And make sure none of us is alone at any time. Pick a partner and stay with them. Hang out with each other at all times. As long as no one is alone, no one will be harmed—"

"And no one will have a chance to do harm," Kapp finished for him.

"Hey, Mom," Fern chirped. "You're with me, okay?"

"But what about Dad? Who's with him? What if something else happens—"

"He can be with us, too," Fern interrupted, darting a quick glance at York. "Right?"

"Right," York agreed. "There's nothing magic about pairs. We just need to keep a watch on each other."

"But why—" Uncle Earl started.

"To give us a chance to think," York stated. "We all need a chance to think. And we can spend time together as we're thinking. We'll protect each other. Each one of us needs to ask if there is anything at all that we know that might help in figuring out who would want to kill Aunt Daphne and poison Pilar—"

"But we don't *know* that anyone was killed," Uncle Earl complained.

"Then ask yourself, what it is that makes you think Aunt Daphne wasn't killed." York pushed on. "What did you notice? What do you remember? You must have a reason for your feeling."

"It'll be cool, Earl," Fern put in. "Like a game. Try and remember everything you know that might be important and hang out at the same time."

"Just as long as you remember that this *isn't* just a game," Kapp warned. "We have to be careful. We need to take the precautions that York has suggested."

"Oh, sure," Fern agreed easily. "I'm cool. Can we start socializing now?"

Something about the lightness of her tone gave me pause. I snuck a quick glance at Victor. He was worried, too. This wasn't Clue. There was no Mrs. Peacock in the library. There were only Lazars and Duprees and a few strangers.

"Begin socializing on the mark," Geneva joked, but her voice was too strained for real joviality. She began a countdown. "Three, two, one, gossip!"

"I think it's so cool that I'm related to Pilar," Fern complied. She tilted her head. "Maybe when everything is resolved, she'll be like a sister or something. We can like, talk and share stuff—"

"About your crazy mothers?" Linda challenged her.

Fern kept her body still, but her eyes widened with hurt. "Oh, Mom—"

"You all think I'm crazy, don't you?" Linda asked the room at large. When no one answered, she went on. "Well, Natalie was the one who was crazy, not me. You all had it so easy. You don't know what it was like. You don't even care."

"Linda, we do care," I tried. "Until today, we never even realized what you were going through."

"Well, you do now, and you still don't like me," she shot back. "I can tell, you know. I don't have to be psychic. You didn't like me then, and you don't like me now."

That was a tough accusation to answer. Honesty? I looked into Linda's squinted eyes and decided against honesty.

"Listen, Linda," Geneva cut in expertly. "How about a little reality therapy? You are making it very difficult for us to like you. Wouldn't it be groovy if you actually gave us something to work with?"

"Huh!" Linda replied, crossing her arms.

York put in his piece. "Geneva's right. I'm not great at socializing either. But I don't blame people for not liking me. And if I truly want someone's affection or respect, I work for it."

Tom Weng nodded as York spoke. His eyes softened. I wondered how York had gained Tom's affection. Probably the same way he had mine, by earnest and honest love. York could be brusque, but I always knew he loved me.

"I don't really know you, Linda," Tom put in. "But I'm sure we could chat. Are you interested in music, art—"

"I'm going to the bathroom." Linda cut him off, and turned away from us all, heading on her way.

An instant later, Fern seemed to wake up. "Hey, Mom, no!" she shouted. "I'm supposed to go with you, right?"

But the bathroom door closed before Fern could join her mother.

We all eyed the barrier. But what could Linda do in the bathroom besides use it as it had been meant to be used?

Uncle Earl shook his head. "I'm going out for a cigarette," he told us. "Anyone want to come?"

"Are you still smoking, Uncle Earl?" Melinda asked. "I mean, how can you stand it after all the smoke you've inhaled firefighting?"

"Maybe I'm addicted," he answered, smiling. He coughed into his hand. "So how are you doing with your comic strip?"

I couldn't believe it. They were socializing. I caught Geneva with my eye and gave her a thumbs-up.

York and Arnot and Tom clustered together, earnestly making plans, manly plans. I could hear snippets from where I stood with Roy.

"Keep an eye on the food and drink . . ."

"No one leaves without an escort . . ."

When Linda finally exited the bathroom, she sat down on the plum couch. Roy gave my arm a little tug and we sidled over and sat down on either side of her.

"Your daughter, Fern, does you proud," Roy began.

Linda was still frowning, but something in her face softened. Maybe she was remembering Geneva's words. Would she give us something to work with?

"She's a good kid," Linda conceded. She paused, then looked Roy in the face. "Are you and Cally going to have kids?"

Roy blushed then. "I'm not rightly sure, ma'am," he muttered. "Cally and I are not even married yet."

"God, Cally," Linda gushed to me. "Where did you find such a sweet man?"

My shoulders relaxed the tiniest bit. "All the good ones come from Kentucky," I confided.

"Book me a flight," Linda shot back, laughing. Then she turned back to Roy. "Do you have a brother?" she asked.

"Sisters," he answered, his blush receding.

"An uncle?" she pleaded.

Roy chuckled.

"How about you, Roy?" Linda went on. She edged closer to him. "Cally doesn't deserve you anyway."

Roy stopped chuckling. He looked across Linda at me for a clue. Was she serious? I raised my eyebrows. I didn't know.

Linda was hard to read at any time, but her friendliness was in another language completely.

"So, you're York's little sister," a new voice interceded. I looked up and saw Tom Weng hovering.

"Pull up a chair," I told him cheerily. "Sorry you had to meet the family in the middle of all of this. I've been wanting to get to know you for a long time."

"It won't work, Cally," Linda cut in as Tom took a nearby seat. "He's gay, remember?"

Tom bent back his head and laughed as if Linda was actually witty. Personally, I was annoyed.

"I've seen your work," Linda told Tom. "It's amazing what people will pay for."

Tom laughed again. "Are you an artist?" he asked her.

Now Linda blushed. *Was* she an artist? As far as I knew, she programmed computers for a living.

"Just a little in my spare time," she admitted. "I sculpt."

"Well, my artistic pursuits were limited to my spare time, too, until I was 'discovered,'" Tom assured her. "I was a waiter for years and years."

"Chinese restaurant?" Linda asked.

"My uncle's," Tom confessed. "How'd you guess?"

Then Linda laughed.

I couldn't believe it. Linda was actually socializing. Or was she? I looked around the room. Melinda, Fern, and Geneva were huddled. And Kapp was talking to York as Arnot and Victor whispered together. Were we socializing or thinking, or both? At least we were communicating.

"So, Cally," Tom broke into my reverie. "Your sister Melinda told me she signed a book contract last week for a collection of her Acuto from Pluto cartoons."

"She did?" I asked, jerking my head back to look at him.

"You didn't know?" Linda accused.

"She never told me," I admitted defensively.

"Oh, right," Tom murmured. "York said you guys never talk much."

"My family is good at secrets," I blurted out. "Secrets and secrets. It's unbelievable."

"Cally," Roy whispered at my side in warning.

"I'm sorry," I apologized. "I get crazy about this. I just wish that Melinda had told me earlier. But a family whose members can't even talk about their own parents isn't going to talk about much else. I—"

Linda was staring at me, her face smug. She was enjoying this. I stopped mid-rant and did a U-turn.

"Tom?" I asked. "Is your family anywhere near as weird as ours?" Dack, I couldn't believe I'd said that.

"Oh, you bet," Tom assured me. "Everyone's family is weird in its own weird way." He laughed. "I can't claim any recent possible murders, but let me tell you, I'm enjoying your get-together more than I would be enjoying my own. You should listen to my aunties. 'Why aren't you married yet?' 'Someday, you gonna get a real job?' 'Your mother would be so sad that you have no children.' 'Why don't you have children?' Then they start over again."

"But does your family talk?" I asked wistfully.

"Nothing but," he answered. "Sometimes I think that's why I paint. At least it's quiet. York told me you guys never talk about important stuff. From my point of view, it isn't such a bad thing. My entire family, all of them, like forty or so, had to hear that I was gay. We took a whole floor of a restaurant for the announcement. And everyone had opinions. Loud and long opinions. I didn't win that election. And yet, we're not really that close. Seriously, I think you and your siblings are close, for all of your secrets. You're just all treading very carefully around sensitive subjects. Think of it as a blessing in disguise."

"Thank you," I said sincerely.

I looked over fondly at Geneva, Arnot, York, and Melinda. Maybe Tom was right—

"Huh!" Linda snorted. "Just because you like her brother doesn't mean you have to like her whole family."

Tom laughed again. Linda's frown disappeared. Around Tom, Linda was passing for a reincarnation of Dorothy Parker. Wit and cruelty were only a hair's width apart, after all.

"So, how's my favorite niece doing?" Uncle Earl asked before any of us could speak again. He smelled of smoke and stood near Tom's chair.

"Oh, puh-leese," Linda commented. I scratched the comparison to Dorothy Parker.

"The Lazars are a very special family, Linda," Earl insisted.

"So are the Duprees," Linda argued.

"Well, of course," Earl agreed, frowning in confusion. "I didn't mean any disrespect—"

Linda stood up in disgust. Even Tom wasn't laughing anymore. He was just watching.

"I'm going into the kitchen," Geneva announced from across the room. "Who'd like to come with me?"

Uncle Victor raised his hand.

"I'll even do some dishes," he offered.

"You're a doll, Uncle Victor," Geneva said and patted his cheek. Victor grinned.

Linda glared at her father. And suddenly I understood why Linda had a special antipathy for Geneva. Jealousy. I watched her watch Victor and Geneva as they headed toward the kitchen.

Earl sat down where Linda had been. "Cally, I just wanted to tell you that I really am impressed by your healing practice. You know, I was a little shocked when you quit practicing law. Maybe I wasn't supportive enough. But now that I see how much good you're doing. Well, I'm just proud, that's all. I don't know much about auras and such. But just because I don't see them doesn't mean that they don't exist. And now your sister Melinda has a book contract. I'm impressed with all you kids."

"Yes, they're your favorite human beings," Linda snarled from where she stood. "We know, Earl!"

Earl's head snapped back as if Linda had slapped him.

"The Lazars are golden," Linda went on, mimicking his pompous tone. "They are perfect. One of them ought to be president of the United States. The Duprees—"

Roy and I rose as one. Neither of us wanted to hear this

again. But Tom watched Earl and Linda with interest in his eyes. Maybe they'd end up in one of his paintings.

I grabbed a stackful of leftover platters from the dining room table. Roy gathered up some pitchers. And together, we walked into the kitchen.

Victor was at the sink doing dishes as promised while Geneva scraped leftovers into a garbage bag.

I tapped Victor on his shoulder.

"May I have this dance?" I asked.

He chortled, then untied the apron he was wearing and handed it to me with a bow.

My arms were in hot, soapy water when I heard Victor ask Geneva where the garbage cans were. Out of the corner of my eye, I saw him lift two bags and head for the back door.

He was only gone for a moment when we heard his scream.

EIGHTEEN

I yanked my soapy hands from the sink and reached for my cane, my mind leaping as fast as my feet. Victor had gone outside alone. He'd broken the rules. And he'd screamed. My cane was soapy in my hand, but my feet kept moving, my mind's urgency dissolving into white noise.

I flew out the back door and skidded to a stop at the top of the sloped, concrete pathway leading to the garbage cans. I used all of my martial arts training not to slip, not to go further with my body as my eyes traveled the glossy, slick trail of darkness that ran down the center of the concrete pathway to the bottom. I stuck out one foot tentatively and touched the surface of the dark trail. It was definitely slippery.

Then I heard Roy and Geneva some footsteps behind me.

"Wait!" Roy shouted.

"Cally!" Geneva added.

Their footsteps kept coming.

"Stop!" I yelled. "Don't run. It's booby-trapped!"

Carefully, I made my way down a side of the concrete pathway that wasn't slick, toward Uncle Victor where he sat in the middle of the whole mess. He looked dazed as he turned to me among the remnants of garbage and torn garbage bags. But he was alive and moving.

"Uncle Victor," I began. "Are you—"

I didn't hear Roy's final steps and his slip as he came toward me, but I felt his body hit mine, and we fell together in a heap next to Uncle Victor. So much for my shout. Still, I didn't take the fall hard. My back connected with Roy's body as he slid underneath me. Roy's body underneath me wasn't an all together bad thing, even under these circumstances. The smell of spoiling leftovers didn't add to the ambience though.

"I'm okay, I think," Uncle Victor was saying.

Then Geneva slammed into us, tumbling instantly on top of the heap that Roy and I had made.

"Puppy pile?" Roy asked softly, his voice muffled from beneath Geneva's torso.

I laughed. I didn't mean to, but I did.

"There's something slick on the path," Uncle Victor went on. "Be careful. It'll make you slip."

Geneva cursed from her prone position, and used her arms to push herself up off of me and Roy. Then she carefully raised herself to her feet, straightened her back, and slipped again. Mercifully, she landed closer to Victor this time, bottom first on a pile of garbage.

Uncle Victor laughed then. He threw his head back and roared. "Are you trying to make me feel better?" he asked Geneva once he'd stopped laughing. "I told you to be careful."

"Are *you* all right?" she asked Victor.

"I think I'm okay," Victor answered, moving his arms and legs experimentally. "I landed on garbage primarily. I suppose it alleviated the impact of the fall."

Together, Geneva and Victor knelt, then pushed themselves into crouches, and finally lifted themselves up into standing positions. Geneva grabbed Victor's hand, and they moved away from the slippery area to the side of the concrete, swaying like elegant drunks as they found their footing among the strewn garbage.

"What happened?" Geneva demanded of Uncle Victor.

I didn't feel like laughing anymore. A fall at Victor's age was no laughing matter.

Uncle Victor took a couple more careful steps to the side, twisted his neck back and forth, flexed his arms and whispered in amazement, "I fell." Then he laughed again. "Pretty good for an old man," he added.

"Are you sure you're okay?" Geneva pressed him.

Victor nodded his head. "I think I was relaxed when I went down. Nothing's broken. I'm sure of it. I read somewhere that if you're relaxed, a fall is less likely to do damage. It's an interesting theory—"

"Should we take you to the hospital?" Geneva interrupted impatiently, putting his relaxation theories on hold.

"No," Uncle Victor told her. "I'm really okay. I'm lucky I landed on the garbage. I've never appreciated leftovers more than I do now. I'm sure I'll be sore tomorrow. But at this moment, I'm fine. It almost makes me feel young again. Maybe I'll try it one more time. Hee-hee—"

"Uncle Victor, don't make me crazy," Geneva warned. "I thought you'd had it." Tears popped up in her eyes.

"Oh, Geneva," Victor murmured. "Don't you worry."

York was out the back door next. Of course, he didn't fall. He stopped right before the slick and centered himself, arms and legs wide, rooted to the earth beneath the concrete.

"Aw, come on!" I shouted, hysteria mounting with the relief of knowing that Uncle Victor really was okay. I moved into a sitting position next to Roy. "Can't you pretend to slip?" But York was too busy to answer me. He walked carefully onto the concrete and squatted.

"What are you doing?"

York still didn't answer me. Instead, he dipped his finger into the dark trail and sniffed.

"Olive oil?" he hazarded.

Geneva walked carefully back to the slick and dipped her finger in, too.

"Olive oil," she confirmed. "The whole can, I'll bet. And I'll bet it was from my pantry. Do you know how much that big can cost me? It was huge. Extra virgin olive oil! Almost a gallon."

Roy sat up next to me. My heart went on red alert. I'd

assumed Roy wasn't hurt by his fall, but what if he was? And I hadn't even thought to ask.

I turned to look at him. But he was way ahead of me. He squeezed my hand and shook his head no to my unasked question, smiling.

"Please, do feel free to fall on me any time your little heart desires, ma'am," he whispered in my ear.

I giggled, knowing we were both relieved to be alive. Joy arrives at the strangest moments sometimes.

Geneva's eyes skewered me.

"This is not funny," Geneva declared, finally steady enough to shake her finger. "Who would do such a thing? I'm not just talking about the cost of the olive oil. Olive oil can be replaced. But someone could have been hurt. Someone could have been killed. This is not cool, not cool at all—"

"Hey, you guys!" a new voice shouted from above. "What's going on? What are you—"

I looked up and saw Fern. She ran forward, and her feet flew out from under her. She landed, still sliding, on her backside and skidded our way. As she reached me, I grabbed her arm and slowed her slide to a stop.

"Wow!" Fern murmured, rubbing her hip. Her eyes widened. "Was that supposed to happen?"

"No," I told her. "Did you break anything?"

"Uh-uh," she assured me and swiveled her head around suddenly.

"Mom, stop!" she yelled. "It's a slide."

Linda stopped with one foot in the air. Amazing. Why hadn't Roy and Geneva stopped when I'd shouted?

Fern turned herself around and made her way on all fours back to her mother.

"Fern, what are you—" Linda began.

"It's cool, Mom, really," Fern told her. "Just don't go any further, and you'll be fine."

Uncle Earl came through the doorway next, frowning at the sight before him. His eyebrows went up. He opened his mouth, but I beat him to the auditory punch.

"Don't move!" I shouted. "Don't anyone move."

Uncle Earl stopped. At least someone was listening to me. Kapp came through the doorway next. I didn't even have to yell his way. He looked at us all and took one careful step backward. Tom Weng peeked out then, but stayed inside the kitchen door. A very smart man York had there, I decided.

Then Kapp stepped just far enough out so that he could see what was going on. He saw the olive oil slick. He saw the two of us still down. Then his brain began to work. I could tell by the movement of his eyebrows.

"Olive oil?" he questioned.

Geneva turned on him, her elegant outfit dripping with oil and leftovers. "How did you know? Did you do this?"

"Holy Mary, I didn't know anything!" Kapp shot back. "I just guessed that it was olive oil since that's what you were screaming about. I thought you might have been just ranting about prices or something."

"I never rant," Geneva stated, gathering all her dignity around her along with the oil and leftovers.

And finally, Melinda and Arnot came shooting out the back door on either side of Uncle Earl. Earl flung out both of his arms, catching a sibling with each.

"Whoa!" Melinda objected. But then she looked down at the rest of us.

"Good catch, Uncle Earl!" I yelled.

"Melinda, Arnot," Uncle Earl warned. "It's dangerous out here—"

But Melinda began to giggle before he even finished. She pointed at us. "You all fell down, and I didn't," she explained. She raised her fist in the air. "A new first for the Lazars! Hooray!"

I joined her in her cheer.

"I don't understand," Uncle Earl said, turning to Melinda.

"Melinda didn't fall," Geneva tried. Her voice was loud but strained, as if she'd hurt it when she'd landed on the concrete. "Melinda usually does the falling for the family."

"And Cally usually does the cane-fighting," Kapp added. He stuck out his tongue. "Betcha you can't reach me from there!"

"Not unless you come here first," I muttered, trying to glare at him but failing.

"Hah!" he snorted. "Good try, Lazar." He pointed his cane in my direction tauntingly.

I pointed my cane back and made menacing sounds. We were all having a pretty good time in and around the olive oil slick.

Then I heard the ring of a phone. Was that Geneva's phone? Kapp turned first toward the kitchen. The phone rang again. Melinda, Arnot, and Earl all turned toward the kitchen. It *was* Geneva's phone.

"Kapp, answer it!" Geneva ordered.

All sense of fun fled as Kapp turned and went back into the kitchen. The phone hadn't meant anything good lately. And all I could think of was Pilar. Had she taken a turn for the worse? Had she named her poisoner?

Slowly but steadily, Roy and I struggled to our feet and walked back up one dry side of the pathway.

I could just hear Kapp's voice as we grew nearer the kitchen. His tone was terse.

"Geneva Lazar's residence," I thought I heard him say. Then he muttered something incomprehensible.

Geneva and Victor were also climbing back toward the kitchen, on the other side of the oil.

"No," Kapp stated.

Geneva looked up toward her kitchen desperately and increased her pace, dragging Victor along with her.

"No," Kapp said again, more emphatically.

Who was on the other end of the connection?

As Roy and I finally reached the finish line, Kapp repeated "No" once more and hung up the phone. Roy and I entered the kitchen with Geneva and Victor a couple of steps behind us. Everyone else was already inside by then, their eyes on Kapp.

"Who—"

"What—"

"Was it Pilar?" Geneva broke in.

"It was a solicitor," Kapp explained. I let out my breath.

"A solicitor?" Geneva demanded. She dipped a kitchen towel into the soapy water and began cleaning herself off.

"I told her no," Kapp defended himself. "What more do you want from me?"

Geneva just nodded, and busied herself dipping more towels in the soapy water to hand out to Victor, Fern, Roy, and myself.

"What was she soliciting for?" Melinda asked as I looked down and saw that my pants were shredded on one knee. My arm was scraped and my hand bleeding. I wondered why I couldn't feel it.

"The phone call wasn't about Pilar?" Linda asked belatedly before Kapp could answer Melinda.

"No," he told us all. "It was about the environment—"

"Oh, that's nice," Melinda cut in. "Earth or Pluto?"

It was hard to tell if she was joking. No one risked a laugh. I looked at Roy. His clothes were dirty, but he looked relatively unscathed. He dabbed at the stains on his shirt.

"I'm not really sure," Kapp admitted, smiling. "Does Pluto have redwood trees?"

Melinda looked out over our heads for a moment, thinking. "I'm not sure," she finally answered. She *was* serious. I was glad I hadn't laughed.

York cleared his throat. "Can we skip the solicitor?" he asked.

"Easy for you to say," Kapp muttered. "But yes, let's skip her."

"I believe that someone purposely poured Geneva's olive oil onto the concrete pathway," York declared. Tom Weng moved closer to him, as if to guard the invincible York.

"I'll second that supposition," Kapp agreed quickly.

"And I'll third it," I added, rolling my shoulders and wiggling in place to loosen up my tight, battered body.

"And I fourth it," Victor announced, staring down as he

tried to clean off the worst of the garbage and oil from his clothing. There was a hole in the elbow of his shirt. But he didn't seem to be bleeding anywhere.

"But why would anyone do that?" Earl asked, rubbing his chin. "It doesn't make any sense."

"To scare us away?" York proposed quietly.

Victor looked up then, his face tightening into a scowl. Even while covered in garbage and oil, his scowl was formidable.

"Dad," Linda cut in. "You said you'd leave if you were at risk, didn't you?"

Victor nodded slowly, pulling a piece of napkin from the back of his pants.

"Well, you could have broken your neck," Linda pointed out. "You are at risk."

"But he didn't break his neck, Mom," Fern insisted. She held her towel out in the air. "And neither did I. Or Cally. Or Roy. Or Geneva. This wasn't any kind of murder attempt. This was something different."

"Everyone was just lucky," Linda muttered wearily. "It could have been worse."

And for once, I was with her. It was pure luck that there were no broken bones, especially for Victor. It could have been much worse.

"Maybe we should call the police?" I suggested.

"To tell them that someone spilled olive oil?" Victor replied. He shook his head scornfully. "If this prank was meant to scare anyone away, it's not scaring me away. Because now we know something really is going on. Someone wants this family to scatter back to their own homes and leave the question of Daphne's death alone. Well, my resolve is just strengthened. I want to know what happened to Daphne more than ever."

"Murder?" Fern whispered.

Victor nodded his head.

"Victor, you can't know that—" Uncle Earl tried.

"Can't I?" Victor challenged, his voice trembling with what I thought was anger, but might have been shock.

"Why else would someone try to scare us away? Because someone did pour that oil. It was real. I know all too well how real it was. And it was dangerous. People don't like to see the truth. We might have left without ever working to find answers. But I say that this incident leads to a reasonable inference of murder."

"Not necessarily, Dad," Linda began. "Maybe—"

"Of course it does!" Kapp barked. He pounded the kitchen tile with his cane. "Mother of God, what's the matter with you people? Even the police suspect murder. Don't you think they're investigating right now?"

The room was silent. *Were* the police investigating?

"How do you know that?" I asked finally.

"Contacts, Lazar," Kapp answered, his voice controlled. "I have a contact in the police department here. And I have a contact in the county. Khashoggi and Rossetti have logged in their notes now. Kaifu feels at fault for his department letting Daphne's death go by the wayside, even though he never knew about it until we told him. When he came here to ask us about Pilar, he didn't know anything about Daphne at all. Now that he's put the two incidents together, he has plenty of reason for suspicion. And he's angry. He thinks Daphne was murdered. And he thinks he almost missed it. He's called in the county for help. It's murder, and murder is beyond his expertise—"

"Oh, come on," Linda interrupted impatiently. "We don't know that for sure—"

"Are you all in denial?" Kapp hissed. "Why aren't you jumping up and down? It was your Daphne who was killed; your Pilar who was poisoned."

I found myself wanting to shout, "Yes!" Because all of the members of my family were in denial on some level or another. And we had been for a long time before Aunt Daphne had died. Facing the truth head-on was not a skill of either the Lazars or the Duprees. And Linda was in her own special form of denial, screaming about how unsafe Geneva's house was at the same time that she was refusing to admit the possibility of Daphne's murder.

"Mr. Kapp," Uncle Earl put in. "You are not a member of this family. You can accuse all you want to, but you have no evidence. Isn't that what you lawyers ask for? Evidence of a crime? Daphne died. Maybe she took an overdose of her medicine. You have no evidence that she didn't." Earl's voice was rising again. How could I have forgotten Earl's special form of denial? I could almost guess what he would say next. "I know all the members of this family. I've known them far longer than you have. And I don't believe there is anyone here who would have murdered Daphne Dupree. Except for an outsider . . . like you."

"And who do you believe poured oil on the pathway then, sir?" Roy asked.

"We don't know for sure that oil was poured on the pathway," Earl argued. "The kitchen has been a busy place. The doors have been opened and shut. The oil could conceivably have rolled out onto the pathway—"

"Along with the clock switching its own chimes on?" Kapp finished for Earl helpfully.

"You're all jumping to conclusions!" Uncle Earl boomed. "And your conclusions could harm this family forever. Linda wants to leave and never visit again. And I can't say that I blame her. Pilar will distrust everyone if she thinks one of us could have murdered Daphne—"

"I disagree," Geneva said. "I think Pilar will distrust us all until she knows conclusively what happened to Daphne. She knew Daphne better than any of us, and she doesn't believe that Daphne's death was an accident or a suicide. And she certainly knows whether she was poisoned or not. If this family is to ever trust again, we *have* to question what's happened here."

"Dad, are you hurt?" Linda asked from the silence.

"No," he muttered. "No. Not enough to matter."

"Then we need to leave right now," Linda insisted.

"Wait a minute," Geneva commanded. "Uncle Victor, what do you mean by 'not enough to matter'? Are you really hurt? I want you checked out by a doctor."

"I'll get medical advice after we've talked," Victor said, and I could tell he meant it.

"Can't we just go now?" Linda screeched. "I wanted to leave before, and you wouldn't listen to me. And I want to leave here now!"

"No, Linda," Victor stated quietly. "That's exactly what we're not doing. I'm finished with being afraid. When you're afraid, you have the opportunity of courage. We're staying."

"Are we done with our time-out?" I asked.

"Yes, it's time to talk," a serious voice declared.

It took me more than a moment to realize that the voice belonged to my sister Melinda.

NINETEEN

"Yes, we're going to talk," Victor agreed, looking at Melinda.

Melinda, my sister. Melinda who thought Pluto was as real as Earth. Could Melinda have killed Aunt Daphne? The shock of even considering the notion was exploded by the relief of remembering that Melinda hadn't arrived until after Aunt Daphne had collapsed. But I'd still thought of my own sister as a murder suspect. My stomach began a gentle rebellion with a sharp gurgle.

"Uh, Mom," Fern whispered. "I smell kinda funky."

The smell of leftover garbage seemed to grow as we all stood in the kitchen. It was as pungent as the fear that one of us might be a murderer. My stomach began to growl in earnest.

"Before we talk, we all need to change clothes," Geneva told us. "I refuse to go through any emotional discussion smelling like turkey."

Victor looked down at himself and let out a snort of laughter. "Being a turkey and smelling like one are two different things," he commented. "But I must agree. We change clothing, and then we talk."

I had a feeling that the clothing change was going to be easier said than done. It was true that Geneva was a clothing designer. But her home was not her shop. And I suspected that her ample closets held clothing made only for her height, sex, and shape.

"Why don't I change first?" Geneva suggested. "And I'll go through my closets for the rest of you—"

"Don't change alone," York warned sharply.

"But—"

"No, he's right," Linda said. I was surprised to hear her agreement. "Dad went out of the house alone, and look what happened to him."

"Oh, God," Victor whispered. He brought a grimy hand up to his face. "You're right. I didn't even think about it. I went out alone."

"It's okay, Granddad," Fern assured him. "Everything is cool now. Except for the smell."

"I'll go up with you while you change," I offered to Geneva.

"Cally, you stink almost as much as I do," Geneva objected. "I don't want this glop all over all of my clothes—"

"I don't stink," Melinda threw in. "I can go with you." She still sounded serious, which added another layer of unreality to the situation as far as I was concerned. Melinda could rarely sustain a serious attitude for more than a few moments.

"Good," Geneva ruled. "Melinda will go with me. I'll be as quick as I can. And I'll pick clothes for the rest of you, too."

Then Geneva raised her chin and strode from the room. Melinda followed her an instant later with a frown on her elfin face. I heard them clomp up the stairs together.

It was quiet again in the kitchen. Maybe it was the smell. Maybe it was the fear. Or maybe no one was going to talk until talking was formally announced. I thought about sitting down, but I didn't want to mess up Geneva's chairs. So I stood for what seemed to be an agony of time. And Roy, Fern, and Victor stood with me, each of us ineffectually dabbing with our wet towels and picking actual pieces of garbage off of ourselves, only to have them land on another part of ourselves. We weren't just covered, we were sticky.

When Geneva came back with Melinda, she looked good. Her hair was wet from what had to have been a shower, and she wore an elegant mauve duster over slinky pants. Melinda was barely visible over the armful of outfits she carried for the rest of us.

"First of all," Geneva announced sternly. "I want you to know that most of my styles are unisex. No one has to feel uncomfortable about wearing women's clothing."

Uh-oh, I thought. Victor and Roy *were* going to be wearing women's clothing.

Geneva turned to Melinda and pulled a cream-colored pantsuit with a simple tunic top from the summit of the pile. It was a nice choice, made from a flowing material that appeared to be crinkled silk. It had a silk undershirt, too, in the same color but uncrinkled. I wasn't wild about the color, but I liked the simple styling. I stepped forward to claim it. But it wasn't for me.

"This is just perfect for you, Roy," Geneva declared and handed the outfit to my sweetie. She softened her tone. "It's right for your coloring, and it's not too feminine."

Roy blushed and took the outfit by its hanger hooks. "I'm sure it'll be just fine, ma'am," he muttered.

"And you're about my height and weight," Geneva added hopefully. "So it should fit you. I'm sorry I didn't have the perfect outfit."

"Thank you kindly for your efforts," Roy tried again. "I know your styles don't tend toward flannel shirts and jeans. And I do appreciate something other than what I'm wearing."

"Thanks, Roy," Geneva said and kissed the air near his cheek. I think she'd been aiming for his actual cheek at first but changed her mind mid-attack.

Kapp snorted. "Be glad, Roy," he advised, laughing. "At least she doesn't make dresses."

"Yes, sir," Roy answered soberly. Roy was rattled all right.

"Cally," Geneva went on, grabbing another hanger draped with layers of lavender. "You're shorter than me, so you'll do better with capris. And I thought a simple folkloric blouse with a jacket?" she added, whipping out a second hanger.

"Sure," I agreed, wondering how simple a "folkloric" blouse could be. When she handed it all to me, I saw the delicate embroidery and mini-mandarin collar. Whoa! It was woven with shimmering shades of pink and lavender that matched the jacket and capris perfectly. Maybe I could take the whole outfit home with me and never return it. I tried to hold the pieces of the outfit as Roy had, by the hangers, far away from my sticky, smelly body.

Uncle Victor was assigned a liquid black velvet jumpsuit.

He took it with a little smile on his face. "I'm going to look pretty sexy in this without my underwear," he muttered under his breath. "Maybe I'll get lucky."

"Dad!" Linda objected.

"Hey, Sean Connery is sexy, and he's pretty old," Victor argued.

"Then give the jumpsuit to him," Linda told him, but her face looked a little softer. "No double-O-seven stuff for you."

Geneva ignored their comments and gave Fern, who was lucky enough to be a little plumper than the rest of us, a purple oversized cashmere sweater with matching stretch leggings.

"Cool," she breathed. "Really cool."

Geneva smiled and blew her a kiss. A compliment to Geneva's art was a compliment to Geneva.

Then we all tried to figure out who would go where, and when, to shower and dress. Geneva's house had two upstairs bedrooms with showers and one downstairs without a shower.

"Victor, sir, I do believe you and Fern can take the first showers," Roy offered. "Cally and I can wait, can't we, darlin'?"

I picked a tiny piece of broccoli off of my sleeve and smiled back at him. I could stand a few more minutes, I decided. If Roy was gallant enough to wear Geneva's clothing without objection, I'd go along with this further gallantry.

"I'll go with you, Fern," Linda told her daughter. "But who will go with Dad?"

"I'll go," Arnot offered. "Gotta keep him out of trouble. He's one sexy stud. He needs a keeper."

Victor chortled appreciatively. Kapp harrumphed. Maybe he was jealous.

And the two pairs went upstairs to the bedrooms while Roy and I continued to stand in Geneva's kitchen. At least Geneva took our outfits back. I don't know how long we could have stood and held them away from our bodies.

"Do you know who it is?" Kapp whispered in my ear as Geneva hung the outfits on the back of the dining room chairs visible from the kitchen. I was surprised Kapp had come that close to me in my fragrant state. He must have been desperate.

"No!" I hissed back.

And the worst part was that with all the food smells, I was olfactorally-challenged. I couldn't smell Kapp's aftershave. Little did he know that he probably could have whacked me from behind with his cane at that moment.

"So, Melinda, tell me more about your book contract," Uncle Earl prompted conversationally.

"Small press," she muttered. "No big deal."

"But I'll bet you're excited," he bulldozed on.

"Maybe I am," she replied, her eyes widening. "Maybe some part of me is. But it's like I can't reach it, you know?"

This was painful.

"It's all right, Melinda," I told her. "We're all under a lot of stress right now. You might be feeling a little strange—"

"I'm off my asteroid, Cally!" she blurted out. "I can't seem to find myself. I'm scared."

"Of course you are," I whispered gently. "I'm scared, too."

"Really?" she asked.

"Really," I confirmed. At least I could tell the truth on that one.

"Remember when Mom and Pop died?" she murmured.

I shivered as I nodded. How could I not remember?

"I felt weirded out then, too." She frowned. "Or maybe weird is normal for me now. I can't tell. But it all changed that day—"

"Now, now," Uncle Earl interrupted. "You're fine right this minute. Just take a big breath. Think of your kids. Think of your work."

Melinda closed her eyes and breathed in so deeply, I almost thought she'd stopped breathing. But her minimalist chest was bulging.

"And let the breath back out," I reminded her.

She did. "Thanks, Cally," she said. "I almost forgot that part."

Then we were silent again.

"So, Tom," Kapp finally threw out. "What do you think of the family?"

York jerked his head around to glare at Kapp.

But Tom was smiling. "Nothing this exciting ever happens at my family events. And men don't get offered women's clothing. I'd have to give the Lazars a ten."

Kapp laughed. Even York smiled.

"Geneva explained that her clothing is unisex," Earl objected.

Tom just raised his eyebrows. Then Kapp and York really laughed.

Roy blushed as his eyes wandered to his outfit to be.

"Think of it as a costume," I whispered in his ear.

"I believe I'd rather play a bunny rabbit," he whispered back.

I giggled.

And finally, Roy smiled.

I risked an arm around his waist. After all, we were equally odoriferous. Roy leaned his head on my shoulder. He was a good man, even if he was afraid of women's clothing.

"Ta-da!" Uncle Victor announced himself as he returned to the kitchen in the black jumpsuit. He executed a model's turn.

He'd been right about the lack of underwear. There were black velvet bulges in places that didn't belong in women's clothing.

"Lookin' good, Uncle Victor," Geneva offered.

"See if you can beat this, Roy," Victor challenged my sweetie, not unkindly. He was probably just as embarrassed as Roy was going to be.

Roy saluted. "It'll be tough, but I'll surely try," he replied.

"To the shower!" I commanded.

Roy and I made our way upstairs to the guest shower, the shower that had been mine when I'd lived with Geneva so long ago. The mirror was still steamy from Victor's stint. I just hoped the hot water wouldn't run out.

Roy and I shed our spoiled clothing as fast as we could and wrapped it all in the plastic bags that Geneva had left for us. Then we climbed into the shower together. Roy. I'd forgotten how good he felt in my arms. The spray from the shower head was weak but hot as I closed my eyes and leaned into him, my thoughts moving from reel to reel. I remembered my teenage years in this shower. I remembered my parents' deaths. I remembered Aunt Daphne's death. And I remembered all the times Roy and I had embraced. I tried to hold onto the last memory as I held onto Roy himself. And finally, the shower went cold.

We jumped out, only to face our outfits.

"Oh, foot!" Roy exclaimed, regressing to his favorite Kentuckyism. "I feel such a fool for frettin' over women's clothing while so much bad stuff is going on. But I do. I was never given much to dress up. But this—"

He reached out for the cream-colored pantsuit.

"It'll be—"

"And your Uncle Victor was surely right about one thing," he went on. "My underwear is as trashed as the local dump. I'm going to be stark naked under this, this . . ."

"Outfit," I offered as softly as possible. "Roy, the tunic is pretty long. Maybe it'll cover, um . . . the embarrassing stuff."

"Maybe you're right, darlin'," he agreed and gave me a desperate hug before he pulled on the crinkled silk pants.

I turned my back as he struggled into his outfit. I put on my own folkloric blouse first, then the lavender capris and the jacket. I wiped a square foot of condensation off the mirror and peered at my reflection. The capris weren't really right, being a little too long on me for capris, but not long enough for regular pants. But I loved the blouse.

I turned to face Roy. He looked like an actor out of a period-piece movie. What period, I couldn't quite place. His shoulders were too wide for the tunic, but it was long enough to hide any real embarrassment. As he moved, the crinkly fabric seemed to pour over him.

"You look sexy," I murmured.

"Don't tease me, darlin'" he objected.

"No, you really do," I insisted. "Look in the mirror.

Roy looked. He laughed. "Okay, maybe I'm an Asian Robin Hood with red hair," he finally concluded. "You're right, Cally. It isn't worth frettin' about, and the naughty parts are covered. What more can a poor boy from Kentucky wish for?"

"A hug?" I offered.

And he accepted.

We went back downstairs. Everyone had reassembled in the living room. Fern, sitting next to her mother on the lilac couch, was a knockout in her purple cashmere sweater. She was even color-coordinated. Victor was in a nearby chair. And someone, my guess was Linda, had placed a knit throw over Victor's lap. Uncle Earl was on the plum couch with Melinda and Arnot. Kapp and Geneva had two chairs across from the lilac couch. And York and Tom were standing.

"Hey, you actually look good, Roy," Melinda sang out.

Roy blushed once more, but I thought he was pleased.

"We saved you a place," Geneva promised, nodding toward the magenta love seat.

Roy and I dutifully took our places. We sat down and clasped hands. The scary part was about to begin, the talk.

"No, I should go," Tom said to York once we'd taken our seats.

From York's frozen face, I had a feeling Tom had already said the same thing before, maybe more than once.

"No," York insisted. "This is a family thing. But you're my family. Just like Roy is Cally's and Kapp is Geneva's."

"But Kapp and Roy were here when your aunt died," Tom shot back. "I wasn't. I don't have any information to offer. I'll just be in the way. Your family isn't going to talk with me around. I've already made them uncomfortable with all my nosy questions."

"Let's talk in the kitchen," York suggested.

Tom sighed and followed York out of the living room.

They returned within moments.

Tom said, "It was lovely meeting you all. I look forward to seeing you again."

And York walked him to the door and hugged him good-bye.

"Call me as soon as you figure everything out," Tom ordered my brother. Then he turned and left.

York walked back to a spot near the love seat, crossed his arms, and stood like a bodyguard.

"Criminy, York. Can't you just sit down like a normal human being?" Geneva asked him.

"No" was all he said back.

Victor cleared his throat.

"I think the time has come to talk," he announced. He reached into his backpack for some sort of capsule, swallowed it dry, and followed up. "We know what happened to Daphne and Pilar," he expounded. "Not as individuals but as a group."

A flutter of fear danced through my chest. And with it a thought. *Did I want to know?*

"I called the police while you two were upstairs," Kapp put in. "They are investigating. Now it's time for us to investigate. Who has something to offer?"

Earl rolled his shoulders and clasped his hands together.

"I've got something to offer," he replied. "I'm not sure how well received my ideas will be, but I feel it's my duty to be realistic about this situation." He looked around the room.

"Go ahead," Geneva prodded.

Earl sighed, then proceeded. "I'm not saying this is *the* explanation, but this is one explanation of the events. I think it's probable that Daphne overdosed on her medication accidentally. And Pilar felt so bad that she tried to do the same thing. She's a young girl. She was angry, and she took her anger out on herself—"

"But—" Fern objected.

"No, let him speak," Geneva directed.

"Then there was the incident with the oil," Earl went on. "What did it accomplish?"

"It didn't scare us away," York replied.

"Yes, it just made you more sure that murder had been done," Earl agreed. "Have you thought that the purpose of the oil spill may have been exactly that? Victor loved his sister, Daphne. He believes she was murdered. But how could he convince us holdouts? I think it's just possible that Victor staged this incident himself."

"Are you accusing my dad?" Linda demanded, eyes narrowing. "Because my dad wouldn't do such a thing—"

"No, it's okay, honey," Victor told her. "Earl is doing just what we all need to. He's thinking and expressing his opinions honestly." Then he turned to Earl. "Earl, all I can say is that I didn't stage the oil incident. I wouldn't have risked the danger to the others. But I can imagine how you might believe it a possibility." He turned back to the room at large. "Anyone else?"

"I think Aunt Daphne might have had a lover other than Bob," Fern put in. "A man who was, like, the father of her child. Someone who she met on the day she died. Someone she never expected to see again."

"Me?" Kapp guessed. Fern looked down at her feet. I

took that as a yes. Kapp went on. "I can only say, not quite as eloquently as your grandfather, that you have a great idea, but it simply isn't true. I'm not sure how to disprove it, but I can tell you that I never met your aunt Daphne until yesterday. And I suspect she would have said something aloud if she'd recognized me."

"I've wondered if Bob did a mercy killing," Linda put in. "But that doesn't explain Pilar's poisoning."

"What if the spirits of the past spoke to Aunt Daphne?" Melinda tried next. "I feel something very strange here. And I think she felt it, too."

"Aunt Daphne knew something," Arnot muttered. "She knew something detrimental to someone in this room. And that someone knew she knew."

"What's your evidence?" Kapp inquired mildly.

"Aunt Daphne was perceptive," Arnot told him. "While the rest of us were sticking our heads in the sand, she was watching. You could tell. She knew something."

"But what?" Fern asked.

Victor brought it up first. The elephant in the Lazars' living room.

"Simone and Hugh Lazar," he whispered. His skin was pale as he said their names. "Did any of you ever wonder about their deaths? I did. Your father was careful. I never believed the explosion was an accident—"

"Now, hold on," Uncle Earl objected. "That was years ago. If Daphne knew anything about that, she would have mentioned it at the time."

"But she was dying," Victor insisted. "Maybe she felt she had to speak."

A silence blanketed the room. I closed my eyes as if to ward away the looming darkness I felt. I willed myself to go to the center of the light I could see beneath my eyelids. I would face this thing, whatever it was.

"Yes," I announced, breaking the silence as I opened my eyes.

York nodded.

Geneva sighed and said, "I concur."

Arnot's eyes were wild as he looked at me. "I always knew—" he began.

"And so did I," Melinda finished.

"I've always had a sense of something . . . ," Geneva tried to explain, "of something not right. But I just thought it was my own loss and grief. I didn't want to hurt anyone else by speaking about it out loud."

"Yes!" York, Melinda, Arnot, and I all agreed as one.

"Could Daphne have been killed for the same reason as your parents?" Victor hazarded.

"It almost seems as if she must have been," Melinda put in, her voice floating in sadness.

"But what is that reason?" York murmured. "I've been trying to put it together ever since Aunt Daphne died. And I haven't found it."

Kapp nodded eagerly. "You all think," he advised. "Think hard. Why would anyone have wanted to kill your parents?"

But this wasn't a game to those of us who were the daughters and sons of Simone and Hugh Lazar. Silence was all that answered him. My mind couldn't think clearly about his question. I wondered if anyone else's could.

"I'm sorry," Victor apologized. "I shouldn't have brought it up."

"Yes, you should have," Geneva argued. "We need to talk, to think, to feel—"

"I've gotta use the restroom," Linda interrupted, and rushed toward the bathroom door.

Roy squeezed my hand.

"Hang in there, darlin' " he whispered. "This is the core of the darkness." I took another deep breath.

Then we were all talking again, talking about love and loss and grief turned inward. All five of us Lazar siblings had felt it. And we had all felt something else: Our parents' deaths had been no accident.

"But how could this have to do with Aunt Daphne's death?" York finally asked once again. "I feel that it does. But I can't seem to—"

York crouched suddenly and sprang into the air, twirling so that he was backward when he landed. His feet were planted firmly on the floor, and his hands were stretched toward Linda.

TWENTY

Linda jumped back, the color leaving her face.

Slowly, York dropped his arms. "Criminy," he muttered. "I forgot about you."

Linda's formerly colorless face began to redden at an alarming rate. She lifted her fist to shake at York.

"What kind of stupid stunt was that?" she demanded, her voice high and angry. "It's a good thing I already went to the bathroom. Or I would have gone right here when you attacked me. You're as sneaky as your creepy uncle Earl. What right do you have to attack me—"

"I didn't actually attack you," York tried to explain. "I just—"

"Oh, you don't call that an attack?" Linda asked in a falsetto. Then her voice deepened. "You jump into the air and come at me like a cat, and you think that you're just being friendly or something? Is this all part of the big scare-the-family-into-leaving scheme? I'm the one who already wants to leave, remember—"

"I was startled," York admitted. "I thought I could see everyone from where I was standing. I forgot that you'd left the circle. Then I heard your footsteps—"

"So you attacked me—"

"I'm sorry if I scared you, but I wasn't attacking you,"

York tried to explain once more. "I was just getting myself into position in case you were a threat."

"Did you think I was carrying an ax or what?" Linda pushed.

"I didn't think anything," York muttered sullenly, clenching his hands by his sides. "I didn't even know it was you."

"Well, for your information, you didn't scare me," Linda told him. She put her hands on her hips. "I don't care what martial arts you do, you still wouldn't hurt me in front of witnesses. So there."

"Keep pushing him, and he might," Geneva interceded pleasantly.

"What?" Linda yelped, turning toward Geneva.

"York is trying to apologize to you," Geneva asserted. "But you won't give him the chance. We're all nervous here. And York is trying to guard us. Wouldn't it be groovy if you would just give him a break?"

"You have some nerve," Linda shot back. "All of you. I felt sorry for you a little while ago, with your parents dead and all. But I forgot how you always stick together to stick it to me. Well, I don't have to take it."

Linda crossed her arms and stomped toward the front door.

"Not alone, honey," Victor put in mildly. "Remember, we're not going anywhere alone today."

"Mom, do you want me to walk with you while you chill out?" Fern asked, standing up from her seat on the couch.

Linda turned back to face her daughter, her eyes filled with tears.

"If you and Dad are so concerned about me, then why aren't you defending me?" she asked softly.

"Oh, Mom," Fern sighed and walked over to stand with her mother, touching her arm. "Granddad and I would always defend you if you were in danger, but York wasn't trying to hurt you—"

"There you go again!" Linda shouted. "You're taking their side against me."

So much for our talk. I wondered if my cousin had derailed our progress on purpose. Fern whispered to her mother as the rest of us froze in position.

After a while, I looked toward York. "Are you okay?" I mouthed his way.

He shrugged his shoulders. I was pretty sure he was more angry with himself than with Linda at that point. And I would have bet he was glad that Tom hadn't stayed after all to witness his performance with Linda.

"York, will you consider sitting down now?" Geneva asked gently, breaking our silence.

York sat, grumbling under his breath for a few seconds. Then suddenly, he went very still in his seat. He stared out over our heads and seemed to gather himself together from somewhere.

"I apologize to everyone," he said finally, his voice normal again. "I haven't been very alert. That's why I was startled. And I didn't see who poured the oil. I meant to watch more carefully. But I just—"

"York, stop!" Arnot ordered. He waved his arms in the air expansively. "You are stressed to the absolute max. So am I. I didn't see who poured the oil either. I meant to keep track of people, but I didn't."

"But I—" York began.

"You're not perfect, York," Geneva finished for him. "Hey, even I'm not perfect."

"You're not?" Melinda asked seriously.

Arnot laughed. But York was still on a roll.

"But it's my job to—" he began again.

"It's your job to teach martial arts," Geneva declared. "Even if you were in the Secret Service, you couldn't have prevented what's gone on here. How can you keep your eye on everyone when they've gone into different rooms? It's logically impossible."

"York," Kapp interjected. "I was trying to watch, too. And I don't know who poured the oil either. I got distracted. Everyone moved around too much. Geneva's right.

There's no way to keep track when people go to different rooms. There are doors that go outside from the living room, the dining room, and the kitchen. And for that matter, we don't know *when* the oil was poured. Maybe it was poured before we tried to pair up."

York frowned more deeply as he took in Kapp's information.

"It'll be okey-dokey," Melinda assured York. "Even Acuto wins once in a while, and he's a total goof-up."

York stared at Melinda and unexpectedly smiled.

"So, I'm not a total goof-up?" he asked her gently.

"Uh-uh," Melinda replied earnestly. "You never fall down or knock things over or anything."

"If anyone's at fault here, it's me," I put in. "I ought to be able to read murder in someone's energetic patterns, but I can't. I've had enough practice, but I never seem to understand the significance of a murderer's aura until after the fact. It's so frustrating!"

"Do you mean you've been trying to read our minds?" Linda asked.

Uh-oh. She was back.

"I've taken a few peeks," I told her cautiously. "But I can't read minds. I can just see colors, sense feelings, that kind of thing."

"Tell me what number I'm thinking about," she challenged me.

"I just explained," I answered, keeping my voice slow and even. "I can't read minds. I just sense things."

"Huh!" Linda snorted. "And you do this for a living?"

"Cally heals folks for a living," Roy spoke up. "There's quite a bit of difference between the sort of healing she's able to do and the reading of minds. She guides people's spirits back on track when their bodies are hurting. Or when their minds are hurting. And she does it kindly, you see? Kindness is part of her practice. That's why she can't see murder."

I turned to Roy, surprised by his analysis. Was he right?

"Never mind," Linda snapped. "I don't care about Cally.

Anyway, I decided when I was in the bathroom that if there was a murder, then Pilar did it. She killed Aunt Daphne, then took some morphine herself."

"Mom!" Fern warned.

"No, it's okay," Geneva told Fern. "Your mother's talking. Her opinions need to be heard just like everyone else's."

"But why would Pilar kill Aunt Daphne?" Melinda asked.

"It's so simple," Linda returned. "I keep trying to tell you guys. Pilar inherits."

No one agreed with her or argued with her. We just waited. We didn't have to wait long.

"See, I know my sister, Natalie, or whatever she was to me, was really strange. Mean, crazy strange. And Pilar's her daughter. All that weird stuff she went though with Natalie as her mother had to wack her out. I mean, come on. You don't grow up that way and come out normal. You all saw how high-strung Pilar is. And that's just what showed on the surface. Maybe Aunt Daphne was trying to help her, but Pilar is probably certifiably crazy."

"I thought you wanted to adopt her," Fern objected.

"I do if she isn't the murderer," Linda conceded. "But first, we have to figure that little fact out. And the more I think about it, the more I think it's her." She put up her hand, flipping up her index finger. "She had opportunity. She was right in the room with Daphne, with access to all her stuff." She stuck out her next finger. "She had the means. She probably understood the morphine dosages better than any of us." A third finger popped out. "And motive? Maybe she hated Aunt Daphne for trying to change her. Or maybe she loved her so much that she didn't want her to suffer. Who knows? But she was the closest to Aunt Daphne. There had to be some pretty strong feelings there." Her pinkie joined the rest of her fingers. "And talk about temperament. You saw her. She was angry and confused. What a mess."

I wanted to argue with Linda, but she had made some

credible points, fingers and all. I thought about Pilar. Uncle Earl's voice interrupted my thoughts.

"One could make a pretty strong case for means, motive, and opportunity for Bob Ungerman, too," he pointed out. "He knew about the morphine, and he controls Pilar's money now." He paused and lowered his voice. "Not that I think it was necessarily murder."

"Remember, I take custody," Victor argued. "I don't think Bob would gain any advantage over Pilar's money. I wouldn't allow that. And he knows it. In any case, either Bob or Pilar could have easily killed Daphne when she was in Oregon and called it suicide. What would be the point of drawing attention to the act here?"

"Maybe Bob was afraid that Pilar would know, or Pilar was afraid that Bob would know," Linda thought aloud. "So one of them did it here to cast suspicion elsewhere." She sighed and shook her head as if to clear it. "And you're not really going to take custody, are you, Dad? Maybe Bob knew that. Maybe he thinks you'll give custody of Pilar to him. Then he'd control the money."

"Pilar needs to be taken care of by her family," Victor said seriously. "Bob knows how strongly I feel about this. And he knows that Daphne wanted Pilar with the family. That's why she gave me custody."

"Then why is Bob at the hospital with Pilar instead of one of us?" Linda questioned.

"We've already been through this, honey," Victor told her. He let out a wisp of a sigh. "Pilar only feels safe with Bob now. Once we figure out what happened to Daphne, she'll feel safe with us again."

"Well, Earl's right anyway," Linda concluded. "Bob could have done it, too."

"Or York's friend, the Chinese artist." Uncle Earl cut back in. "We keep forgetting that he actually knew Daphne. That's suspicious. I've said so all along."

"Criminy, Uncle Earl!" York shouted. "Tom wasn't even here! How much do you need to convince yourself that it's not one of the family? How can you accuse someone who couldn't have possibly had anything to do with Aunt Daphne's murder? Why don't you just accuse the local homeless guy or something?"

Earl's face paled. Hurt showed in his puffy eyes. York was usually quiet. I don't think he'd ever shouted at Uncle Earl before. I don't think any of us ever had.

"I'm sorry, York," Earl muttered. "I was just thinking aloud." He coughed into his hand. "I suppose you're right."

York closed his eyes for a minute before replying. But Linda spoke just as he was opening his mouth.

"Well, Zoe knew Aunt Daphne, too," she started in again. "And Zoe didn't like her. Remember?" I saw Geneva flinch as Linda continued. "It doesn't have to be a member of the family. Why are you insisting it has to be? You guys are so weird. It's like you want it to be one of us—"

"Mom, chill," Fern ordered. "Please?"

"You can't keep telling me to chill," Linda snapped back. "You're the child. I'm the mother."

"If you act as if you're a child, it shouldn't be a surprise to you that you are treated as one," Uncle Victor murmured. "Please, Linda. Try to think about what other people in this room might be feeling."

"But—"

"Everyone in this room has been sympathetic to your feelings," Victor went on, more loudly. "Can you give back some of that sympathy now?"

Linda looked around the room. I tried to send her good thoughts.

"Honey, I know you're capable of good character." Victor pressed on. "I've seen how well you did raising Fern. I've even seen you show kindness to strangers. Please, can't you be just as helpful now? We need to reason now, not argue and emote."

"Please, Mom?" Fern added in a whisper.

Linda turned and embraced her daughter as if she hadn't seen her in a very long time. Maybe she hadn't. Then mother and daughter returned to sit on the lilac couch.

Earl cleared his throat.

"Linda might have a point about this Zoe," he put in. "She was very hostile to Daphne. Very hostile—"

Kapp dissented. "With no offense to you or to Linda, may I ask just how Zoe could have poisoned Pilar when she wasn't here to do it?"

"Couldn't she have had the morphine mixed in with something ahead of time?" Earl attempted an answer.

Kapp just shook his head. "How would Zoe know Pilar was going to drink a super shake? What would that 'something' be that she mixed the morphine with? If it was any of York's ingredients, then why didn't *he* get sick?" Kapp tapped his cane on the carpet. "No, it had to be done after the shake was made, on the spur of the moment."

"It's connected with our parents' deaths," York insisted. "We all really know that. I certainly do. Zoe was Cally's age when our parents died. So let's stop accusing outsiders. It's one of us."

"York," Fern said quietly. "Are you sure Aunt Daphne's death has to do with your parents' deaths? Mr. Kapp said we needed evidence. I'm not saying you're, like, wrong or anything. But how can you be sure you're right?"

York shrugged.

Fern had a point. Emotionally, I was with York. But logically, there was no proof. When bad things happened, I always thought of my parents' deaths, connection or no connection. It was just an emotional association.

"Let's stop and think for a moment," Victor suggested. "What do you really remember? What facts do we have? Not suppositions, but facts."

I leaned back in the love seat and closed my eyes, trying to think. But my mind was full. Memories assaulted me. I remembered Mom and Pop: Geneva was trying to teach them how to dance free-form like hippies while they laughed and undulated; my father told a joke and forgot the punch line, turning to my mother, who happily supplied it; my parents were eating my first effort at a pumpkin pie and ignoring the burned crust; my mother was kissing my forehead; my father was hugging me. Then the funeral—

"They're in the room," Melinda announced.

"Who?" Geneva demanded.

"Mom and Pop," Melinda told her. "Can't you tell?"

The hair went up on my arms. But there was something—

"How do you know?" Kapp prompted.

Finally, I smelled it, the fragrance my mother had worn. A hint of vanilla, jasmine, violet. And I smelled something else, too, besides the perfume . . . something . . .

"What's that smell?" York whispered, standing again.

"It's Mom's perfume," Melinda answered easily. "And I can smell Pop, too."

Earl jumped up off the couch, practically knocking over Melinda and Arnot. Did he smell it?

"Stop that!" he shouted.

"No, she really smells it," Geneva interjected. "I can smell it, too."

"Mom and Pop," Arnot murmured. "Yeah, I smell them."

He was right. We were all right. It wasn't just Mom's perfume, but that particular metallic, oily smell Pop always had from his workshop. It was in the room. I put my hand over my heart, trying to stop it from racing.

"Okay," Earl growled. "Who's playing games here? I know that scent. It's Simone's. Which of you is trying to rattle us?"

We all looked at one another in fear and awe.

I held up my hands to show I wasn't concealing anything. And each of the Lazar siblings followed suit.

But Earl wasn't satisfied. He sniffed the air and paced like a bloodhound, trying to place the source of the smell.

"This can't be happening," he rationalized.

"But it is," Victor argued the point.

"Then someone is doing it!" Uncle Earl insisted. "And I want to know why." He turned to Geneva. "Are you wearing your mother's perfume?"

"I don't wear perfume," she answered. "I don't even own perfume."

"Then where is the smell coming from?" he persisted.

"I don't know, Uncle Earl," Geneva answered. "I really

don't. There aren't any hidden perfume ducts in my house as far as I can tell. I can't explain it any better than you can."

And suddenly, I realized that the smell was gone. There wasn't a trace left in the air of my mother's scent or my father's. I sniffed hopefully, but only smelled a mixture of food, furniture polish, sweat, and Kapp's aftershave. My heart tightened. As frightening as the phenomenon had been, at least I'd felt my parents' presence. I wanted them back then as much as I had when I was fifteen years old.

Roy squeezed my hand again. I remembered him saying that we were at the core of the darkness. Were we?

"It's gone," Melinda announced.

Earl looked around suspiciously. He stuck his head out and inhaled.

"I smelled it, too," Linda said in a voice too small for her.

"Thank you, Linda," Geneva murmured. "It's good to have your validation."

"But where did it come from?" Earl demanded, his voice high and loud.

"Could be mass hypnosis," Kapp theorized. He looked pale himself. "But I smelled something, and—"

"No," Earl insisted. "This wasn't mass hypnosis. Somebody staged this. And I want to know who."

No one answered him. He turned on Victor.

"I want to look through your backpack," he said.

"Please do." Victor obliged him. He took his pack off and handed it to Earl.

Earl opened it and stuck his nose in. "Nothing," he finally concluded.

"Give it up," Kapp advised gently. "It's frightening, but I don't think we're going to find out the source of the scent. Not in this world."

"You would say that," Uncle Earl groused.

Kapp just shrugged his shoulders. He stood up and leaned on his cane. "Look, I'll make some calls," he offered. "See what's up with the police."

"I'll go with you," Arnot declared and jumped off the couch.

The two of them headed toward the kitchen.

I didn't blame them for leaving. I didn't want to talk about my parents. I didn't want to talk about the perfume. I was too afraid. Because I had a feeling that Earl was wrong. The perfume wasn't a trick like the oil and the clock. It was real. It meant something.

"They were telling us their deaths were connected to Aunt Daphne's," York posited. And we all knew who he meant by "they." Our parents.

"You don't really think so, do you?" Linda asked, fear in her protest.

"It was the evidence," York insisted. "We asked for evidence, and we got it."

I twisted my cold hands together. Roy took them in his and let his own warmth heat them.

"I want to know—" Earl began.

No, I definitely didn't want to talk about the perfume.

"Who knew about the morphine?" I asked instead.

"I didn't," Geneva offered.

"Why should we believe you?" Linda asked, less fearfully than a moment before.

Uncle Earl rebuked her. "Geneva is ethical, always has been. She wouldn't lie."

Uncle Victor complimented me. "This is a good question," he said. "This is the kind of question we should be asking. Who did know about the morphine? Let's each answer in turn. I'll go first. I knew."

"You did?" Fern whispered.

"Daphne told me last year," Victor confirmed. He turned and looked at Earl. "What about you," he asked. "You kept in touch with her, didn't you?"

"I kept in touch with her, but she never told me," Earl answered. "I wish she had. Maybe I could have done something."

Kapp came back from the kitchen before anyone else could offer up their knowledge or lack of knowledge of Aunt Daphne's use of prescription drugs.

"The police now believe your aunt Daphne died of a

morphine overdose," he announced. Arnot was at his side. "They haven't done a full autopsy, but a gross autopsy shows enough evidence for further investigation. They've taken samples and sent them to the forensics lab. They're strongly considering the possibility of murder. Kaifu is on the case like a dog on meat. You'd better figure this one out quick—"

The bell rang, interrupting his lecture.

Geneva got up and walked toward the door cautiously. When she opened it, Zoe Jackson stepped into the room.

"Hey, you guys," Zoe opened cheerfully. "What's happening?"

TWENTY-ONE

Zoe's smile left her face gradually, the corners of her bee-stung lips finally tipping down in her fragile, pale face.

"Are you cool?" she asked, turning to Geneva.

"No," my sister replied, shaking her head. "I'm not cool at all, Zoe."

"Why, what's going on?" Geneva's assistant designer pressed her.

"As if you didn't know," Linda muttered.

"What?" Zoe asked, clearly confused by Linda's comment.

"What did you have against my aunt Daphne?" Linda prodded her.

"Linda!" Geneva warned, seeming to grow taller where she stood next to Zoe in the doorway.

"Are you talking to me?" Linda mocked her, raising her brows. "Are you talking to Linda, the cousin that everyone can stomp on for asking questions during question-and-answer period?"

Linda had a point, I thought.

"Zoe had nothing to do with Aunt Daphne's death—" Geneva began.

"Your aunt Daphne is dead?" Zoe asked, having heard the critical word.

"Ms. Jackson," Kapp suggested. "You might want to take

a seat. A lot has happened since the last time that we saw you."

Linda pushed her head forward. It looked like she still had something to say. But Fern put a finger across her mother's mouth.

Zoe sat down as per Kapp's suggestion. Geneva closed the front door and took a chair next to her.

"May I sum up?" Kapp asked the group at large.

"Yes, please," Victor answered. No one argued with him.

"After you left our gathering yesterday, Geneva's aunt Daphne Dupree collapsed. She was taken to the hospital, where she was declared dead. Her young ward, Pilar Vaughn, believed that Daphne had been poisoned from her own store of medicinal morphine. Daphne had been given the morphine to control the pain of her cancer. So Daphne's significant other, Bob Ungerman, called the police. Do we all agree on this?"

Kapp surveyed the room. Linda shrugged her shoulders angrily, but most of us nodded.

"Two police officers came and paid us a visit last night," Kapp went on. "But the two officers apparently neglected to log in the visit or Pilar's accusation of poisoning. Then this morning, Pilar herself was poisoned. She, most happily, was given an antidote for the morphine and will recover. The chief of police arrived today to question us about Pilar's morphine overdose and learned that some of us believed that Daphne Dupree had also been poisoned. The police are currently investigating both Daphne's death and Pilar's morphine overdose. Preliminary findings seem to support Daphne's death by morphine, though the method of delivering that morphine has not been ascertained. Those of us who were present at the time of both incidents are under suspicion by the Estados Police Department."

"So you say," Linda put in.

"So I say," Kapp agreed genially. "I think that about sums up the events."

"Uh-uh," Fern objected.

Kapp looked at her, surprised.

"You forgot the clock, and the oil, and the perfume," she reminded him.

"Ever think of a career in law, Fern?" Kapp asked, smiling.

"Actually, I did," Fern told him. "But Mom said attorneys were a dime a dozen on this coast. Anyway, it costs too much to go to law school."

"With all due respect to your mother, *good* attorneys are not a dime a dozen."

"Attorneys!" Earl barked.

Kapp turned his head slowly, readying himself for attack.

But Zoe was still absorbing her shock. She didn't care about attorneys. "They were poisoned?" she asked in a very small voice.

"Well, I'm not sure I'd say—" Uncle Earl began.

"They were poisoned," Geneva interrupted him.

"Were they poisoned by mistake?" Zoe asked then, her eyes round under her jeweled glasses.

"Quite possibly accidents—" Earl tried.

"Mother of God, you can't believe that, can you?" Kapp asked.

"Why can't he believe that?" Linda challenged.

"Aunt Daphne was murdered," York stated decisively.

"Murdered?" Zoe repeated, her voice even smaller than before.

"One murder, one attempted murder—"

"We don't know that for sure—"

By one of the family—"

"No, *not* one of the family—"

"Oh, come on—"

"Possibly suicide—"

"Murder!"

"Everyone stop this instant!" Geneva commanded.

And they did.

"Zoe," Geneva said quietly. "We all have our opinions, but we don't really know yet what happened. Just that Aunt Daphne is dead, and Pilar is in the hospital."

"Oh, I'm so sorry, Geneva," Zoe murmured. "And I'm sorry I was rude to her. Jeez. And now she's dead."

Geneva patted Zoe on her sinking shoulder.

"That's okay," she assured the younger woman. "None of this is your fault. You're cool."

"Maybe," Uncle Earl put in. "Maybe not. May I ask you something, Zoe?"

Zoe turned to Uncle Earl, her eyes still round.

Earl asked away. "Why were you so hostile to Daphne Dupree?"

"I . . . I . . ."

Earl followed up eagerly. "Under the circumstances, it doesn't seem to be too personal a question."

"I didn't poison anyone," Zoe objected.

"Of course you didn't, young lady," Uncle Earl conceded. Or maybe he was just pretending to concede the point. "But we still don't know why you were so hard on Daphne. And right now, we can't afford the mystery."

"Yeah!" Linda backed him up.

"But the last time I saw Geneva's aunt was when I was a teenager," Zoe argued.

Even my ears began to prick up. Why wasn't she answering Earl's question?

"Then why were you angry when you met her again yesterday?" Earl persisted.

"Uncle Earl," Geneva objected. "There's no reason to attack Zoe. She had nothing to do with this."

"But she didn't like Aunt Daphne," Linda pointed out. "We all saw that."

"Zoe," Geneva murmured. "Your personal life is your own. There is no reason—"

"The police have Zoe's name," Linda pointed out.

"The police?" Zoe questioned. There was fear in her voice. I was sure of it. "Why would the police have my name?"

"Because you were here before Aunt Daphne died," Linda told her.

"Now, listen—" Geneva began.

"No," Zoe told her. "It's okay."

"But—"

"I understand why they need to know," Zoe said.

"So, tell us," Linda demanded. She was bent forward in her chair, triumph in her eyes.

"Well," Zoe tried. She breathed in through her nose and sat up straighter in her seat. "My mother was a single mother. And we were poor. I didn't even know who my father was. We were on public assistance." She clenched her hands together. "One of the charitable institutions, or so they called them, sent visitors to spy on us. Oh, they said they were there to help, but they were checking up on my mom. She had a drug problem. She had an everything problem." Zoe laughed harshly. "So these ladies would come over with pies and cookies and glare at my mother's cigarettes. They tried to be nice to me. Maybe they were trying to be nice to Mom. But see, I loved my mother, no matter what. And your aunt Daphne . . . well, she was one of the ladies who thought I should be placed in a foster home. She didn't understand. It was like my mother and I were made of one piece. I wouldn't have left her for anything. And social services let my mother keep me. But I was so afraid when they were investigating." Zoe took a deep breath. "And when I met your aunt Daphne yesterday, I remembered all of it. I'd forgotten how much it had hurt, how afraid I'd been. She called me by my old name. I changed my name when I turned eighteen. My mother understood. She liked Zoe better than Zelda anyway. But hearing Ms. Dupree call me Zelda brought it all back for a moment."

"That must have been hard," I said to soothe her.

"It was," she agreed. She shut her eyes for a moment. "I felt like I'd shed all that garbage from the past, and it came back and ambushed me. Geneva knew about my past. But I hadn't realized she was related to someone who was there then. I explained about your aunt to Geneva yesterday. I apologized to Ms. Dupree, too. I'm sorry she died. But I didn't have anything to do with it. I was just angry for a moment, remembering."

"You know, Zoe." Uncle Victor jumped in. "Daphne wasn't a staid church lady at all. She'd given birth to her own illegitimate child and given her to relatives for adoption. Perhaps that's why she thought you could be better brought up by someone other than your real mother. She'd given up her own child. I'm not trying to invalidate your feelings. But I want you to know that Daphne went through her own adversity, too. Visiting you might have brought up some of her own issues—"

"Ms. Dupree had an illegitimate daughter?" Zoe whispered in amazement.

"Yeah, my sister," Linda added to the confusion.

"Your sister?"

"It doesn't matter," Linda claimed. "What matters is how angry you were with our aunt Daphne."

"I told you," Zoe shot back. "I was angry for a moment. It's all in the past. My mother's dead now anyway."

"Oh, Zoe," I murmured. "I'm sorry—"

"She died of a drug overdose," Zoe explained. She didn't sound cute and funny like she had the day before. She sounded tired.

The room was quiet for a moment as the word "overdose" reverberated.

"Morphine?" Arnot asked finally.

"What?" Zoe asked back, squinting her eyes. "Why would she have anything to do with morphine? She died of a heroin overdose. She screwed up. It happens."

"Thank you, young lady," Uncle Earl said. "In your story, you've given us a little perspective. An overdose can happen by mistake."

Zoe shrugged uncomfortably. "My mother used street drugs, not prescribed medication. Street drugs are harder to judge, and she misjudged."

"So, that's enough about Zoe," Geneva announced.

"Oh boy, back to murder," Melinda sang out.

Zoe looked at Melinda as if trying to place her. And I remembered that Zoe had no reason to recognize Melinda. Melinda hadn't been at the house at the same time as Zoe on Thanksgiving day.

"Zoe!" Geneva blurted out, clapping her palm on her temple. "I never even introduced you. Melinda, Arnot, this is my designer, Zoe. Zoe, this is my sister Melinda and my brother Arnot.

"I'm Arnot," my brother announced. "I'm the boy." Melinda giggled.

"Do you really think your aunt was murdered?" Zoe asked Melinda. "I mean, it's hard for me to believe—"

"That's why it's good to get an outside view," Earl reminded us. "Even Zoe finds it hard to believe that Daphne was murdered. An accident or suicide is much more likely—"

"But what about Pilar?" Fern put in.

And they were off to the races again. As everyone argued, Zoe's eyes got wider and wider. "Who do you suspect?" she finally asked Geneva.

An odd sort of silence permeated the room, a silence made of unasked questions and unexpressed accusations.

Geneva sighed. "I believe it had to be a member of my own family," she finally answered. "A Lazar or a Dupree, but one of us. I don't know who—"

Linda snorted with disgust and made her way to the bathroom once more.

Zoe flinched. "But how could you really think—"

"Our parents were killed many years ago," York answered for Geneva. "We think Aunt Daphne's murder was related to theirs."

"Oh, my God, Geneva!" Zoe blurted. "I didn't know about your parents." She reached over to pat Geneva's shoulder. "I go on and on about my own troubles, and you never told me about your parents. What happened?"

"An accident, we always said," Geneva murmured,

shaking her head. "But now, now we're not so sure. At least *I'm* not so sure."

"What kind of accident?" Zoe pressed.

The room turned claustrophobic. My chest felt too tight for my heart as Geneva answered Zoe.

"My parents were in the basement," Geneva said. "They were in my father's workshop. He used it as a laboratory to do experiments. He was an inventor, you see, a successful one. He was working on something to do with fuel. The basement exploded. Both my mother and my father were killed."

"Oh, Geneva," Zoe whispered. "How awful."

Awful didn't even begin to cover it, I thought uncharitably. No wonder we Lazar siblings didn't share our feelings very often. Then I reminded myself what Zoe had been through. At least I'd had good times with my parents before they died. We all had.

"So when Aunt Daphne died, and Pilar was sure she'd been murdered, I asked myself if there was a connection." Geneva kept going. "I asked myself if Aunt Daphne knew something about my parents' deaths."

Linda came back into the room as Geneva was finishing up. She shook her head.

"Why does this have to be about your parents?" Linda asked. "Why is everything always about the five Lazar kids?"

"Not everything," York corrected my cousin. "Just Aunt Daphne's murder and Pilar's poisoning. Can't you see why we might wonder about a connection?"

"No, I can't," Linda shot back. "You keep attacking me. At least you didn't jump at me this time."

"I didn't mean to jump at you, Linda," York muttered. "If I'd meant to, you wouldn't still be standing."

"Oooh!" Linda cooed. "Is that supposed to scare me?"

Maybe it didn't scare Linda, but Zoe looked frightened as she viewed York's angry features. I didn't blame her. York in a sullen mood could scare people just by looking at them.

"Linda is only teasing York," Geneva was quick to explain. "York scared her with a martial arts demonstration."

"A martial arts demonstration?" Zoe repeated. She pressed back in her chair as if she was trying to make herself invisible.

I squirmed in my own chair as York squirmed across from me. I was sure we were sounding weirder and weirder by the minute to Zoe. And the bad thing was that we were as weird as we sounded.

"I teach martial arts," York said. He attempted a reassuring smile at Zoe. When she didn't respond, he went back to his well-worn scowl. "In my opinion, the murderer must not only be one of our extended family, he or she must be someone old enough to have been there when our parents died. Me, Geneva, Cally, Arnot, Melinda, Earl, Victor, Linda—"

"Wait one minute," Linda stopped him. "I didn't have anything to do with this."

"I didn't say you did." York sighed. "I'm just talking about the possibilities. Think about it. If the events are connected, then it helps us to rule out people. Like your daughter, Fern, for example."

"But we don't know that the events *are* connected," Linda said for the umpteenth time. "You just seem to want them to be."

"Why do you think you smelled Mom's perfume?" Melinda challenged her.

"Perfume?" Zoe asked. Dack, she was beginning to sound like a parrot.

"We all smelled my mother's perfume," I divulged.

"It was a sign," Melinda reasoned confidently.

"It was a trick," Earl maintained. "Like the oil and the clock."

"The oil and the clock?" Zoe said. I almost mouthed the words with her as she spoke them. Yep, a parrot.

"Never mind the oil and the clock," Victor advised. "We all smelled the perfume. It had meaning."

"I smelled the perfume," Linda admitted. "It's weird,

but I did. Still, the perfume doesn't mean the events were connected. Not necessarily. I'm serious now. I know maybe I just don't want to believe that there's a murderer in the family. But unlike the rest of you, I'm keeping my mind open. There are other possibilities. Like Pilar and Bob, for instance. I still think that they have better motives. You people think you're reasoning on the basis of some kind of special Lazar intuition, but you're fooling yourselves. You just want to explain your parents' deaths because you're all still freaked out about them. Fine. But don't act like you're thinking logically, because you're not."

York looked stunned by her words. And for good reason. She might well be right. Just because she was Linda didn't mean that her logic was necessarily faulty.

"I'm not a Lazar," Kapp pointed out. "And I don't believe that Pilar would poison either Daphne or herself. Intuition can be a result of experience, and I've had years in the California court system. And I 'feel' that Pilar didn't do it. My feelings are based on—"

"I know," Linda cut him off. "And you don't 'feel' that Bob had anything to do with it either. Well, there are other possibilities. One person may have poisoned Daphne." Linda paused and directed her gaze toward Zoe. "And someone else may have poisoned Pilar."

Zoe couldn't miss Linda's look. "Do you still think I had something to do with your aunt Daphne's death?" she demanded.

"Did you?" Linda pressed. "Why'd you ask me if you aren't still hiding something?"

Zoe rose from her chair, thin but suddenly dangerous looking. "I saw the once-over you were giving me, that's why. What kind of con job are you trying to put over on these guys anyway? Huh?"

"If you have nothing to hide, why are you so upset?" Linda prodded.

"Linda!" Geneva tried again. But Zoe was rolling.

"I had nothing to do with your aunt Daphne, not since I was a kid!" Zoe snarled. "I've made peace with my past. If

I wanted to kill someone from my past, it wouldn't be a female, believe me." She laughed harshly. "You wanna know what I'm hiding? Well, it has nothing to do with your aunt."

"What does that mean?" Linda asked, more softly than before.

"*Men* abused my mother. *Men* abused me. I think the real reason I was angry with your aunt was that she started me remembering. Do you know how many years of therapy I've had to get over those memories? Do you?"

"I—" Linda began.

"Your aunt was nothing to me in the scheme of my messed-up life!" Zoe hissed. "Nothing. I don't need your accusations. They're a bunch of lies. I don't know what your game is, but you can count me out."

"Oh, Zoe," Geneva whispered. "I'm so sorry. No one here really suspects you—"

"Thank you, Geneva," Zoe muttered, but she didn't turn away from Linda.

Linda finally dropped her own stare. Her neurosis might have pushed the rest of us around, but she was outgunned by Zoe's life.

"Zoe, ma'am," Roy broke in. "I do believe that Linda here is merely frightened. She most certainly doesn't want to believe that anyone she knows could have done these terrible things. So she accuses others. Don't fret on it, please. No one else suspects you of anything but being a good, kind friend to Geneva."

"Really?" Zoe asked, searching the room with her eyes.

"Really," I confirmed. Even Linda didn't argue the point.

"Zoe." Victor chimed in. "We were all discussing the possibility of murder when you came in the door. I'm afraid we got carried away. Please accept my apology."

Zoe squinted at the elderly man. Maybe she wondered why *he* was apologizing. But she nodded finally. Then she graciously made her good-bye rounds and left Geneva's house.

I heard her whisper to Geneva on the way out. "They're wearing your clothes, Geneva. Do you know that?"

Geneva rolled her eyes and whispered back, "I'll tell you about it someday."

Once the door shut behind Zoe, Roy stood up.

"I feel I must speak out now," he declared, clasping his hands in front of him. He raised his head to stare at us each in turn. "Some of you know that I have had the experience of sensing darkness near my Cally. It has been a most frightening and confusing experience. But I believe I have found the core of that darkness. It is here. It rests with the deaths of Cally's parents. It rests in this family—"

"That's enough!" Uncle Earl shouted. "I won't have you upsetting Cally. Why do you say these things when everyone is already afraid? Are you crazy? What are you to Cally? How can you claim—"

"Can't you see that Roy loves Cally?" Kapp demanded. His face flushed. "What kind of man are you, that you don't recognize love when you see it?"

TWENTY-TWO

I was stunned by Kapp's words, not because I disagreed with them, but because sentimentality wasn't normally in Kapp's repertoire. And the most emotion he'd ever displayed toward Roy before had been amiable condescension.

Earl was stunned, too, but only for a moment.

"I know about love," Earl huffed. "You just don't know anything about me. I've known a true love that no one can take from me, a pure passion. What have you known? Billable hours?"

"Okay, okay. We're both old men with our own precious memories," Kapp declared. "I'm not going to try to match mine with yours. But if you claim to know love, how can you miss the love of these two young people before you?"

"Kapp," Geneva whispered, a grin on her face. "I always knew you were an old softie."

Kapp blushed all the way up to the bald spot on his head.

"And I'm not as old as you," Earl added, crossing his arms. "I'm seventy-five. You've got to be at least eighty."

"And?" Kapp prompted, actually looking confused for the moment.

"You said we were both old men," Uncle Earl muttered.

"Well, excuse me all to pieces," Kapp growled back. "Beauty before age, by all means."

"Thank you kindly for your incisive words, Mr. Kapp,"

Roy offered softly. "You were most certainly right about my love for Cally."

"Don't let it go to your head, kid," Kapp told him. But he was smiling.

The bell rang. I wondered if Zoe had come back to fight with Linda some more.

But it was Bob who stood in the doorway when Geneva answered. He looked worn but not as unhappy as the last time that we'd seen him.

"I thought you'd want to know that Pilar is doing better," he told us.

"Oh, I'm so glad," Geneva murmured, taking his hand.

He didn't move away. He gripped her hand back with his trembling one. That was surprising. "I just wondered if you folks are any further in figuring out who poisoned Daphne and Pilar."

"Huh!" Linda snorted.

"I do believe we are, sir," Roy answered at the same time.

"Oh, they have some goofy theory that Daphne was killed because of their parents, and Pilar was poisoned because of that," Linda accused, rolling her eyes. "Don't ask me to explain. It doesn't make any sense. But they aren't being logical."

"Who exactly are 'they'?" Bob prodded.

"The Lazar siblings," Linda expanded. "Who else? The precious five children of Hugh and Simone Lazar. Geneva, York, Cally, you know."

"And Arnot and Melinda," Arnot added with mock indignation. "Don't forget us."

"Our parents were killed in an explosion more than twenty years ago," York explained. There was no mockery in the seriousness of his tone. "We think that Aunt Daphne's death was connected to our parents' deaths in that explosion."

"But how would Daphne's death be connected?" Bob asked. His words held no challenge, just curiosity.

York scowled anyway.

"We don't believe that our parents' deaths were an

accident," Geneva answered for York. "Aunt Daphne may have suspected something or witnessed something about our parents' deaths. Or she might have been killed for the same reason that our parents were killed. We haven't gotten that far yet. But Roy is right. We are further than we were. And we are going to get to the bottom of this."

"Right," Linda snapped, rolling her eyes some more. "About the time that world peace becomes a reality."

"And we're going to find out what really happened without accusing outsiders to our family," Geneva proclaimed. She let go of Bob's hand gently and turned to face Linda. "How could you accuse Zoe of murder when you know that she couldn't have had anything to do with it?"

"I told you," Linda tried. "Zoe could have left an overdose of morphine for Aunt Daphne. And maybe Pilar was poisoned by—"

"You don't really believe that, Linda," Geneva reasoned coolly. "You aren't that stupid. Zoe didn't even know about the morphine. But I know you. You made Zoe suffer to get to me. I'm not sure why you hate me, but you didn't have to take it out on an innocent bystander. That's not groovy, Linda. It's not groovy at all."

Linda's face paled. She turned to her father.

"Dad, are you going to let her talk to me like that?" she demanded.

"Linda," Uncle Victor answered. "You're a grown woman. I saw how you treated Zoe. I don't understand it. She answered Earl's questions, but you kept twisting your knife in her. Maybe Geneva is right. Maybe she isn't. But I'm not going to fight for your right to exercise cruelty."

"And you wonder why I hate you!" Linda screamed at Geneva. Her pale skin reddened. "He's taking your side against me, even now. You're perfect. You can do no wrong. All I was doing was exploring the truth. Isn't that what you said you wanted? All of you? Well, you can't have it both ways. Zoe is still a suspect as far as I'm concerned. And so is Bob. And so is Pilar."

"Pilar?" Bob questioned.

"Yes, Pilar." Uncle Earl weighed in. "And you, Mr. Ungerman. Yours and Pilar's motives are the strongest as far as I'm concerned."

"But Bob and Pilar can't be suspected any more than Zoe can be if Aunt Daphne's death is connected with our parents' deaths—" Geneva began.

"Geneva, I love you like the eldest daughter that I never had." Uncle Earl cut her off. "But you're blinding yourself with your assumptions. Linda is right. You're assuming the same person poisoned Pilar and Daphne. That's not necessarily true to begin with. You're assuming these poisonings tie in with your parents' deaths. That's not necessarily true either. And you're refusing to consider all the options. Suicide, accident. They're still possible, but you've shut your mind. I'm not saying you need to agree with my views, but at least keep an open mind."

"Um," Fern muttered. "I think Mom and Earl might be kinda right. Aunt Daphne could have been poisoned by accident or on purpose. But that doesn't mean that Pilar couldn't have taken an overdose on purpose herself. She wanted to get attention, you know. She wanted everyone to believe that Aunt Daphne had been murdered. Taking the overdose made that happen. I'm not saying she did it, but it's possible. Or maybe it wasn't the super shake at all. Maybe both Aunt Daphne and Pilar drank out of the same glass or something like that in their bathroom. None of us, like, really knows. That's all I'm saying."

"She has a point," Kapp admitted, rubbing his chin. "I think it's a family member, but I wouldn't bet my life on it. And it's just possible that there's an explanation that doesn't involve murder."

"But I'm here, so it must be murder," I put in, affecting a light tone. But my body didn't feel light. It might have been made of lead, it felt so heavy.

"My sweet Cally is making her joke because she is hurting unbearably," Roy translated then. "But I assure you that I am not joking about the darkness. I know not everyone will believe me, but there is a darkness here today that is worse than what I've seen before. And it is most surely associated with the death of Cally's parents. That's why Cally's been drawn to so many murders. I can see that now. Cally sees auras. I see darkness. She is a kinder person than I am. And she doesn't want to see the darkness. It's too hard for her. But if we can figure this out and get past it—"

"I'm not going to listen to this," Uncle Earl rumbled. His voice rose in pitch as he continued. "I don't know how Daphne died, but I'm not going to listen to the insane ramblings of a man who should be locked up. It's not normal to see darkness. I don't even know what he means—"

"I do," York asserted. "Roy is saner than a lot of us are."

"Maybe you know what he means, son," Earl tried in a gentler tone. "But you need to let the police do their business. They'll find out the truth. We're all just getting each other upset. It can't be good for any of us."

"It will be good for us when the truth is discovered," Victor argued. "And that's what we're going to do, discover the truth. The only question is how we are going to do it. I still think we'll get to the truth if we each speak. We each know different details, details that may seem unimportant by themselves. But if we put all these details together, the truth will be formed organically."

"Please, do that," Bob said quietly. It was not an order, but a simple request from a tired and sick man.

"Yes, sir," Roy promised. "We will."

"Then I'll leave you to it," Bob told us and turned back toward the doorway, keeping his spine straight in spite of the Parkinsonian tremors that traveled through his body. How much had the last two days' events escalated his disease?

"Let me walk you out," Kapp offered, pushing himself up from his seat with his cane and hobbling Bob's way.

"I'd appreciate that," Bob muttered.

Good-byes were shouted out as Kapp reached Bob and escorted him out the door. What was Kapp up to?

The sound of crying reached my ears. Linda sat with her daughter on the plum couch, weeping softly. Fern just held her mother, her eyes serious and troubled.

Geneva walked to the plum couch slowly. "Linda," she enunciated carefully. "I'm sorry that I've hurt you. I never meant to. And I know your father loves you. If I've taken anything from that love, I apologize. I don't feel perfect. I hardly feel adequate most days. But maybe I look better to you than I feel to myself. I was angry with you because Zoe is so vulnerable. I forgot that you are vulnerable, too. You've made some good points that I hadn't thought of. I'm listening. I know I can appear arrogant. Maybe I am arrogant. But I don't want to cause you pain."

Linda slowly looked up at her.

"Are you serious?" she finally asked.

Geneva nodded.

"Well, thank you," Linda muttered. "Maybe the truth *will* set us free."

Geneva reached out a hand. Linda took it and squeezed.

"So, do I have to slip in oil to get one of your 'groovy' outfits?" Linda asked.

Geneva's bark of laughter was a surprise.

"No," she answered. "You can pick one out for yourself anytime. You're family. And anyway, you'll look better in one of my outfits than your father does."

"I heard that," Victor announced, trying to scowl over the spark of happiness that lit his face.

Then Linda laughed.

Kapp walked back through the front door and closed it behind him. He looked at Geneva and Linda and looked away.

"So what are we going to do now?" he asked.

"It's gotta be us," York announced. "The daughters and sons of Simone and Hugh Lazar. We have to figure it out. Cally can help us search our memories. Let's go upstairs."

"Can Roy come, too?" I asked softly. The words slipped out before I could stop them. But I knew the truth would be too hard for me to face without Roy's presence. It might be too hard even with Roy's presence.

"Of course." Melinda granted her permission. No one else argued.

"How about me?" Kapp asked.

"No." Geneva nixed him. "You'd probably want to put everything we said into a book, you old fraud." But she smiled at him as she spoke, then crossed the room and kissed his cheek.

"I'll wait," he offered, blushing. I felt a wave of warm comfort in his friendship.

"But why you six?" Earl asked. "I've been a father to you kids. Why not me instead of Roy?"

"Oh, Uncle Earl," I tried as I stood with Roy. "It just has to be this way, I think. We have to face the truth together. And Roy can help us to see it."

"But—"

"We have to do it alone," York insisted, also standing.

"Perhaps, you could stay here to talk while the rest of us remain silent," Victor suggested as Melinda and Arnot rose. "Maybe we could support—"

"No, Dad," Linda told him seriously. She turned back to the group of us that had gathered. "Go," she ordered with a regal wave of her hand. "Find out the truth, and put us out of our misery, for God's sake."

"Thank you, Linda," Geneva murmured. Then she turned to the rest of us. "Let's go," she commanded.

The six of us walked up the stairs and into Geneva's bedroom. York shut the door behind us and locked it.

It was lucky that Geneva had a queen-sized bed and a couch. Geneva, Melinda, and Arnot sat on the side of the bed that faced the window, looking like dolls in a showcase on the lavender comforter. York, Roy, and I sat on the periwinkle couch that was positioned beneath the window. The three of us on the couch could see the door. That seemed important, even though the door was locked.

"Okay, what do we know?" Geneva started the ball rolling.

"We know Aunt Daphne died of a morphine overdose," York answered. "We know Pilar ingested morphine. We know our parents were murdered—"

"We don't actually know that," I cut in diffidently. "We believe it."

"But do we all believe it?" Geneva asked.

All six of us nodded.

"Then the question might fairly be, why do we believe it?" Roy commented thoughtfully.

"My belief isn't based on any great psychic insight," I admitted, my ideas unfolding as my mouth moved. "I think I believe Mom and Pop were murdered because of many things I know, consciously or unconsciously, that lead me to that conclusion."

"Come again," Arnot requested, lifting up his hands in confusion. "I don't get what you're saying."

"Okay," I tried to explain. "Pop was careful. That's one thing I know. A fact. But there are other facts, too. Maybe facts that I've been denying. But when my unconscious adds them all up, they tell me our parents were murdered."

"Oh, I get it," he murmured. "It's like designing a piece of woodwork. I couldn't tell you why it'll work, but I know it will."

"Yeah!" Melinda added enthusiastically. "It's like knowing what people will like in a cartoon—"

"Fine," Geneva broke in sharply. "All of us have added up the facts in our brains. But what are the facts?"

"There was the perfume," Arnot put in.

"Um," Melinda muttered guiltily. "I sat on my purse."

"Keerups, Melinda!" York blurted out. "What does your purse have to do with this?"

"I keep a little bottle of Mom's perfume, or maybe it's cologne, in there, you know?"

There was a brief silence. I didn't know. I didn't think York or Geneva or Arnot or Roy knew either. Only Melinda knew.

"It has one of those bulb thingies, an atomizer, maybe," she went on. "But I barely sat on it. I hardly squished it at all."

"You squirted a shot of Mom's perfume?" Arnot demanded, looking at her.

"Just a little," she defended herself. "Hardly any."

Then Arnot frowned, looking amazingly like York for a moment. "But I smelled Pop, too."

"We all did, didn't we?" I asked.

"I didn't," Roy told us. "But I don't actually know what your papa—your pop smelled like, so I had no reference."

"You mean the rest of us smelled Mom and automatically smelled Pop?" I hazarded.

"It makes sense," Geneva concluded.

"It does?" I wasn't so sure.

"Absolutely." Geneva steepled her fingers under her chin as she spoke. "We really did smell Mom's scent. I think it was Evening in Paris. Pop actually bought it for her in Paris. Anyway, when we smelled Evening in Paris, our minds took us to the next thing associated with that smell, Pop's smell. The actual scent of Melinda's perfume was probably in the air for less than a second. The rest was in our minds."

"It was still a sign," Melinda insisted.

"We don't need signs," Geneva declared. "We need facts. And we need facts now. So first—"

"One more thing before the facts." Arnot stopped her, holding his hand up. "Roy, what did you mean about the darkness?"

"Oh my, the darkness." Roy sighed. Then he spoke very softly. "This is so very embarrassing. You see, the darkness first appeared to me some years ago as a sort of shadow moving from me to Cally. But after a period of time, I began to realize that the darkness was really more centered around Cally than me. I'm sorry, darlin', but it's true." Roy turned to me, his eyes begging for forgiveness.

"It's okay," I whispered and smiled. It wasn't a time for smiling, but Roy's need drew it from me. He was working so hard to do the right thing.

He went on then. "I thought it was some sort of witchy, other-world, dark force right out of a science fiction novel. I'll admit it, I wasn't quite sane on the subject. But you see, I thought it would harm Cally. And I was certain that it was my fault for the longest time." He paused and his voice grew a little louder. "But since I've been here, I've seen it on all of you, whenever you speak of your mama and your papa. Whenever you speak of their deaths. It's curling around each of you now—"

"Oooh, I feel it." Melinda cut him off. She smiled, feeling around her in the air with her hands. The hair went up on the back of my neck. "I do, I feel it. He's right."

"But this sense of darkness isn't a fact, ma'am," Roy reminded her. "It's just what I see. And you feel. I imagine it's more in the category of belief. And Geneva's most certainly right about facts and beliefs. The question is what we know, not what we believe."

"So what do we know?" Arnot asked, his voice more serious than I could remember.

"I want to talk about the day our parents died," York told us. "We've never talked about it. We probably remember different things."

"Everyone still lived nearby," Melinda offered. "Uncle Victor and Linda and Uncle Earl. And Aunt Daphne."

"Good," Geneva said approvingly.

"Pop was working on a fuel experiment," Arnot remembered.

"No one knew Mom was going to be there," I said slowly.

"What?" Geneva questioned. "You're losing me here."

"The man at the deli told me," I explained. "York and I ate there a few months later, and the man at the deli told us how sorry he was about Mom and Pop. You know how Mom usually spent weekdays at her studio? Well, the man at the deli said he remembered the day . . . the day they died because Mom had come in and ordered two sandwiches to take to Pop for lunch as a treat."

"I remember!" York cried out. "He was romantic about the whole thing. But that meant that whoever killed them thought only Pop would be there."

"Maybe . . . ," Geneva murmured.

"And if Mom was there, Pop would have been extra careful," Melinda put in. "Remember how he always warned us about safety stuff when we visited him in his shop?"

"And Aunt Daphne knew . . . ," I began, but I couldn't finish.

"What?" Geneva demanded.

"She said . . . ," I tried again, remembering the Thanksgiving meal the day earlier. "She said, 'You always loved Simone.'"

My head filled with darkness. As my eyes closed, I wondered if this was the darkness that Roy saw. But this darkness hurt. I wanted it to stop hurting.

Then I heard two voices.

"Cally, darlin'," one said.

"Did you pass out?" the other asked.

The second voice was York's.

I shook my head, trying to remember. I must have passed out. But why? Then I knew. I knew who'd murdered Aunt Daphne and why. I hadn't wanted to know, but I did.

I looked at my brother York.

"Yes," he told me. "I know, too."

TWENTY-THREE

A half an hour later, the bedroom door was unlocked. Roy and the five of us Lazars all tromped back down the stairs to Geneva's living room.

"Are you ready?" Kapp asked us. He and the others were all standing at the bottom of the stairs.

Geneva nodded.

"Wait a sec," he commanded, lifting his cane for emphasis. "I'll call Bob on his cell phone. He's waiting just down the street."

I smiled in spite of everything as Kapp moved toward the phone in the kitchen. No matter where I was, he was always one step ahead. Except for the practice of cane-fu. But then again, I didn't wear aftershave. He couldn't smell *me* coming.

We all took our seats as we waited for Bob. York, Roy, and I sat on the plum couch, the one nearest the front door. Melinda, Geneva, and Arnot took the lilac couch, next to the entrance to the dining room. Without discussion, we'd arranged ourselves to cover the exits. Then Fern and Linda made themselves comfortable on the magenta love seat. Uncle Victor settled next to them on a stuffed chair. And Uncle Earl lowered himself into an easy chair near the three of us at the front doorway.

"Why do we have to wait for Bob?" Fern asked. She

grinned. "Is this like one of those cool Nero Wolfe scenes where the true criminal is exposed by the great detective?"

"Yes," York answered her seriously.

Fern's grin faded along with the color in her face.

"It'll be all right," her mother assured her. That was a turnabout. Linda was acting like a mother.

Kapp walked back in from the kitchen.

"Bob's on his way," he told us.

"Thank you, Kapp," Geneva said formally.

Kapp executed a half bow in her direction.

"I don't understand why you've called Mr. Ungerman," Earl grumbled.

"You will," Melinda promised. She wasn't giggling after speaking anymore.

"Well, I trust you kids to do the smart thing," Earl assured us. "Still, it would be nice to keep these decisions in the family." He didn't glare at Kapp this time. Maybe he was just too tired.

"Thank you, Uncle Earl," Geneva murmured. "We're doing our best."

Victor reached into his backpack and took out a bottle. He opened it and poured two tablets into his hand before popping them into his mouth and swallowing them dry. He looked tired, too, and pale in his black jumpsuit.

"Ginkgo leaf is said to be good for the mind," he explained.

"Then maybe we all should take some," Linda suggested, a half smile on her face.

"Too late," Melinda announced. She wasn't joking.

The doorbell sounded less than a minute later. Kapp let Bob in, and the two of them sat in the chairs between the two couches after strained greetings all around.

I closed my eyes and took a deep breath in lieu of any ginkgo. We were ready to begin. The only important person missing was Pilar. As York began his speech, I decided that her absence was probably a good thing.

"Aunt Daphne was murdered," he declared. "And her murderer is in this room."

He looked around the room, locking eyes with each of the people who sat there.

"We would like to be as clear as possible in sharing our reasons for reaching this conclusion." Geneva took up where York had left off. "To do that, we must question the motives of everyone here." Linda, Earl, and Victor all opened their mouths to speak. Geneva held up a hand to silence them before continuing. "We are not necessarily accusing anyone. We'll try to do this without rancor. So please, just listen."

Arnot took the verbal baton. "Okay, first off: The same person killed Aunt Daphne, killed our parents, and tried to kill Pilar," he disclosed.

Mouths opened again.

"Listen and learn, you guys," Melinda advised. "It'll be worth the rocket ride."

Linda and Uncle Earl looked restive but said nothing. Victor bent forward, his face intent and sweating. Fern leaned into her mother. Bob looked at Kapp, squinting. Kapp nodded his assurance.

"Every single one of us is a suspect," I carried on. "We'll explore all the possibilities so that no one is unfairly singled out.

"Are we in agreement?" Geneva demanded.

No one argued with Geneva. Still, I could feel the unexpressed disagreement from more than one quarter; and I could feel the tension, too. The whole room seemed to tremble. Or maybe it was just me.

"Five of us here are the children of Hugh and Simone Lazar," I began. "We all had motive to kill our parents—"

"No!" Fern cried out. I saw tears in her eyes.

"I only said that we each had a motive, not that we did it," I told her gently. "We all inherited after our parents died."

Geneva nodded. "I used the money I inherited to start my own design business."

"But you didn't kill them," York put in.

"No, I didn't," Geneva agreed. "And presuming, as we

are, that each murder was carried out by the same person, we can exclude both Melinda and Arnot. They couldn't have poisoned Aunt Daphne. They weren't here. And they weren't here when Pilar was poisoned either."

"Cally didn't do it," Melinda reasoned. "Cally was fifteen when Mom and Pop were killed, and she'd barely passed chemistry. The goofball didn't have the necessary science, believe me."

"And York was in his first year at the University of Pennsylvania when our parents' basement exploded," Arnot added. "I know he was there." He closed his eyes and took a breath. "I know because I was the one who got to call York to give him the news."

"I suppose we have to talk about Zoe and Tom." York moved on, his voice thick with what might have been tears or anger. I didn't turn to him. I was looking at someone else. "Neither of them knew or had anything to do with our parents. They are excluded."

"But how do you—"

"If Zoe or Tom had known our parents, we would have met them," I cut in, quelling Linda's objection before it could fully form. I knew my argument wasn't entirely logical, but it seemed to stop her. And we needed to keep going. We had a murderer to psyche out.

She frowned, then nodded uncertainly.

Melinda followed up. "The same for Roy and Kapp. They didn't know Mom and Pop. They're out."

I waited for another objection, but none was forthcoming this time.

"And we come to Pilar and Bob," Geneva said. "Both Pilar and Bob had motives to kill Aunt Daphne, but again, they didn't know Hugh and Simone Lazar. Pilar wasn't even born when our parents died. And Bob lived in another state at the time."

"What?" Uncle Earl asked.

"Kapp checked him out" was all that Geneva had to say.

Now Bob looked at Kapp with indignation in his eyes. I didn't blame him. This was news to me, too. When had

Kapp and Geneva conferred? Had Geneva known all along that our parents' deaths were connected to Aunt Daphne's? Then I sighed. I'd known all along, too. I just hadn't admitted it to myself or acted on the information.

"Which brings us to Fern." Melinda kept the ball rolling. "Who also wasn't even born when our parents were blown up."

"That's right," Linda murmured eagerly. "I was pregnant when they died."

"If I understand your reasoning, Geneva," Victor began slowly, "you're saying that only Linda, Earl, and myself are truly viable suspects. Is that correct?"

I hesitated. York didn't.

"Maybe," he replied.

"Uncle Victor, I'm still a suspect," Geneva took over. "But we've talked about that. Now we're talking about you. You inherit now that Aunt Daphne is dead. You've said your bookstore isn't doing well. You have a motive for Aunt Daphne's death. But did you have a motive for our parents' deaths?"

"No!" Fern burst in. "You're wrong. Granddad doesn't have a motive for Aunt Daphne's death at all. Granddad's just cheap. He's totally rich. He just doesn't spend money. He buys his clothes at thrift shops. He thinks it's, like, extravagant to eat take-out burritos. He bought the bookstore for fun, and so I'd have someplace to work, you know? He doesn't need any more money."

"Dad's so cheap, he reads the books really carefully and puts them back on the shelves," Linda added.

"I only read the used ones," Victor objected. "It wouldn't be right to pre-read the new books."

"Linda, you also inherit." Geneva jumped back in. "And you have more interest in money than your father does."

"Mom didn't do anything!" Fern objected.

"We're just talking like we said we would," I assured her. "We're not to the accusation stage."

"Yet," York added. He turned to face Uncle Earl. "And

we come to the last person in the room, the person we all trusted."

"The person who was freaked out by the smell of Mom's perfume," Melinda put in.

"The one who could always leave a room to go for a smoke," Arnot offered.

"The one who tried in every way possible to convince us that Daphne wasn't murdered, or that if she was, it was a stranger who murdered her," Geneva declared. "The one who wanted us to believe that Pilar poisoned herself."

"The person who tried to convince us that our parents' deaths were accidental," I blurted out. I snapped my mouth shut tightly after speaking, tasting bile.

"And the one who tried to scare us away," York pressed.

"With a clock," Melinda expanded.

"With oil," Arnot growled.

"But it backfired," I whispered.

"So then he tried to turn the logic around, saying the prankster wanted us to stay," Geneva said.

"There is one person in this room who had the skills to set up the explosion that killed our parents and make it look like an accident," I concluded. "A fireman. Uncle Earl was a fireman."

All five of us were staring at Uncle Earl then.

"The man who loved our mother not as a sister-in-law or a friend, but with a 'pure passion' that would be unrequited as long as our father lived," York stated.

"He didn't know Mom would be with Pop on the day he set up the explosion." Melinda pushed on, her voice shrill. "He thought she would be at her studio."

"Then Aunt Daphne spoke of Earl's love for Simone, our mother, in front of us," I said. The words hurt as I spoke them. They burned through my stomach, my esophagus, and my throat.

"Daphne was dying," Bob threw in, his voice wavering. "She felt she needed to speak the truth wherever she went."

I looked into my uncle Earl's puffy eyes.

"Aunt Daphne said 'You always loved Simone,' and you were afraid then, weren't you?" I demanded. "Afraid of losing our respect? Afraid of going to prison? Afraid—"

"No!" Earl cried. "You just don't understand—"

"Then Pilar said she 'knew stuff.'" Geneva kept at him.

"No, listen to me," he tried. "I love you kids like you're my own."

He must have seen it in our eyes. We didn't believe him. And even if one of us had believed him, none of us could have forgiven him. Not then.

"I did it for you, for you kids!" Earl insisted, his voice rising. "And for your mother. I knew Hugh abused you all."

"Pop did no much thing!" Melinda shouted.

"But I—"

He looked into each of our eyes, one pair at a time. And finally, he seemed to break. He shrunk down into his chair, looking older by the second. But he wasn't finished.

As York opened his mouth to deliver the final verdict, Uncle Earl leaped from his chair and ran for the front door.

I stuck out my cane automatically. Earl tripped and hit the floor. York tackled him even as he connected with the carpet, pulling my uncle back into his seat with a surprising gentleness.

"I did it for you!" Earl cried. He was really crying. "I did it for Simone."

I stopped hearing my uncle's voice after a while. But I could still hear Kapp calling the police.

Roy had been right. I had known who the murderer was. I just hadn't wanted to.

TWENTY-FOUR

It was Saturday afternoon, the day after my uncle Earl had confessed to three murders and one attempted murder.

Our whole family was together, getting ready for one last meal before everyone headed home. We stood outside as the brave November sunlight filtered down on Lazars, Duprees, and everyone who finally felt as close as family: the sons and daughters of Hugh and Simone Lazar; Victor, Fern, and Linda; Kapp and Roy; Zoe and Tom; and Bob and Pilar. Of course Pilar *was* family. She was a Dupree like our mother. I watched, feeling an ache of warmth and longing, as Geneva put her hand on Pilar's shoulder. Even the Turkey Sisters were there, peeking around the hedges.

"So did you guys really know he was the one?" Fern was asking.

"We knew," York answered.

Pilar tilted her head and stared at him, puppy love on her young face. York looked around for Tom.

"But they didn't have proof that would stand up in court," Kapp reminded Fern as Tom strode up to stand with York. Pilar just tilted her head to the other side and continued staring. York blushed.

"So we just decided we had to trick Uncle Earl into confessing," Melinda explained. A hint of her old grin was coming back into her elfin eyes. Though it hadn't made it to her mouth yet. "He should have just kept his yap shut, but he's such a stupid bozo on top of everything else. He makes Acuto from Pluto look smart."

I shook my head. Criminy. I wanted to laugh. I wanted to cry. Though I'd done enough crying since Earl's confession already, maybe enough for a lifetime. I squeezed Roy's hand and turned my face up to the sun, reminding myself that there was always light. I heard the hum of cars on a nearby thoroughfare and smelled fireplace smoke. There was still life after murder.

"Earl started out trying to kill his own brother," Geneva lectured, her finger extended and shaking. "He seemed to feel that killing his brother was excusable, even appropriate."

I closed my eyes for an instant, feeling the mixture of warm sun and cool air on my face. Uncle Earl had still been trying to explain why he had to do what he'd done when the police arrived the day before. It was hard to know just when his self-defense had spilled into confession. But it had, luckily for us.

"I just don't know what was going through your uncle's bedeviled mind, rattling off the way he was yesterday," Roy commented. His quiet voice was uncharacteristically angry. "Is it truly possible that he believed those police officers would just say, 'There, there,' when he told them that he killed your poor mama and papa to protect your mama and you kids. It just makes no sense, no sense at all."

"But he really thought that Pop was an abusive bully." I couldn't believe I was defending Uncle Earl. Still, there had been a method to his madness. "He even thought that Mom reciprocated his love. He was deluded. He still is. He actually thought he was doing the right thing."

"Grandfather Lazar was a tyrant," Geneva said slowly. "Mom told me about it. He beat Pop and Uncle Earl every day when they were boys."

"Those poor kids," Zoe murmured under her breath. I wondered if I was the only one who heard her.

A long past memory of Grandfather Lazar surfaced in my mind. He'd been an unpleasant man, unsmiling, who'd even smelled of anger. I shivered in the sunlight.

"So Uncle Earl projected the behavior onto Pop," Arnot mused. "He figured that if Grandfather Lazar had been horrifically abusive, then so had Pop."

"It worked for him to believe Pop was a bully," York pointed out. "He was in love with Mom. It gave him an excuse for his actions to think he was saving her, saving us."

"But Mom wasn't in love with Uncle Earl," Melinda objected. "Keerups! She was in love with Pop."

"Mom was kind to everyone, remember?" I reminded her. "Uncle Earl may have taken her kindness for love." I shrugged my shoulders. "Or maybe he just *wanted* to believe she loved him."

"Killing Mom is the only thing he's sorry for," Geneva informed us, her voice hard and even. She and Kapp were keeping tabs on the continuing police investigation through one of Kapp's many sources. "He's not sorry for killing Pop. He's not even sorry for killing Daphne. He said he only helped her along. And he insists that he was just trying to keep Pilar quiet, as if that was enough reason to poison her. But he's sorry about Mom, not for what he did, but that she died. He feels he made a mistake there." Geneva gave a bark of bitter laughter.

I remembered my uncle's compartmentalized aura. Was that how he could kill someone he loved and not feel guilty?

"Remember when Earl's wife, Ingrid, died?" Arnot asked.

I nodded along with most of the Lazars and Duprees.

"Mom comforted him then, I think." Arnot threw up his hands. "If only she'd known what scum he was. She was too good. He got closer and closer to her. But Pop had to be cut from the scene for Earl to really have Mom to himself. So Earl decided to kill Pop. He knew Pop was experimenting with fuel ignition in the basement, so he injected pure oxygen into the fuel chamber. When Pop set it to ignite, it exploded."

"But Mom was downstairs in the basement with Pop," I remembered. "Earl had killed her, too. He hadn't meant to. It preyed on him. No wonder he'd tried so hard to be a good godfather to us."

No one spoke for a while.

"Did you know he'd proposed to Mom first?" Geneva whispered. She put her arms around herself as if she was cold.

"Oh, no," Zoe objected in disbelief. "Did he really?"

"I remembered a lot last night," Geneva continued. I didn't even think she'd heard Zoe speak. "It just all splashed out from my memory. Mom told me once how sad a man Uncle Earl was. That Grandmere Dupree had always favored Pop, and Earl hated it. And Mom married Pop after refusing Earl." She laughed bitterly again. This time, it was Pilar who reached out a tentative hand to touch *Geneva's* shoulder. "All these years I've been trying not to think about it. Earl acted like a godfather to us. How could I think it?"

"But you surely have fond memories of your parents," Roy put in gently. "Cally's told me what fine folks they were."

The five of us siblings all began to speak at once, wanting to share those fond memories. The sons and daughters of Hugh and Simone Lazar talked and talked, and even laughed, remembering our fine, foolish, fearless parents. Even Linda and Victor began to praise them.

"I wish I'd, like, known them," Pilar and Fern said at the same time. They looked at each other and giggled.

"They're going to prosecute Earl," Kapp announced. "They have more than his confession. They found morphine residue on his clothing. Hooboy. No fingerprints on the tote bag, but Earl wasn't sure about that."

"Is that why he made a grab for the tote bag?" I asked.

"Yep," Kapp agreed, smiling. "But he wasn't fast enough. York stopped him from touching it."

"My hero," Tom cooed. York blushed again.

"Oh dear," Uncle Victor put in. "As I remember, I grabbed for it, too."

"Yeah," Kapp shot back. "But you stopped when I said 'fingerprints.' Earl was determined to put his hands on that bag, to obscure any fingerprints that might have already been on it."

"Your uncle Earl was in totally over his stupid head," Pilar proclaimed. "He lied. Daphne *had* told him about her hoard. She liked to tell uptight people. And Earl was so totally uptight."

"Now Earl's confessed to the police that Daphne even told him the amount for a fatal dose and how she always carried it in the tote bag in her suitcase," Kapp added. "Holy Mother! He told the cops that Daphne was threatening to let the family know that he'd been in love with her sister, Simone. That she'd always wondered about the accident that killed Hugh and Simone, but wasn't sure whether to let the family know about her worries."

"She was really trying to do the right thing before she died," Bob agreed. "I didn't know what secret she was worried about revealing, but I knew she was worried."

"I thought so," I whispered. "She was working up to it when she said, 'You always loved Simone,' working up to expressing her doubts. Earl couldn't bear for us to even consider the idea. He needed us to love him. He thought we did." I paused, trying to remember. Had I ever really loved my uncle Earl? There'd always seemed to be a cloud where affection should have been.

"Well, *I* didn't love him, even before," Melinda pronounced, crossing her arms. "No, really. I'm serious. He was always so icky. And he wanted to replace Pop."

"But how could he risk poisoning Aunt Daphne?" Linda asked.

"Hah!" Kapp responded. "He might have gotten away with everything. Remember, he'd gotten away with murder once. When Daphne talked about his love for Simone, Earl decided to act. So he waited in the dining room. Then he took the crème de menthe out of the cupboard, whisked it upstairs to doctor it, came back down and slipped it back in the cupboard, wiping off his fingerprints as best he could. In the hubbub after Daphne left for the hospital, he retrieved the bottle and dumped its contents, washed it, wiped it down, and put it back. But when the police were coming, he began to worry about it. So he went out for a smoke and buried it in the neighbor's glass recyclable bin. Amazing."

"And then Pilar wouldn't chill," Fern recollected. "She started talking about knowing stuff."

"It was too intense," Pilar said quietly. "I mean, I didn't know anything about him murdering your parents and that stuff. I just knew he knew about Daphne's stash of morphine. But, duh, lots of people knew."

"Still, you scared the stuffing out of Earl," Kapp told Pilar with a smile. Pilar smiled back. "Earl decided he had to act again. He still had the morphine. So he waited; then he poisoned your super shake. He thought no one saw him."

"I thought it was him," she muttered. "But I was so totally spaced at first, I couldn't remember anything. When I started feeling better, I thought I remembered seeing him fooling with my drink. But I wasn't totally sure. At first it was like, I gotta do this thing, call the cops or whatever. But then I started wondering. Did I really remember that? I didn't like the dude. But I didn't want to say he poisoned me if he didn't."

"Pilar's a good kid," Bob put in. "She called me and told me what she thought she remembered. And she asked me to check and see if any of the rest of you suspected Earl. That's why I came back out yesterday. I wasn't sure enough to tell anyone what Pilar suspected. But Kapp seemed to know why I was there. He told me to wait down the road until you five kids talked. He told me you might have something to say." He chuckled faintly. "You did."

"Once Bob was gone, I told myself I really had to, like, focus," Pilar let us know. "Then I was absolutely, totally sure it was Earl I'd seen. So I got the nurse to call Chief Kaifu. He was, like, totally stressed when I told him what I remembered. But he believed me."

"So, Pilar was fingering Earl from the hospital at the same time you Lazars were interrogating him here," Kapp concluded. "I'll bet they were happy to hear he was running his mouth!"

"And he thought he could scare us away," York put in scornfully.

"It must have been easy for him to tamper with the clock," I guessed. "But the oil? We were all watching each other. How'd he manage that?"

"He probably was desperate," Arnot answered. "He was such a rabbity man. He was always afraid. He panicked. And Victor said he'd leave if he was at risk. Even with all the pairing up, it was easy for Earl. He just snuck off to the kitchen while everyone was talking, got the oil, went out the back door and poured it. He was back before Geneva went to the kitchen. If anyone had asked, he would have said he went out for a cigarette."

"The rat probably even smoked a little so we could smell it," Melinda put in. "I smelled smoke on him. But then, I always smelled smoke on him. I hope they won't let him smoke in prison."

"He was going in two directions at once," I thought aloud. "He wanted to scare everyone away with the clock and the oil. But he just made it look all the more likely that a murder had actually happened. So then he tried to pretend the oil pourer had wanted all of us to think it *was* murder. Remember, he accused Uncle Victor."

"Without his confession, the prosecution would have had a hard time making a case against him," Kapp declared. "Even with Pilar's identification. But he didn't want us even thinking about murder. Like Arnot said, the man panicked. He could have gotten away with it. He almost did. All that talk about Daphne's doing it herself almost had me convinced at times. A good defense attorney could have come up with a reason that the crème de menthe bottle was missing. But with every step Earl took to lead suspicion away from Daphne's murder, he lead suspicion to it."

"And he didn't say he knew first aid, and he was a firefighter," Fern pointed out. "I wondered about that at the time. I should have said something."

"We all knew things we should have said." Linda comforted her daughter. "It's okay. The Lazars kicked his sorry butt."

"Mom!"

"Well, they did," Linda insisted, grinning. She turned to Pilar, who still stood next to Geneva. "So, are you gonna call Geneva 'Mom' or what?" she asked the girl.

Geneva was taking Pilar in just as she'd taken me in more than twenty years ago. She was going to raise another teenager through the worst years of her life. My heart went out to both Geneva and Pilar.

"'Aunt Geneva' would be just groovy," Geneva answered for Pilar.

Pilar giggled, and enunciated in a robot tone, "Yes, Aunt Geneva. Groovy, Aunt Geneva. Your wish is my command, Aunt Geneva."

Geneva laughed, and this time, there was no bitterness in it. "It's been a long time since I had a teenager in the house," she murmured diffidently. "But look at Cally. She turned out to be very cool in my opinion."

I crossed my eyes and stuck out my tongue at her. Then I rushed her with a hug that included Pilar.

"Geneva is the best," I whispered in Pilar's ear before sidling my way back to Roy. I looked up at the sun again and realized that I was happy, genuinely happy.

Minutes later, Pilar and Geneva were eagerly chattering. Victor joined them. And then Fern. And Linda. Kapp, Bob, Tom, and Zoe grouped together to gossip.

I smiled at York, Arnot, and Melinda. They all smiled back. Finally, I took a deep breath of cool, November air.

"The darkness is gone," Roy proclaimed quietly. And it was. Forever.

The mystery series with great karma
by
Claire Daniels

Cruel and Unusual Intuition

Dr. Aurora Hart's negative vibes have
returned to her—in a lethal way.
It's up to Cally Lazar and friends
to divine who set the late doctor's
aura-maker on "fry."
Then, just when time is running out,
Cally tunes into some killer karma.

0-425-20158-9

"A HEROINE THAT IT IS IMPOSSIBLE
NOT TO LIKE."
—MIDWEST BOOK REVIEW

"CALLY IS A DELIGHT."
—RENDEVOUS

Also available from
BERKLEY PRIME CRIME

Dead Men Don't Lye
by Tim Myers
Benjamin Perkins thought he had his hands full taking care of his family's specialty soap store and keeping his quirky clan in line and out of trouble. But he's about to learn that when it comes to murder, there's no such thing as a clean getaway.

0-425-20744-7

Death at Blenheim Place
by Robin Paige
Kate Sheridan is at Blenheim Palace to research King Henry's mistress Rosamund, said to have been poisoned there by Eleanor of Aquitane. But her visit takes a strange turn when her hosts unwittingly begin to relive the legend.

0-425-20237-2

Theft on Thursday
by Ann Purser
A friend has asked working-class mother and house-cleaner Lois Meade to help crack a case. It looks like the handsome new choirmaster may have been poisoned. Soon, Lois finds herself untangling a web of secrets, bigotry, and intrigue—and can't let the culprits get away clean.

0-425-20747-1

Available wherever books are sold or at penguin.com